SHARPENED OUT

OF EXISTENCE

ERROL ZOOG

37 Celsius

Copyright © 2013 by Errol Zoog

37 Celsius, LLC
www.37cpublishing.com
P.O. Box 782
Pickerington, Ohio 43147

Cover Artwork by Amber Moore

First Edition
First Printing January 2013

ISBN 978-0-988-245402

To my family,
I am blessed.

For Brittanie
When no one gets the joke,
I look for your smile on the horizon.

PENCIL NUMBER TWO

Isaiah sharpened his pencil out of existence.

The grinding vibrated his elbow as he deliberately turned the pencil sharpener handle round and round. Pencil shavings undulated in gusts from an impatiently fanned notebook to mix with small piles of dirt kicked in by student's entering homeroom. Like powdered chocolate it seemed to mix with his snot, and he attributed it to the smell that contaminated every breath.

He was blindsided by a bear hug. The cologne Barrett had tried to cover his cigarette stink up with was as strong as testosterone's grunting residue. Barrett rocked back with Isaiah engulfed in his strong arms, hair gelled so thick it felt like plastic on the side of his neck. He lifted Isaiah off the ground six inches before rocking forward and dropping him.

"How I've missed you so," Barrett squealed.

Hot moist ashtray breath invaded Isaiah's ear canal.

"You're never going to believe what I just heard," Barrett continued with mocking excitement.

Isaiah left him to the mercy of his short attention span and finished sharpening his pencil. Barrett continued louder.

"Another ripped hymen. Two psalms as wide open as her thighs, shrieking with forgotten prayers as she truly gave herself to something for the first time."

"Barrett."

In this predictable exchange of the morning Mr. Stigler's stern voice interrupted. Quick as a neuron firing Barrett turned to face him. His biceps twitched underneath a tight t-shirt advertising Visene eye-drops. Mr. Stigler, a short humpty dumpty of a man, eyed Barrett in return with his meaty arms crossed over his hardened Jell-O gut. Pale light from the television reflected off his polished desk.

"People are trying to watch Channel One."

"It's just a Pepsi commercial," Barrett said.

"Sit down and be quiet."

Mr. Stigler's thin-lipped grimace concentrated his ugliness below a mustache that seemed to gray in the middle with every exhaust of bad breath. Isaiah had been humming bullshit to the melody of the commercial that pickled them, but he quickly became silent and lowered his head, feeling vulnerable in association with Barrett.

"Stupid cunt," Barrett whispered under his breath.

He dismissed Mr. Stigler's presence as he sat to join the rest of the class staring impassively at the television. Channel One echoed from the corner of every classroom and hallway.

"What?"

Barrett ignored Mr. Stigler.

"What did you say boy?"

He glanced at Mr. Stigler as if annoyed at the interruption.

"I. Did. Not. Say. Nothing."

Mr. Stigler clenched in momentary indecision before his anger could exert its full force. Isaiah even thought he saw amusement flitter underneath his stern expression, but it probably was just the cheerful light of the McDonald's commercial reflecting off his desk.

"Be quiet."

Isaiah pressed the tip of the pencil against his finger. Barrett's jolt had caused him to sharpen it unevenly and the lead was loose. He tore it out of the wood socked and stuck the pencil back in the sharpener. Every subject had a pencil labeled for its use, and he sharpened each of them every morning. He completed all notes and homework with the same pencil so on tests the power of his subconscious would help him measure another A. Isaiah pressed the pencil stub, barely more than an eraser, against his finger until he felt a prick of pain.

He sat down, the chair-desk's steel arm dug into his side, and rested his chin on crossed forearms on the laminated desktop to stare at the television; the commercial drained all their complaints of emotions, drowned out the sarcasm at this mundane interruption grating in his throat, until he sat passive like he was in packaging. The television went blank with a pop of static. It left a reflection of his classmates' dull stares.

The morning bell rang its dull electric monotone, all other sounds lost in its elongated vibration. The noise of the P.A. system screeched on with background static like the voice of the walls themselves.

"Let us take a moment of silence today on the anniversary of Chris Collie's passing away to remember him."

The class roused from their stupor. Barrett looked at Isaiah with eyebrows raised and his mouth opened to form conceit. But it seemed he remembered being in Isaiah's living room when Isaiah had told him the news, for this first reaction smoothed into the same solemnity he had that day. There was a slight release of tension in his eyes at being able to relate outside the cellophane layer of sarcasm that covered everything in Goldenwood.

At the funeral many a young faces had paled with grief. In the church girls who had never spoken to Chris had left tear tracks for him in their makeup. There were made up stories told to remember him. But here in the classroom hints of cruelty tugged the corner of many expressions as they remembered the jokes that echoed down the hallways. Finally they acquiesced with bowed heads with the rest of the respectful class.

"Let us also remember the other friends we have lost."

The silence was not perfect. The electric drone of the lights became noticeable. The building groaned and the ventilation system seemed to sigh in boredom. Chair-desks scraped and squeaked. Velcro and zippers were pulled apart. Coughs were unsuccessfully muffled. A runny nose was politely snorted. Mr. Stigler shuffled papers. The shroud of silence that had covered Chris's life continued in his death, dragging on as torturously as when a teacher would unexpectedly call on him. Passing away, as if Chris had not even felt the razor blade's surgical slice, his life dripping away just the anticlimactic final moments of a lifetime of dripping away.

"Chris you are missed."

The silence passed like the boy in the corner back to the business tone of the PA. Isaiah knew the paparazzi of widened eyes were not for Chris in particular. They looked at each other in a voyeur's game, the story had been told by cell phone, in Internet chat rooms – it was a ghost story whispered with flashlight illuminated faces in acres of suburban backyards, heartbeats pounding adrenaline in the blood like a drug – the curse of the Goldenwood High School millennium class.

"Counselors will be on hand to help you with the grief. Have a wonderful day."

The PA screeched off and Mr. Stigler barked out the role.

"Isaiah Templeton."

From the doodled lines circling inwards on his notebook Isaiah raised the limp hand holding the pencil stub.

"Here."

SANCTUARY

There were no clocks in this room. This was Isaiah's sanctuary. Here time and space curved for him. Outside the progression of bells he was free to humor contemplation. His AP Physics book was open to a page by chance. Glossy diagrams blended with the sentences as an incantation of the spell Mr. Quinn had cast upon his imagination the previous period.

His crooked pinky upon the page was a reminder of the universe aligning for him. When the quarter was flipped he had called tails and an eagle had shimmered in the atmosphere. He had caught the winning touchdown and a hero's adulation had lifted him from the nondescript of eighth grade. He had not even realized the finger was broken until the next day. Here he was still the chosen one. Upon his throne still sat God's lucky prince. But his mind was upon further universes now.

Mr. Quinn, his personal Merlin with his beakers and Bunsen burners, had scrunched his eyes in Physics like he was sharing an intimate part of himself.

"Stars, my rickety old Honda, a cat named Peaches and nuclear bombs are subject to the laws of thermodynamics. When plants absorb sunlight entropy is increased, when we consume this energy entropy is increased, life itself increases the entropy of the universe, a theoretical end of the universe can be linked to the continuance of these laws, even as I talk about the entropy of the universe I am adding to the entropy of the universe. Irreversible, scary word, like Michael Jackson's nose job, the increase of this irreversible energy in the universe is entropy."

The bell had interrupted Isaiah's laughter.

"God what a science fair dork, when he jerks off he increases the entropy of the universe," someone had said.

But he had not humored mockery's normal path to the lunchroom. Instead he had abandoned himself to picturing red, blue, yellow particles like billiard balls spinning in the solar system of atoms. They formed the molecules in the walls of the hallway. They shaped the stained grout and the tiles crisscrossing in a diamond pattern to the pubic hairs at the basin of the porcelain. They were bonded in the urine he had cleaned off the toilet seat using thick wads of toilet paper with arms like giant Q-tips. A mush of particles he had flushed down the toilet with the tip of his forefinger, relieved that a wave of brown turd water hadn't overflowed the rim in a molecule soup.

The confessions scribbled on the wall of one who sat broken hearted because he came to shit but only farted were not his. He sat meditating on the toilet bowl with his pants around his ankles so if caught skipping lunch he could claim diarrhea. In between the usual people to call if you needed a blowjob or homosexual encounter were lines written in thick red marker:

From room to room
hall to hall
can I write my way out of this hell
if I start at the bathroom stall?

He erased stick figure genitalia and breasts drawn over the words. He repeated them in his mind, Om, like a chant. He imagined words scribbled down the hallway, past the rooms of lectures, rulers and chalkboards, the busy work done with cramped hands and sore eyes. Words burst open the heavy doors with letters shooting up into the vista, flaring out through the clouds, up past airplanes, sentences into the blue, blackening into conceptualized outer space, past the sun, past our solar system, past other stars, comets, our galaxy, other galaxies. Isaiah's imagination expanded out to the edge of the universe. Maybe too fast, eventually dispersing in time-space into a meaningless ratio, maybe too slow, eventually crushing into a sweaty arm pit traffic jam, somethingness becoming so dense it was nothingness in an eternity of time folded inwards. But the theoretical end of the universe did not scare him. He did not feel insignificant. Here in his sanctuary he was immortal seventeen. The universe was a potential vastness scaled down to the non-omniscient limits of his mind, and depression was just an insignificant neuron misfiring in his little toe.

VIOLENT THUNDERCLAPS IN THE NIGHT

The summer sun enveloped Isaiah in an eternity of childhood. Wet grass stuck to his feet and he dripped from running in the sprinkler. He giggled thinking of his mother's reaction to the mud splattered all over him. He watched her from the window of the garage where she had been working the last hour, power tools filling the garage with noise and dust. The unfamiliarity of seeing the crooked goggles balanced over her delicate nose gave him a pause. Disconnected from association he saw her like a well-intentioned stranger. Her brown hair was pulled back as she leaned forward with her neck angled stiffly, her face serious in concentration. Thick motherhood was pressed against the counter, the shapely breadth of her arms wobbled in creative manipulation of the wood.

The pleasantness of this voyeurism ended with a pang. Something was gone. He was not sure what it was, but he hurried to her for knowledge of it, so she could help him possess it again.

"Mommy."

She looked up from her work. Electric fangs sank into his foot. The jolt sent him airborne. He intuited into sight impossible angles, seeing the flash of horror in both their gaping expressions. His hair stuck straight up as if in a cartoon. He whelped, electricity escaping its boundaries of cords and hairdryers to become a monster. He landed away from the extension cord with his whole body tingling. They stared at each other. Then relief replaced their fear with hysterical laughter.

Her laughter cut off. Their previous fear expanded into dread. She grabbed him and pulled him outside. Beyond their chain link fence a nuclear bomb descended in slow motion. Their garage and the neighbor's tall pine trees framed it so it filled his sight like it was on a movie screen, a bloated satellite filling the sky, its shadow growing to cover *their whole backyard. She put her arm around his shoulders.*

Shadow became nothingness.

Then blackness became outer space. Ahead and behind was a line of transparent souls, ghosts glowing single file as they traveled through the pulsating stars, more stars than he had ever seen before shimmering and surrounding them. He was calm. He could sense his mother somewhere ahead, stronger than when she had been beside him. Like the scents in the evening after she bathed, lavender, vanilla, posy, which accentuated her clean scent, her kind face was just the residue tingeing what he could feel of her glowing inside. All throughout the line the glow of their souls transmuted brightly as far as he could see. They were as bright as the stars bleeding into the darkness of outer space. He had no vision of earth or heaven but he was aware of both as their translucent light traveled forward.

thunder rumbled

his spirit's calm was juxtaposed

with awareness of his heart clenching. He had never awoken, he had never fallen asleep, his eyes opened as if changing the channel. Lingering in the dark was concentrated emotion, like the sizzling smell of a recent lightning strike. If he closed his eyes long enough the channel would shift back. Further blurring the distinction was that part of his dream had been a memory, déjà vu superimposed. Eyes open or closed there was the texture of the tunnel surrounding him, always the darkness surrounding. The thunder became distant as consciousness increased, the memories of the dream fading into the undercurrent of mourning that remained. He wiped its wet remnants from his eyes.

The thunderstorm had left cool humid air in its aftermath. In its thickness his house was as quiet as a tomb. It creaked as it settled, as if it rose a bit every morning with its inhabitants. He released the pillow he was clutching. He did not need the clocks heavy tick reverberating downstairs to remind him of time, insomnia had taught him these contemplative hours after midnight.

1:37.

It was just another stupid nightmare. He attempted to slow his brain waves back into the gentle roll of sleep like a matador avoiding the rushing thoughts of a big dumb tomorrow. But even as the murk pressed his heavy lids with an empty darkness, even as it pinched in until his room seemed the last flickering faint light in the world, sleep would not come.

1:49.

These were the hours when as a child the monster under the bed crawled up to breathe hungrily in his ear, causing him to run to his parent's bed.

1:55.

In a room like this, with a lion upon his t-shirt and a stuffed animal cradled in his arms, Chris Stone's life had slowly dripped out of his veins. "Even this, my sad friend, is entropy," he imagined Mr. Quinn whispering scared into the night. In the coffin Chris had looked like they had pumped the blood back into his veins. Isaiah had wanted to check his breath, as if he could perform CPR until Chris finally coughed and sputtered into life, his eyes opening with wonder.

2:08.

He knelt beside his bed with his face in his mattress, piling all the blankets and pillows upon his head. God please, he prayed, God please, but he didn't know what to ask for. Recitation failed him. All those Sunday school mantras were lost to heaven's entrance exam, God please, as he calmed, God please. In the silence he stayed supplanted. The children of Jehovah still huddled in the night in this modern age, waiting for immortality to tame the beast so they could walk in the eternal morning. His prayer was in the rough carpet against his knees, in the curve of his spine as his face pressed into his bed. In answer the breeze cooled by the thunderstorm came through his screen, its touch fresh on the sweaty skin behind his knees and underneath his boxers. It sent a shiver up his spine. He pulled his head from underneath the mound of bedding so it could refresh his moist hair and the sweat running down his face.

He walked over to look out his window. Their backyard glowed exotically. He craned his neck to stare up at the night sky he hadn't studied in a long while. He had no perception of what stage the moon was in as he fruitlessly searched for it. He looked out like looking down from a Shakespearean balcony; boyhood legends seemed to be ghosts on this breeze. He pictured Tecumseh rising up out of the ground a thousand feet high, stomping over freeway overpasses, buildings, fences, because he did not need to come in stealth.

He opened his bedroom door a crack and looked down the hallway at his parents closed door and listened. All he could hear was the electric whine of appliances downstairs. He paused after the first step, then the second, before tiptoeing down the hall like a stalking cat. Taking the first step down the stairs he flinched at the noise, frozen with his leg flexed for a few pounding heartbeats. Courage grew with each additional step, until he made it down and bounded through the first floor. He peeked through the blinds at their sliding glass back door, then inched them open. It caught halfway and seemed to cause the foundation of the house to shudder. It took their wooden clock ticking off two minutes for his heartbeat to subdue. He stuck his calve out into the cool air, the rest of his body still behind the blinds. He set his foot down on the wood of their deck like he was testing the temperature of a swimming pool. The wood was slick with rainwater, its finish like a layer of slime. He shivered pleasantly up to the top of his spine. With another quick powerful step he was standing on the deck.

The sky was clear. The moon he hadn't been able to find from his window was directly above full and glowing. If there was a man in the moon, aglow in the brilliance of the sun he stared wide-eyed towards the Ohio heavens, lunatic mouth agape as he serenaded the earth. The storm had left the world silent of the sounds of nature he listened for, but in their lack was water dripping all around them, and a gush from an unseen source was as loud as a hose.

Lunatic mouth agape, in rapture Isaiah took off his boxers and threw them back in the sliding glass door. The breeze rustled hairs and tickled up his inner thigh to places unaccustomed to it. Its chill pared him bare to his senses. He tiptoed across his deck down the steps. The damp grass was cold. He moved across his yard with animal instinct, aware of every muscle. Every tentative step contracted and retracted with dormant energy ready to explode into movement. Wild, his movements were his thoughts, soft and alert like a deer. His pace was his mood. Every step he felt more alive. His backyard seemed larger. The chain-link fence barely existed. Further on the darkness diminished the privacy fences of the neighborhood, and he felt like he could hop over them as the plain spread out before him in the night. Childhood memories held fewer fences, when he could see the trees lining the creek running through their neighborhood unobstructed, and many times he had adventured its banks into the enchanted night.

Isaiah longed for the full moon to reassert illusion. David had brought along a new friend, Chris, to their venture. Isaiah was starting to wonder why. Chris just stood rigid at the creek, silhouetted formally in the moonlight with his blond bangs blocking his eyes. Isaiah had tried to engage him in conversation all night, but he only seemed to communicate in shrugs and nods. His silence mocked him and made him aware he was just a child playacting. He had tried to make Chris believe with his whispers that they must escape from an enemy encampment, silent and swift with danger all around them. He wanted Chris to feel as exhilarated as David and him as they snuck out of their tent in his backyard, crouching through moonlit backyards, free to explore the mysteries of the curfew forbidden night. But his sense of adventure was losing momentum as David and he stood in the darkness of the trees watching Chris stand mute and dumb. Enemy campfires had become just glowing windows from the Sunderhill's backyard, this river of adventure just their neighborhood creek. As his silence continued Isaiah looked at the electric light from the windows and started to wish he was in his room playing Final Fantasy. David's patient smile was even starting to annoy him.

"We must not be afraid, even though they are wearing polos made out of our grandfathers' skin, and if they catch us they will get drunk on our blood while we watch, we must not be afraid."

Unprompted Chris uttered the first complete sentence Isaiah had ever heard from him, looking around as if he channeled the words out of the night's sounds. Reflected moonlight widened around David's pupils as he shared a look with Isaiah. Chris swept his blond bangs out of his eyes. Otherwise he did not move. Now Isaiah waited alert. He became aware of his breathing. The wind rustled leaves behind his ears, brushing his cheek with a wooing whisper. He waited. Soon he could differentiate between individual insect's noises in the rhythm of their chorus. The creek was a vein of liquid moonlight and watching it flow he could feel the power of magic within him. Power built as it pooled with each heartbeat.

"Tonight under the cover of darkness we must follow this river through enemy lands."

Chris conjured up every book of fantasy David had shared with him that summer. The suburban porch lights and lampposts through the trees were torch lights from an enemy village; this out-of-the-way path traversed the fields of Tolkien and the dark mysterious Frost woods, they were escaping from enslavement, not boredom, tip toeing in the dewy grass past curfew and into the freedom of the charmed night.

"Waiting for us are three great armies, even now war horses breathe mist into the cold northern night, and they are hoping for their three kings. We the princes of these beautiful lands, we must fulfill our destiny, and our duty, to return to be our people's kings. Then we shall lead them like a torrent down upon the evil of this place."

He moved as sudden as he had started talking and smiled at them as they followed. David and Isaiah crouched down behind the trees when they heard a car in the subdued noise of the suburban night. Headlights appeared on the road parallel to them.

"Crap," Isaiah said.

Chris remained confidently upright.

"I am not afraid. You do not scare me, scout of the devil, scourge of hell. I will bring the light from the north and we three shall cleanse our motherland of you and your demon army."

Chris turned to them. The force of his will enchanted them as he thrust their fantasy onward into the night.

"Come my friends, they are waiting for us, they need us, and we must save our people. I know you have not forgotten in all this time the way our land looks, even now as winter comes to it, this river journeys to the great falls of Grandalter. That is where the magic of our people begins. The woods will communicate our coming by shuffling their leaves, and the news will spread through our forest paradise, everyone will rejoice at our returning; the tears of joy will run down their faces."

Fantasy was on the breeze, as real as the ripples it caused when it made the moons reflection shimmer.

A scream came out of the night.

"Woo Hoo!"

Isaiah stood statuesque, his skin glowing pearl in an untamed dimension. He allowed eyes to absorb him, an exquisite alien, to misunderstand him, extraterrestrial to imaginations limited to zoned and fenced acreages.

"Woo Hoo!"

Louder and more boisterous, the sound was aimed at him like he was a prize for the mantel. He stood frozen, a target exposed, until shame came over him. He pictured the lunchroom tables at school and everyone leering at him as they laughed with ridicule.

He turned and his muscles exploded into a sprint, his exposed genitals flapping. He leaped up the steps and into the refuge of his house. He grabbed his boxers, not even taking the time to put them on until he slammed the glass door in a thunderous grind. He covered his cold shrunken penis and rushed up the stairs quiet as possible. Any noise he made was subdued by the beating of his heart. Interaction with any other human being, especially his parents, in this state of humiliation would be unbearable. He rushed by their room covering the bulge in his boxers with his hands. He crawled under his blankets and buried his face.

The dark mood massed.

It was just hormonal melodrama from sprouted pubic hairs. It was just teenage angst sold in various shades of black in the mall. Isaiah tried to reason it away, but it was like rationalizing with a force of nature. He could not repress it anymore, it was heavy in his thoughts and memories; the dark mood had massed all throughout the day with geological force.

He would lie thus entombed until sleep took him to the numb relief of the morning. The morning bell would come. He would stare upon his study guide in homeroom, his thoughts trained rote upon the runes of calculus lining the pages. Equations would wrap around him like the arm of his chair-desk, squeezing him in a tunnel that propelled him to the test. He would write his name in short leveled strokes, down the progression of numbers and symbols, the little flourishes of his 6's and 9's always curling inwards. His knees would swivel together towards the front of the classroom like the quivering tip of a compass and his whole torso would move with furious pencil strokes, till he was numb to the metal arm of his chair-desk pressing into his side. The minute hand that was ticking now in the empty darkness of the classroom would pull him forwards then into the equanimity of tomorrows; his machinations would leave no error on the other side of each reckoning equal sign: every answer would be a culmination of the control of his routine.

Still the dark mood oozed.

He detested the smell of his own damp sweat. But he could not escape as he uncovered his face to look around his room in the faint light. There was eeriness to the familiar in faint contrast to the utter darkness. The glow of his alarm clock branded time's chronicle in miniature red coal dots that left a halo. His computer light blinked off the leather back of his desk chair. This bland roomscape stretched with each blink of green alien light out into obscurity, in the darkness between it pressed inwards in all planes of direction. He pictured the walls of Chris's coffin, where he lied in a brown suit with makeup so thick that it protected the mind's need to be reassured of its own immortality.

"God maybe give me that."

This prayer he mumbled as he tried to picture Chris glowing in the line of souls in his dream. Instead he imagined vaporous tracers of light from the chemical goop on his face decomposing. He could not imagine him looking out with pondering brows knit. Gone were the smooth elven features they had shared in the moonlight of boyhood. There were no words that could make that come back. He concentrated on the warmth in his center. He needed to feel it inside as the fruition of his childhood faith. He was desperate for that star of energy that slow burnt coursing assurance even in the darkest loneliness of a sleepless night to burst the coals of his alarm clock until the love that comforted him from hopeless time to apathetic time filled the vastness within. The world and its people were so very far away from this room, and he gave up his place in it for the warmth. If there really was a universe he was going to show it what God saw. But his body did not acquiesce to the warm presence of God within him. Everything curled around the center where the dark mood condensed. Drip drop, drip drop, it seeped. Drip drop, drip drop, thick and gooey. Drip drop, drip drop, down his spine. It accumulated in his chest until like a black hole it distorted anything that came close, bending his thoughts, pulling his emotions in, leaving nothing but a vacuum surrounding.

THE YAWNING WORMHOLE

Dramatized wormhole openings always had tremendous displays of energy. But they had it wrong, for they weren't earth shattering anomalies of the ages. They opened quietly, lost in day to day existence, and thus this wormhole had opened with the creaking jaws of his yawn. His mouth open wide, the long episodic history of this particular yawn crisscrossed into this morning's epoch. Driving to school through the tunnel of headlights reminded him of the previous night's dream. Wakefulness undulated again with tranquility contrasted with his heart clenching. It was hard to imagine the lights leading to Goldenwood led to heaven, or that where he was going was even significant enough to be considered hell. Either way it was useless to ponder or attempt to escape the yawn, there was nothing to do but let it carry him forward. He was numb by the time the red brake lights flashed in Goldenwood's parking lot. Classes would pass like posters on telephone poles seen while driving somewhere he had no interest in going.

The obnoxiousness of the bells elongated tone did not jolt him; it was just a tongue-less moan filling the yawn. Every morning he became acclimated to the alien atmosphere in Goldenwood, as if there was increased air pressure that tightened his orifices from his ears to his anus. The yawn built seismic pressure upon his temples. With his mouth wide open his eyes watered and he worked the muscles of his jaw to equalize the pressure in the building.

Life was but a joke, and throughout the morning he tried to cram happiness in between the bells. In the moments before History class Emily was his hope of diversion. He stared at her, trying to catch a glance from her green eyes that would cause everything else to waver. He stared from behind her just as he did in church. She spread her things out in ordered fashion upon her desk and settled her skirt past her knees.

"How's it going Emily?" Isaiah asked.

"Good. How are you?"

"Good."

She gave him a serious smile and then turned back around. It was not like waifish her head was going to turn askance with all the softness of her small-featured face to look upon him with an invitation to her ethereal world. Her eyes were no beacons; they offered him the same patience she offered everyone. His sister Rachel's friend, he could never discern if her practical responses were because she didn't notice him or didn't like him. But the reality of her thin frame underneath her clothes he could perceive from her dollops of creamy skin. Her hips pressed against her chair. She could not hide the gap of pale skin as real as pornography above her bottom no matter how her lower back shot confidence through her delicate hatchet blade shoulders. Fine hair nourished by pale blue veins traveled from her upper lip, down her arm, leading a vision down the slight extant of her body to where he imagined a translucent matt. But she never wavered into an angelic image in this building. Shame per association with the lord and his sister caused him to look away. The bell rang.

The yawn continued like a glacial scream.

His awareness was forced on shuffling dittoes. Ronald Crown poked him in the back with last night's homework. Mrs. Jones had a stack of dittoes to replace the stacks she collected. A pleasant woman, she was everyone's aunt in her sweater embroidered *Go Saints* and her maternal smile. Her ankles anchored her wide hips like the thick flagpole in the corner of her classroom. The flag it held was much finer than those in other classrooms. She had told them the first day of the year that she had bought it using the first paycheck she had ever received, and that made it especially expensive considering a teacher's salary. The rich cloth held the most robust color in the room, and its bold pattern did not have the plastic sheen of the rest of the flags in the building. Despite her kindness it still seemed malicious the way she passed out dittoes like a plow horse back and forth. Her middle-aged rump ruffled posters and the barrel of a World War II tank fluttered. Isaiah was a constant swiveling cog in the machinery processing the never-ending paperwork. He didn't bother to look at Ronald as he grabbed the stack of homework from behind him, and Emily looked only at his hand as she took the stack from him. Mrs. Jones refused to count the dittoes she passed out, and at the mercy of the process he was always forced to turn back and forth. She separated pile after pile of papers as she moved down the rows on the factory line, going back to get another pile to feed at the same rate. Phwap, phwap, phwap, her thick fingers multiplied dittoes around the classroom. As it had in so many foreign lands, the energy of manufacturing put all folktales to rest. Emily was not a fairy, but a girl with a solemn expression who didn't even grace him with a dusting from her eyes as she handed the dittoes back. Finally when he had accumulated a thick stack the dittoes stopped. He returned Mrs. Jones' good-natured smile.

When he dared to relax a ditto jabbed his back and he flinched. He twisted in his chair to take the ditto from Ronald Crown. Ronald's open mouth was aimed at him as if Isaiah had created the whole process to annoy him and had not paid attention as an affront. Isaiah took the dittoes thrust in his face. The haughtiness of Ronald's pale pumpkin spiced face was an inelegant intrusion reminding Isaiah where he was. Isaiah glared at him with the threat of all his frustration igniting. The animal fear of Ronald's soft doughy body overcame his will. He looked down and mumbled to protect his ego.

"I was just trying to get your attention."

"What?"

There was power in Isaiah's whisper and he drew the word out with Ronald under his control as his plaything. There was pleasure in letting his repressed anger flare upon Ronald.

"Nothing, nothing, just saying I am sorry," Ronald whined.

Mrs. Jones' back was turned as she prepared for her lecture. Isaiah rolled his stack of papers up. Like a horse stuck in quicksand and violently pulling free he whacked Ronald along the side of the head. Ronald cowered, defeated, and tried to hide.

"If you jab me like that again clown I will break you," Isaiah whispered.

He turned to pass the ditto up to Emily. She averted her eyes and pretended she hadn't been watching. He tickled the side of her hand as she grabbed the ditto. Her glance felt as if he had pressed up against the breadth of her. Heat rushed through his veins. She turned back around. He revved his knees and squeaks came from his tennis shoes as static built up in his jeans. Then he stopped and bumped his knees into the cold steel bar of his chair-desk to stare forward again in dull seriousness.

SACRIFICES TO ROYALTY

A's were mere byproducts of his routine = on the other side of the equal sign Isaiah was absent impetus. He felt disconnected from the youth surging in the momentary freedom of the bells. Trying to refocus eyes word logged from overhead projections, all he saw was a blur of insignificance as he sought friendly faces. Snippets of conversation and boisterous laughter contrasted the thick pall of nothing. But every voice Isaiah turned to held a face of familiar indifference. The bustle of all the borrowed minutes concentrated in the middle of the day here in the cafeteria, both the architectural and biological center of the building. Light from skylights above the surrounding roofline made this the brightest chamber, even with the cloudy October skies.

When he spotted Hoss, towering affably with his football jersey draped from his shoulders as if molded in the shape of shoulder pads, he hurried towards him in the lunch line. He pushed through a group of kids wearing hemp jewelry and t-shirts advertising their ability to make bongs out of oranges and toilet paper rolls. Goldenwood's most fashionable druggie, Dave Manchester, English they called him because of his name and floppy schoolboy haircut, stared at him as a school day corpse.

"Chill out man."

His laid-back tone belied lifeless eyes awakening momentarily with living dead intensity. Isaiah ignored him.

Standing next to Hoss, Barrett was transfixed upon the swaying movements of the three girls in front of them. Carrie Ann Winter's butt cheek pendulum swayed in the center with her hips wrapped tight in a skirt the fabric of a Ziploc bag. It inched provocatively past the rulers mark. Her white blouse had no superfluous design, the only adornment her bosom swelling its bounty. Her blonde hair was controlled by red ribbons. She mimicked shaking pom-poms, and in unison Stephanie and Erin shared her veiled look and laughed at the table of cheerleaders in game day outfits. Her makeup perfectly brought out pupils of cold reason.

Isaiah became self-conscious of his gait as his rigid legs swung in a straight line. It was an odd sensation. He tried to mimic Barrett's predatory prowl. As if there was a rip in his tighty-whiteys he swung his legs in weightless job. He bounded to grab Barrett's shoulder so hard he spun him around. Barrett reacted with a strong hand upon Isaiah's butt cheek. He was surprised to see Isaiah but he did not shy away, squeezing even harder in a battle of chicken that led them staggering forward. Isaiah's cheeks separated with cool air contrasting the sweatiness. Isaiah squeezed his solid shoulders with both hands to push him away, slow at first and then hard at the resolution.

"Get off me fag," Isaiah said.

The force of his shove barreled Barrett into the stoners. Like unobservant bowling pins they tottered amongst themselves and microscopic ashes filled the air. Barrett regained his balance with one athletic step. They ignored the stoners' muttered curses.

"Oh stop it Isaiah," Barrett moaned and slapped him with a limp wrist.

He made his voice deep and pre-pubescent and mooed like a cow in a herd.

"What, the library closed?" Barrett asked.

"Sign the contract yet meat?" Isaiah responded.

Barrett bayed like a sheep. He stared blankly at a girl walking by until she looked away. Then he bayed even louder in her direction.

"Were seniors in high school, it's about time you loosen up for Christ's sake and enjoy the moment."

Barrett nodded towards the girls.

"The joy and wonder of Goldenwood," Isaiah said unenthusiastically.

"Exactly, the joy and wonder of being surrounded by blossoming females learning to deal with newfound sexual energy."

"Pointless for you then, a?"

"You don't want to go there virgin boy."

"Speaking of blossoming, have you seen Carrie Ann Winter's breasts today?" Isaiah knew this topic would immediately change the subject.

"You kidding me, she is all I saw in boring ass history class. I am going to make her mine."

"She is the reason God created sheep, sweaters, and the color white. In my bedroom darkness she is the light. She is my Jergens grunt every night."

Isaiah had thought this line up when he should have been day dreaming, knowing that it would make Barrett laugh. He pulled Isaiah into the congregation of football jerseys as he chuckled. They caused a back up in either direction. Those left out of the laughter slid past with a mix of envy and irritation. Isaiah reveled with his friends in the full ruddy glow of youth. Their hair spikes scalped the recycled air, and they were the only ones who felt something in the stagnant world.

"Will you guys tell Isaiah he is living his life for a bunch of ribbons?"

Carrie Ann's annoyance at Barrett's interruption of her conversation with her friends caused her to grimace.

"You're just jealous because you're retarded."

"He is living life for a bunch of ribbons, pats on his back sending him on his way."

Barrett pulled at the ribbon in Carrie Ann's hair and with his other hand smacked Isaiah's bottom.

"Don't touch me." She pulled back with aversion. "I aint your rabbit George. What the hell is Gretchen wearing?"

Carrie Ann's eyes rolled to the whites. Stephanie and Erin snickered bereft of amusement out of the back of their throats.

"Ha."

"Ha."

They appraised each other. These were girls who knew how to apply makeup and turn a sarcastic laugh.

"You girls are cruel," Hoss said.

His good-natured brown eyes looked away from her and up at the skylights unabashed. Isaiah stopped laughing and also let his eyes float up. Usually he wasn't comfortable inside Goldenwood even considering the brief transitional moments between buildings he looked forward to every day. But following Hoss's stare everything dissipated for a moment as Isaiah considered that morning. He had not been able to communicate his delight when Barrett had asked him what the hell was wrong with him. That morning he had been struck more than normal by the eastern horizon as it slowly lightened, contrasting the dark phantom clouds over the parking lot and adjacent cornfield. To the west the suburbs had rested comfortably beneath the stars.

Only Carrie Ann's ridicule could ignore Hoss's calm. She stood at the country giant's shoulder staring up into his brown face. It took a while of him stroking the fine black fuzz of his beard before his kind gaze was pulled back down to her sarcasm. Only she did not try to impress Hoss, who was both more exotic and native than them with his John Deere hat covering his nappy hair. The force of her ridicule she did not want calmed by the laid back honesty of his twang.

"I can't help it she looks like a dumpy ball sack," she said.

That morning Carrie Ann's bubblegum Honda had jerked into a parking spot with beads and lays swinging from her rearview mirror so hard she had to untangle the accoutrements from her hair as she checked her reflection. Her presence had caused Isaiah to look down and walk into the building as the earth spun its morning greeting with the sun in Technicolor grandeur.

"This monster knocks the crap out of people on the football field but is really a gentle man-child. He is always talking about the damn clouds when we stretch before practice," Aaron said.

Aaron's cynical laugh was barely more than a loud exhalation as he kept his permanent straight face. Lucky number 7, seven in your program but not in your hearts, it was hard to imagine he cared about anything, let alone the result of a football game. Hoss looked at him content, a slow rumble starting in his chest to thunder out a rich hee-haw.

Isaiah yearned to share with Hoss that which he was unable to share. The light bathing them, becoming them, the sun diffused through the clouds and burning away the polluted puffs of sarcasm to warm these scared children into bouncing particles alive with movement, an eternal gift eight minutes in the making. But this he did not have words for. In Goldenwood it was dangerous for him to even admit these kinds of weird thoughts. So he just made a joke.

"Take Halloween a bit too seriously douchbags?"

He sacrificed to their attention two kids walking past with their trays trying not to be noticed. Rail thin Andy, boots, pants, nail polish, and hair dye all black, with COUNTERCULTURE spelled in big white letters on his black t-shirt, hissed at them.

"It is all cliché."

But Andy could never quite repress his good nature and there was a playful twinkle in his eyes as he grimaced back at them. Dusty, his more somber partner in combat boots, a trench coat and black TOOL t-shirt, was large and dangerous looking with a lot of chin pressed forward, and also a bit prodigious in the forehead. People would have stopped testing him long ago if not for the flowing blond hair that bounced in waves behind him with each step. Such a luxurious mane betrayed even his hardest stare.

"Um, ok."

The girls shared a look and Carrie Ann's crooked smile even allowed an approving glance for Isaiah. Dusty swiveled his gaze side-to-side ahead of him and sped up towards the outskirts of the lunchroom where he would find the humanity of his table. Barrett was excited in a frenzy of irony as he wailed zombie at them walking away. Aaron feigned a lecturing tone and spoke with mock earnestness.

"Goth. Cliché to counter a cliché. We try to be unlike previous generations, but our generation is just as competitive as those that proceeded, just our generation competes in God damned woe is me misery."

"In America, even the lepers and freaks are allowed to dine," Barrett said.

Barrett watched them retreat with a hint of fondness and then focused again upon Carrie Ann's scorn. He punched Isaiah's arm as a reward for giving them this humor. Hoss was not smiling. Admonished, Isaiah hurried into the grotto in the wall to access the kitchen. Solemn in single file he slid his tray along from station to station, a Mexican pizza put on his plate like an octagon Frisbee, the metal tongs disappearing into piled french-fries to make the whole writhe before a serving was put on his plate. He shuffled this joyless step in the eating and crapping of survival, grabbing prepackaged items from the vast trays of sustenance by past routine. Without greeting he had the correct change ready for Doris. In a hairnet, and her pasty face that hadn't changed since the days of black and white television. She took his money with a forgotten expression.

"The special spice of lunch ladies armpits."

Barrett sniffed his pizza right in front of Doris. As they exited the line he hopped to a congregation of sophomore girls to say something before hopping back to continue chattering at Isaiah.

"There is my lady. How are you doing today honey?" Hoss said

They turned in surprise at the enthusiasm in Hoss's voice. Doris was beaming at him. It seemed to Isaiah like she had gained color for the first time. Her giggles were those of an awkward girl, who along with them was stuck in these walls and waiting to escape at the end of the day. He now understood why she hid in a coat and scarf in the stands during football games. Instead of talking of nothing more than the colorless routine of every day, when her friends asked her about her job she could tell stories about the kind boy who made her laugh.

Boom, boom, boom. Greg Lumpinsky's fist thumped like cannon fire against their lunch table. People surrounding their table in the prominent center of the lunchroom paused with glances at the bulging baron of Goldenwood before the buzz resumed. Isaiah felt like he almost had to smack them away to pass through as they flitted around the tables like bees testing flowers before they finally settled into their seats. His tray made a plastic clink on the table as he squeezed in between Barrett and Sanders, claustrophobic elbows tight to his sides.

Boom, boom, boom, his fist thumped again. "To his fucking face."

He stared from above the shiny fat deposits of his cheeks. They were where his nickname Lumpy was derived from, although he assumed it was from his name or his overweight offensive lineman's frame. His large eyes, the blue green gem of his iris compressing the calculating intelligence of his burnt coal pupils in animosity, were upon Isaiah. Light reflected off his condiments and the oil on his forehead. A monstrous whitehead peaked on his nose.

"You're actually joining us today Mr. Valedictorian?"

False laughter held time as Isaiah looked around. Always he had to think of bumper sticker sized jokes to fire off in fast propulsion, pop, pop, pop, to reassert his place.

"It's that time of month Lumpy. I needed a Tommy Hillfigure wrapped tampon."

He grabbed Wadsworth and pulled his head towards his crotch. This dandy made an easy target for Isaiah. He was a nervous stork trying to peck quips into the conversation. A braggart of classical lineage, Sir Jonathan Wadsworth Kleinhauser the 3rd, he spluged the Mountain Dew he had been gulping with jittery head movements on the floor.

"What the fuck?"

His skinny neck wobbled. He readjusted himself like a thin wisp of a balloon string cut off and receding onto the dirty floor. Lumpy did not smile as the rest of them chuckled. Isaiah looked down at his tray, not bothering with ketchup as he methodically put fries in his mouth.

"God damn it."

Isaiah flinched. Lumpy set his jaw like a howitzer as the anger shook his double chin.

"I can't be uncomfortable when I am trying to eat."

"Shouldn't you be on a diet anyways?" Barrett said.

Lumpy put a fist full of fries in his mouth and gave an open mouthed grin as he chewed. Isaiah knew it was because of Barrett that he aimed his antagonism on Sanders instead of him.

"My elbow is getting pressed in between my fat rolls by this ogre next to me," Lumpy nodded towards Hoss. "Get your ass up Sanders."

Nondescript Sanders drew all his animation from the practical amount of anger reddening the cauliflower enlargements of his ear cartilage. He flexed towards Lumpy as he got up but still walked away with his middle finger as his only argument. Lumpy focused his attention on the ranch dressing he sucked out of the middle of the two pizzas he had stacked. They didn't as they began to eat. Taste filled the need to feel something, anything, which Isaiah teased with the first small bites. He caressed his hunger, tortured the need, before scientifically appeasing it with a thick mush of salty syrupy thickness filling his throat in a constant flow into his stomach.

"Titties, tit, tit, tit, for tatties."

"Big flappy tatties."

Frank and Bean were large good-looking blank faced schoolboy canvasses. Their short bangs each were parted opposite the others, above eyebrows raised as they waited for Lumpy's reaction.

"Will you idiots shut up?"

But Lumpy gave a halfhearted rebuke. They still hungered; fed they were still ravenous to feel something, anything, in the time they had left. Isaiah let the last rich sip of his chocolate milk sit upon his tongue. They leaned back to aerate the stick between their thighs.

"Move it girl, I like it, slide that nice clean Christian thang," Wadsworth said.

"Your filthy mouth shouldn't even utter Emily's name," Isaiah said.

"The only virgin left on the cheerleading squad," Aaron said.

"Whatever. With Jesus's permission Emily would be a slut just like the rest of them. At least Carrie Ann's honest about being a slut," Barrett said.

"Oh God, are we never going to stop hearing about one drunken make out session. Enough already," Lumpy said.

"I don't care if she has a dirty crotch, I would eat turds out of her asshole the way she shakes that thing."

Wadsworth's large Adam's apple moved up and down in his thin neck as he drank a second Mountain Dew.

"Wadsworth, you would be lucky if Allison Haute said bonjour," Barrett mocked Allison's thick faux French accent. "And let you join her conversion of bible camp boys. Oh my god, oh my god, oh. My. God. I will convert you to the lord."

"Yeah right, with her dress pants stuck like a concrete slab to her lard butt."

"Zit faced, puss on her lips, her long mantis arms pulling you into her wetness, puss in the friction of your lips as you kiss," Isaiah said.

"Puss-ee pussy," Aaron practiced phonetics in a matter of fact voice.

"Why do girls with no tits always have such anger?" Wadsworth said.

"The small tittie committee is in league with the lollypop guild, and oh, do they have such angry rallies," Isaiah said.

Lumpy smirked at Isaiah and then held his hand up to silence them. He shook his head to show he really had something. Cruelty twisted his countenance before smoothing to a deliberate smile that raised the fat lumps of his cheeks.

"So Chris, that is sad huh?"

He put two hands in the air pretending to press them against a wall like he was a mime. Then he frowned and put his fist to the corner of his eyes and rotated them to signify crying.

"We should have had a prayer for him before eating," Frank said.

"A moment of silence perhaps?" Lumpy said.

It was cruel laughter, monsters around a stirred pot discussing how to devour the weak. Lumpy took out a large container of pudding and with each small bite slowly pulled the plastic spoon out his pursed lips. The purple-garbed giants next to him, Frank and Bean rolled in laughter. Lumpy scratched at his neck just underneath the large nape of his jersey, where Isaiah there probably was another whitehead.

"Why did he do it Isaiah?"

Lumpy turned to him and stared unblinking.

"Well, he was picked on of course, tortured really, even though no one can remember why anymore. But at one point or another isn't everyone tortured?"

Isaiah's laughter was hallow.

"But the more important question is who is it going to be this year?" Lumpy asked.

"We could all place bets, put money in a pool—" Frank finished Bean's sentence, "and if our horse crosses the finish line collect up."

"Who will it be, who will complete the circle, who will be the subject of the speeches, the moments of silence, the grief counselors, the why, why, why?"

"Will they take the coward way out like Chris with slit wrists?" Aaron said with contempt.

"Or," Lumpy responded with a smile.

Wadsworth finished his Mountain Dew with one last gulp before he spoke. "Or die violently like Josh Cantwell who sent a bullet rocketing through the unexplored space of his brain."

"Or is it going to be someone no one expected, someone popular and happy, someone who had it all, including one of the hottest girls in school on her knees, like Toby Speezio, who must have been possessed by Satan himself, red eyes glowing in his mind, maddening whispers in his ear, to kill himself so brutally," Barrett said.

Toby had failed at hanging himself first. Then he had not cut his wrists deep enough. But he had been just building up momentum, experimenting with his intentions. From his bathroom a trail of blood led through the house to the medicine cabinet covered with blood. There were pills strewn across the floor from capsized bottles coated in blood. But the pills were not what had done the trick, although the cocaine they found in his system may have delayed their effects. The pink water in the bathtub and bloody corded hairdryer lying in the water showed that even that attempt had failed. But Toby was committed, and the shotgun blast that turned his kitchen into a slaughterhouse had finally finished the act.

"I put my money on Joe from the trench coat mafia," Frank said.

Joe Hazard sat at Dusty's table with Andy, a chunky mothball of a kid who shopped at the same military surplus stores.

"Isaiah, write this down." Lumpy said.

"Hey, how about his freaky little friend, I pick him," Bean said.

"Andy. He is a weird dude. Today he hissed at us like he was in some kind of horror movie," Barrett said.

"All those guys are weird dudes," Aaron stated this truth, and then looked at Wadsworth. "Your spoiled rich ass better pay me when I win. I'll take Ronald Crown."

"Good choice. I hate that kid, who would have believed the mass produced ridiculousness of his name would fate him for pale white skin and heavy footed clown incoordination. He—"

Wadsworth interrupted Isaiah. "What about that one kid, the one with the fat rolls on his back who is always breathing like he just ran a marathon?"

"Stanley Steamer," Lumpy answered.

"Yeah I take him."

"What about you Barrett, who do you take? Who, who, who."

Lumpy hooted like a large lard owl and blinked at Barrett.

"I think you guys are being a little sexist. What about the ladies? I think I will take Dixie Winn, she can't have much to live for."

"Even the fattest ugliest girl can find someone to have sex with her, so why would a girl commit suicide?" Wadsworth asked.

"Well, then why don't you go have sex with her?"

"Right."

"Ok, I get it, I get it, Barrett you can have Dixie Winn. Isaiah, write that down," Lumpy ordered. "I take that kid that smells like a skunk's asshole, Howard whatever his last name is. He would be doing us all a favor. What about you Hoss?"

The first rumblings of an angry avalanche entered Hoss's voice.

"I bet that someone comes to school with an AK 47 and you are the first one they take out."

"Jeremy's spoken," Barrett said.

"Good song."

"Before MTV."

"Ooo, ooo, ooo," Barrett sang.

"Seriously? Don't be a buzzkill. Just pick someone. We are just joking. Fine. Fine Hoss. What about you Isaiah?"

Hoss made him ashamed of the names he had been writing. It had seemed insignificant, the names nothing more than prototypes for their entertainment. But now he looked down embarrassed. But it seemed like cowardice, and he could feel them staring at him. Desperate to get their eyes off of him, he scanned the lunchroom.

David didn't stand out because he sat alone, hunched over with barely the top of his head visible over the thick hardback book in a tunnel going nowhere. It was because of his total disregard for the solitude. Even as Isaiah grinned at his friends he was jealous of David's immunity from this place, for he had seen that chubby cherub face animate and knew he still felt wonder as he contemplated a world Isaiah no longer recognized. They breathed their hunger of amusement and Isaiah knew this was the sacrifice they demanded. He wondered at how cafeterias were similar everywhere, at his mother's work, at Rachel's college, society always pressed into circles of gossip, that most brutal form of human communication.

"Guys, I am going to be the winner. David McCormick."

It wasn't like they were really going to put him in a pot of their entertainment. But when the entire table followed his gaze he knew they saw him as a coward afraid to face the ugly faces of reality leering at him, escaping into fantasy like a drug. David was oblivious to the sudden stares Isaiah had brought upon him. He sat hunchbacked and weak necked in a ball of chubbiness, emotionally uncoordinated in his false Neverland.

"Good choice. I forgot about him. You're horse may be a winner."

The fat deposits of Lumpy's cheeks bulged red.

"A loser amongst losers," Aaron said.

"Suicide is hilarious," Barrett said.

Their laughter was contagious, and even Hoss added a disbelieving chuckle.

"Stop guys, I am going to overdose on these endorphins, stop, stop," Aaron said breathlessly.

They laughed over the bell and only in its echoes was David's name in his head like a curse. Isaiah knew evil was upon David as he walked with slumped shoulders ahead of them. He was unaware of their looming mirth as he navigated with only peripheral vision, focusing nowhere with heavy lidded disinterest. Isaiah did not have to see his apathetic expression, for it was a constant commentary that could annotate the days. Dressed in clothes the same size as middle school, his faded polo still fit his rolled shoulders but it exposed the pale love handle above his pair of old sweat pants with every step.

"Isaiah, trying to end up like this loser?"

Quick like a knee jerk reaction Barrett swung his leg. He swiveled his whole body like kicking a field goal, and his tennis shoe crumpled the loose fabric of David's sweat pants as he kicked him hard in the butt. Barrett raised his eyebrows, his humor even more intense because he was surprised himself he had done it. David slowly turned to face them. Despite their laughter they faced him as straight as coliseum pillars. Behind him Carrie Ann's haggard bile duct laughter led the girl's giggles, David scorned by the fairer of their species, the songbird fanning out and coughing at him, wretch, wretch. But he barely glanced at them. Isaiah could not stifle his chuckles when David's eyes flashed at him without his heavy eyelids lifting from their bored perch. His cold disdain caused Isaiah a shiver of self-doubt. Then even that retreated back into David's opaque depths. He focused blankly beyond them. Unhurriedly he turned around and walked. Isaiah's laughter redoubled in retaliation to his cold stare and he had to hug his stomach to keep from bending to the ground.

"Boys."

Mrs. Dronomine, Karen as she asked students to call her, laughed nervously from outside her classroom and pretended to be in on the joke. David walked into her classroom and the recently misplaced sorority girl gave them a slight conspiratorial grin. When she turned to enter Barrett's lips parted slightly as he stared at her behind with feral concentration. Isaiah glazed in their faces to relish in the afterglow but they dispersed with Barrett's attention. He was left alone, and his grin faded into the smoldering ruins of his pleasure. He entered Karen's class and the curse echoed with his voice – David McCormick.

WASP WINDOW

The blinds in Karen's classroom glowed with sunlight. October had habituated Isaiah to them being faded gray. Like sprouts sensing the first hint of spring the class collectively leaned towards this first sign of an Indian summer. Sunshine coming underneath the crack beneath the blinds illuminated dust motes in a swath to Isaiah's desk.

His legs started to twitch from side to side.

He swept his hand through the dust motes. They swirled, like floating specks of Attention Deficit Disorder as contagious as the common cold, and more breezed in behind.

"Please turn in last night's essays."

Furious scribbles stopped mid scrawl from some of them as Karen collected the homework. She stood perky at the front of the class with a smile full of teeth as white as aspirin. Blonde hair flowed onto her black blouse, buttoned tight to the top button, making it even harder to ignore her bosom. A white gold chain was visible above her collar. He could not help but imagine its charm underneath, the white gold absorbing her warmth.

He forced his legs to stop moving.

Matching bracelets dangled a charm from each of her wrists. She pulled down the handle of the overhead projector screen. When she let go the screen fluttered back up. She turned in a flustered whirl of blonde and grabbed the handle again, pulling down slowly. It did not stick. She let it roll back up halfway and then with two hands methodically pulled it down and it caught. She spread her arms out theatrically, the charms on her wrists sparkling as they bounced.

"Aha."

She turned the projector on. Wadsworth and Frank raced un-beckoned to turn the light switches off for her.

"This will be on the test."

His left leg started to sway.

The light left shadows in the time-honored formality of roman numerals, linking the sentences together like strands of computer data. As she read aloud her sweet voice was dulled to the humorless cartoon monotone in a final redundancy. He ignored her stretch of exposed neck that enchanted the boy's imaginations so he could tune her out. He willed his concentration through the void and speedily copied the entire overhead. He then waited for her to turn to the next page devoid of though. When her voice rose playfully again with her feminine sweetness he pulled his attention away from the slight rise and fall of her bosom lest she said something testable.

"The first time I read Catcher in the Rye, the ducks annoyed me. I thought, why the..." She paused with the implied curse in her mischievous grin. "Obsession with ducks. Shut up about the ducks already. All I wanted to do was have duck tartar served up on a plate. But for college you will need to pick up on the meaning of these things, and soon I'll make you also able to devour symbols."

It was just another ill-timed joke in her persistence for attention. A pleased giggle heaved her bra.

His right leg started to sway.

As he filled a third page a violent buzzing rattled the blind. Words vibrated out the periphery and he glanced at the window. He had to force his attention back to the overhead. He could not allow frustration or the void would swallow him line by line. The buzzing stopped in unison with him finishing the page. He searched for the insect source but was distracted by the sunbeam. He opened his palm underneath energy that had sped through space as four hundred eighty bored seconds passed in the classroom. Each one of his fingernails had jagged skin at the corners torn to the crimson tips of miniscule blood vessels. His thumb was especially raw where his index finger had been picking at it.

He surveyed the class as he waited for Karen to finish reading. Forgotten in the corner was David slumped with his shoulders rounded. Isaiah expected to see the dull apathy forming a rigid mask above his double chin but instead he was enraptured by his notebook. He held his pencil in the air like a conductor's wand in a moment of vital silence.

Isaiah looked at his own notebook page lest he had missed something. Her resolved monotone had already regurgitated for them the family, coming of age novel, the genus, J.D. Salinger, its kingdom of English and its class of fiction, like vice grips twisting it like a sponge and letting its juice evaporate on the grime of the floor. There was a thumbprint of blood on his paper that had cemented a strand of his hair. It took three tries to pull it away. Karen had started the next page of notes without him noticing and he copied so fast his hand ached, skipping conjunctions, writing over the spiral thumbprint of blood. He actually read the sentences he copied to try and figure out what David found so intriguing. Karen's vigor inspired throbbing testosterone, yes, it sprouted acne and put pressure on the loins, but if other lectures increased the entropy of the universe, than her bored lecture must increase it exponentially, fading the world away so fast that the act itself was a blurred nothingness evenly distributed—

at the tip of each of her nipples.

He looked away from Karen and studied David again. He noticed finally that he was reading one his hard backed novels hidden behind his notebook. So that was the somewhere else that made Karen's classroom not exist. Isaiah remembered the worlds of fantasy they had lost themselves in that summer when he had borrowed book after book from David to fill the time in between. The colors of the cover's artwork bled out and Isaiah imagined them washing through the room, the richer hues making the chairs seem farther apart, and making David with his disheveled hair and clothes seem at place inhabiting that boyhood world, as the rest of the class stared vacantly forward.

His legs were swaying so hard now they bounced.

"So any questions about your assigned reading from last night?"

Today someone else could earn participation points. He stared at the pattern of the fake wood of his chair-desk. He doodled circles, then squares, then circles, then squares. A glance at the clock unwittingly brought upon him a curse of time, the second hand heavy with gravity trying to keep it static. There was no way a mere second could take that long. He was convinced the clock ticked louder in this room than any other in school, torturing him by forcing his awareness upon every seconds passing.

He finally gave in and cocked his head to glimpse outside. When he did he noticed two motionless yellow jackets on the dusty windowsill. They looked ready to be reincarnated by a breeze and glide away. Possibly the buzzing had been a yellow jacket in its death throes trapped in the stale lifeless air of the classroom from an unreachable paradise of pollen and warmth. He hesitantly brushed his pencil across each body. They did not move. He pushed one harder but managed only to twist its carcass unnaturally. He tried to manipulate it into its original state of petrified motion.

"Come on guys," Mrs. Dronomine cooed.

He raised his hand.

"Isaiah."

"Could we open the blinds?"

Her expectant smile soured with a hint of annoyance, her soft upper lip thinning as it pulled up into a rodent snarl towards her button nose. Then she went back to the flirtatious full-lipped smile. The classroom resounded with flapping blinds. The stripe on his desk disappeared into a wash of sunlight. He was not the type of kid to stare listless out windows, but today he would not help himself.

Another yellow jacket was very much alive, its yellow stripes vibrant as it moved along the windowpane illuminated in the sunshine. Its front legs rubbed its rounded spade face rapidly towards the tip facing out the window as if searching for the scent of its hidden hive. Was its pocket of geometric wilderness honeycombed in the corners of this landscaped world, in a fence post, a gutter, the roof of an administrative building?

Along with the yellow jacket he gazed longingly out the window to Potter's park. It lined the entranceway to Goldenwood High School with flowers and Legoland trees standing in attention on either side. The architects had aimed one's vision towards Goldenwood from the road, suggesting the collaged beauty continued through the walls to young minds in vigorous full bloom. The effect also tempted Isaiah outwards.

Two more yellow jacket corpses were stuck on the glass at the top of the window. He could find no hidden hive. How had they gotten in, why had they been drawn to this never opened window as a means to escape? He pressed his hand against the cool glass of the window, sliding his sweaty palm against it to smear a handprint.

"So what do you think?"

The yellow jacket began again to buzz against the window. Isaiah felt claustrophobic, like there was a pressure on his nostrils. He concentrated on his fingertips as if he could transfer energy through the glass. Karen stood at the front of the class like a spurned adolescent, her hands on her hips and her foot tapping, the jiggling going all the way up. The buzzing intensified as the yellow jacket went back and forth from corner to corner in frantic confusion. It moved away from the glass then went back with a loud concentrated buzz. Finally it slowed again to a quieter humming. Karen's chest swelled with a deep intake of breath.

"I will close the blinds."

He removed his hand from the window. His smeared oily handprint ended in clear fingerprints. His legs twitched forcefully from his hips until his whole bottom half was moving. His elbows joined in.

The buzzing intensified until it crackled and then buzzed pop with a climactic stop. It searched the glass again with its antennae. Could its insect brain remember that it had tried this? Or was instinct pushing it forward as it forgot the hours of continuous failures, stunned and trying to get through the wall of solidified air, nightmarish visions of those who had failed before, their carcasses frozen in air. Yet it tried again and again, inching back and forth like a prayer to find passage out to the world. But however hard it pressed all it felt was the constant cool of the frozen air against its body.

His legs slammed together.

He grabbed a ditto and the staple went flying when he ripped the pages apart. He created a closed funnel out of two pages and scooped the yellow jacket up, taking the last piece of paper and closing the top. It rattled against his hands, frantically bouncing around with all the force of its small body lightly pressing the paper into his fingertips.

He stood up in an awkward hurry trying not to get stung through the paper. Standing in the middle of class with a yellow jacket caged in paper he was paralyzed with self-consciousness. Karen and the class looked upon him with faces yet unmoved from previous expressions. It took their confusion starting to show on their faces to get him moving. He almost tripped over his chair-desk. Even David looked at him with slight astonishment. He hurried to the door and pressed his elbow against the handle. The handle jingled and slipped as he slammed against it with a loud grunt.

"Isaiah…"

He desperately pressed again and the handle clicked. He shut the door as fast as he could, flinching as it slammed. The yellow jacket was moving so fast it sounded to Isaiah like a rattle as it bounced against his hands. He ran through the hallways to the entrance. When he reached it he backed through the heavy glass doors and out into the sunshine. He extended his arms out away from him and took the top sheet of paper off. The yellow jacket did not dart out as he expected. He swept the dittos from side to side gently. It rubbed itself with its antennae. He thrust the container outwards with quick movements. Finally it darted out, raising its altitude until it was outlined in the trees as it faded away.

PHOTOSÝNTHESIS

Impulses scrambled, as if his life was a boring movie and a frame had been removed, Isaiah stood immobile in the alternate dimension where that frame had existed. Impressions were as concentrated as thoughts. Leaves flickered from top to bottom, yellow to green, in the spheres of the Legoland trees. Holdover summer sounds of insects and bird chirps were the backbeat to the wind increasing in a stream of consciousness. Leaves fell in a tottering descent, green to yellow. The breeze ruffled flowers and sent stiff waves through the luminous grass.

A car popped bubbles of flatulence from the highway. The tread of its tires played on the fixed point of his vision like it was a record needle, and a static of thoughts crackled. Goldenwood's mass was oppressive behind him. He hurried to his car. At the stop sign he looked back. Goldenwood looked like one of God's children had discarded blocks in the surrounding park. What could be so valuable in those tombs to keep them inside away from the sun reflecting off its steel roof? His tires screeched as he pulled onto the highway. Absent the pull of destination he drove uninhibited by the speedometer.

His tires screeched and absent the pull of destination he drove uninhibited by the speedometer. The hint of vegetation brewed in the air like tealeaves and he snorted to spit out school contaminated snot out the window. The road sliced through cornfields and the endless buffer of the suburbs to the frontier of their borough, where it rolled with the start of hills through patches of woods.

"Hye ya ya."

He hummed the rhythm of a song he did not know the words to.

"Hye ya ya."

For extra credit in history class he had attended a powwow on Columbus Day held in the gymnasium. He had sat amongst the onlookers complaining of the heat, watching a sickly man with a potbelly and pockmarked face dance the circle so quick and graceful that his boots skipped like granite in low gravity, barely seeming to touch the ground as he sang with intent gaze focused beyond the gymnasium. The lingering melody Isaiah yelped out wordlessly in rising crescendos.

"Hye ya ya."

A red pickup truck filled his rearview and came inches from his bumper. It forced his attention again on his speedometer to make sure he was going ten miles per hour over the speed limit. Isaiah almost stopped completely before turning. The obligatory honk and middle finger ensued as the truck swerved past. He read its bumper sticker.

What Would Jesus Do?

Certainly not flip him the bird and almost run him off the road.

Impulse had led him to the arboretum his mother had taken Rachel and him as kids. Its entrance was a covered bridge that crossed the creek that formed one boundary. The functional museum piece seasoned his footsteps. Even the most violent graffiti carved into its old wood seemed part of an organic pattern. One hundred years ago as today his solitary gaze looked out its window at the calm creek with plant particles and lathered bubbles flowing past to mark time. Geese honked in clown laughter from the pond in the center. Unlike Goldenwood's monorchard the path on the other side of the bridge was lined with a variety of trees, a UN gathering of distinct ancestral characteristics opening his imagination to other worlds. Knobby troll trees stood next to smooth silver barked trees from the middle of elvish forests, tall oaks towered next to the exotic domestication of fruit trees. Some had green leaves; others were starting to turn with the green of photosynthesis drained in corresponding hues of yellow, orange, and red, to create a glorious display. He put his face close to each one to take in its scent and offer back his exhalations. Each footfall crushed leaves to quicken their decomposition and richen the soil to be born again someday in the sun. He ran his hands along bark, caressed waxy leaves, intimate like one would be with be with family pets.

"Hello."

The common tongue sounded harsh. He cleared the remnants of it from his throat by humming the wordless chorus again. He removed his backpack and took his shirt off to tie it around his waist. He wanted to synthesize the warmth of the sunshine like the trees and store it for the musty hallways. He closed his eyes and faced the sun, squeezing his lids till specks of saline spun in crystalline flowers, boiling orange shadows spread through the white glow like spots on the face of the sun.

He took out his notebook. A bright spot centered in his vision on the absurdity of scrawled notes he paged past to get to a blank page. Years spent studying yet he did not know the most obvious clues to differentiate trees. He shouldered his backpack and strolled to a giant on the creek bank. American Sycamore, *Platanus occidentalis*, he copied from its plaque, writing underneath, plates of gray bark peeling off to leave white underneath. Catalpa, Elm, Maple, Red Oak, when you breathe out I breathe in, Ohio Buckeye, eyes of the deer never focused, Aristocrat Pear, sitting fat on a couch, Legend American Linden, American Beech, trees of World War veterans, the Latin, *Ulmus Americana, Ostia virginiana, Cercis canadensia*, flowed with meaning for him gleaned only from sound, *Ailanthus altissima, Quercus rubra*, magic evolved from the melodious past, *Ailanthus altissima*; Tree of Heaven.

The geese barked out a short succession of honks as he approached through the underbrush blooming with small yellow and purple flowers, printer white they scurried into the water orange clown feet first and looked back at him distrustfully. He stood at the bank blocked from where they had been sunning by thickets of tall cattails and corn puff topped reeds.

Mallard ducks padded more calmly towards the water, their emerald green hoods held majestically stiff as they eyed him with wet pebble eyes, their brown-speckled females in tow. He imagined Mrs. Dronomine salivating as she read a menu, prepared to devour their symbolic flesh with caramelized red sauce dripping down her chin. She always cawed in class that the first rule of describing beauty was to never use the word beautiful.

But how to synthesize the waterfowl moving in swirls of color across the fall foliage mirrored on the pond rising up into the reflected light blue sky? B, E, A, U, T, I, F, U, L, his thoughts stuttered, w-w-w-words, words, words, he spent lifetimes in a building of words, spooning up regurgitated textbooks, digesting caskets of dead words from bookshelves always forcing him inwards, he had words piled millions of miles of crumbled notebook pages high in his head, still he had none to define even this one moment of b e a u t y, to store it in his mind's eye, like a painting to be hung in the blandest of formal classrooms, w-w-w-words, forcing them he scribbled out clichés, trailing multi syllables like a centipede crawling out of a pile of rotting vegetation.

The effort left his hand aching. He sat on a bench under a tree with no sign. It was hardy with knotted bark and stubbornly its leaves still held all their green, with little red fruit like cherry bomb clusters. He tried to decipher the purpose of ants meandering on its bark. Birds chirped at each other and rattled the branches in bursts of short flight, sending hard little fruits raining. A squirrel hopped from branch to thinner branch, and then stopped, twitching with eyes trained nervously on him. For a moment they pondered from what habitation the other came from to meet in this stare. Then it bounded off into another tree to disappear. The wind intensified and sunlight and shade recreated their boundaries in a dancing light show. It fingered his hair with the first caress he had allowed in a long time, cooling the sweat on his bare chest.

He was tempted to try and write a punch line for the perpetual laughter of the creek. He tried to follow an individual water molecule in the undulating waves, trying to stay with it as it flowed around a big mossy rock to speed towards miniature rapids. He wanted to catch its individual reflection and refraction of the constant torrent of sunlight in the diamond mine his eyes registered like a thought that would explain the metaphysical implications. But it was impossible. Answers were lost past the small rapids in the calmer shadows beyond.

Bong, a church bell rang the new hour off in a distance. Bong, echoes filled the spaces between the precise rings. Bong, echoing in the silence after their conclusion. As if they had awakened the gears of the world into movement a lawnmower started its instant incessantness. A train horn came from far off. It warned of its inevitability like a traffic jam synchronized, leading a heavy chug a chug towards him from the same direction the other boundary of the arboretum flowed. The tunnel of sound amplified right before the engine passed, the horn blast beside him went right down into his nervous system. Its weight settled every rotation with each cars unique metal rattling, until the machine sound of the caboose passed to leave the world deafened. Always there was a dog barking off in the distance.

Miniature rockslides fell as he climbed up to the tracks. The train was a painful bright spot reflected on the far-reaching view. It disappeared into the small dot of horizon between blurred trees so far away they seemed to lean their tips in a shrinking triangle. On the other side of the tracks were the empty castles of suburbia, with boats, pools, parked cars, but not a person in sight. After the noise of the train it seemed as quiet as a movie about the end of the world. The horn rang like a lonesome ghost. The other direction of tracks undulated in elevation along with the telephone poles and there was a road in the distance. Vehicles slowed down at the pinnacle of the tracks before speeding back up. A big yellow school bus stopped. He pictured its stop sign as the door clunked open, and Mr. Winkler, his former bus driver, peering out mole-eyed. He would accept this pause in his monotonous life as a view in each direction of the recurrent symbol of desolation in photographs and movies. The door closed and the bus drove away. But if far gazing eyes from either blurred horizon stared upon this point, and saw nothing, he was still here unknown upon these endless tracks looking down upon beauty ignored. A boy could not press a page full of words describing it against Mr. Winkler's blurry spectacles, screams would just tell him to return to his seat. But it was here, it was beautiful, and that was enough.

FOR A WHILE NOTHING HAPPENED

Pussy, dick, shit, butt cheese, fuck, ass, cunt."
Out of the houses three freshman truants meandered sucking on cigarettes with short demonstrative puffs. Medieval torture devices worth of metal dangled from chains hooked to their jeans and adorned their black leather chokers and wrist slitters. They crossed the field yelling, mocking the boring world for not being a video game. They laughed in amplified false emotion without looking around.

"Dick, dick, dick, dick, dick, dick, shit, cunt, ass shit dick cock and balls."

The small one in front with the largest mass of metal spikes jostled the other two. As he did so he glanced up at Isaiah. He did not shrink into embarrassed silence as Isaiah expected. Two-thirds Isaiah's size yet disconnected from consequence, he uttered a mock scream and pointed. They did not hide their cigarettes. Before even focusing on Isaiah the other two mimicked him and competed in obnoxious shrieks.

"Wierdo, fagot, homo, fag, dickweed, pervert, rapist."

Isaiah looked at them in stiff disinterest to show he was not intimidated. They walked towards the tracks. He stepped down, not out of fear, but only because his sanctity was ruined. The short one's puberty broke for a moment in a high-pitched whelp, but instead of stopping in embarrassment he squealed even louder at Isaiah's retreat. Isaiah stopped to watch them from behind a tree. He put his shirt back on. A native to the arboretum he eyed them as intruders. They climbed the tracks, kicking and throwing stones at each other, missing the stones crashed into a pine tree grove. All three were dressed all in black with COUNTERCULTURE spelled out in different fashions of white block letters on their t-shirts. The small one, adorned further in black nail polish, took a few steps forward and launched a stone down the railroad tracks where he though Isaiah might have been. The other two sent a barrage in the same direction.

"Choo, choo, I'll run a train on you."

The small one stopped and pulled his pants down, wobbling in the middle of the track. He forced out a turd like an uncoordinated animal. The other two ran away in mock horror. He walked down to the other side with his pants still down and ripped a thin branch off a tree to use the leaves to wipe his butt.

Isaiah stalked them as they walked through the park ripping and clawing and spitting deep snorted phlegm at trees. He wanted to rush full speed like a brave and smash violently into them before they even had time to react. Through the covered bridge their trudging footsteps echoed.

"Got a sweet tooth me candy man," their leader said.

They kicked gravel in the parking lot on the other side of the bridge. Isaiah walked onto the covered bridge with stealth to watch them from the window unobserved. They walked quietly now in stiff formation with the small one leading them towards a white SUV. Two doors opened. The small one got in front, the other two climbed in the back. Cigarettes flared up in the cloudy interior. Isaiah watched them puff, hungry demon fire filling the air with poison smoke. It took a while before he realized they were passing a joint. They stepped out and the small one pocketed something as he nodded at the SUV. They squinted as they looked around, nodding at each other, the birds, the squirrels, their imagined spectators, practicing cool they had seen in a movie. That disappeared when they heard a car approaching. Isaiah chuckled at them as they ran in the opposite direction. The SUV shot rocks out as it accelerated out past the car that slowly pulled into the parking lot. The driver of the incoming car seemed to pay no attention to it speeding by. It parked and a heavyset woman wobbled out. She pointed a camera towards the bridge and took four pictures then wobbled back to her car and left.

Driving home he was stopped by the light in front of Goldenwood. Whistles pierced the air as the football team and marching band practiced in the large adjoining fields. Mr. Stigler stood on top of a platform with his arms conducting in military stiffness. He controlled the ebb and flow of youth that surrounded him by yelling through the bullhorn at the marching band.

"Now, now, now, yes, great, great, yes, yes, great," this was the only time his voice was ever this emphatic.

The brass swelled and undulated as the drums pounded in precision. Footballs arched in parabolas that almost defied gravity before spinning down with a blur of laces into the waiting arms of the only acceptable embrace of American boys. He had not missed football since Barrett and he had quit after sophomore year, the boyhood joy of the game had long since been weighed down. But he longed today to be with them at the end of practice, circled around coach on one knee with a teammates arm pressing his pads down on his shoulder as his hand rested upon another teammates' mesh jersey, in their bulky armor with helmets in hand like crusading knights, listening to coach yell and froth of their manifest destiny, waiting to bow their heads together in prayers for victory.

Even Mr. Stigler had his home team. Even those little turds in an SUV smelling of butt crack juice, tasting the world's sweetness as a synchronized chemical, huddled together against their rivals.

At home he was drawn to the living room usually reserved for formal family occasions. He opened the thick billowy curtains and sprawled on the black leather couch. Sunlight reflected off every Windex'd surface, casting glare on family portraits and making the sculptures his mother collected seem like polished piles of scrap metal and driftwood. Even the concentrated woodpeckers peck of their stately oak clock seemed less haughty and refined. He studied Rachel's crooked grin in their most recent family portrait before she had left for college as he dozed off.

He awoke to the syrupy glow of the sunset seeping in. He hurried outside. Like an embracing promise of the eternal welcome of the morning the sun cast soft color as the earth turned away. Over neighbors' houses the blanket of water molecules glowed orange and pink with white undertones. Low flying scruff clouds spun by like smoky sky tumbleweeds. As emerging space replaced the softer undertones and white darkened to gray at the cusp of the earth, he watched intent, as if maybe he could recreate the same effect as watching the ticking clock at school, slowing time as stars plopped out and the soft evening became illuminated by the emerging moon. A middle-aged couple walking their dog smiled and waved. He politely waved back then walked inside.

The living room had regained its ceremonial solemnity. The clock chimed the hour. One golden hand pointed past the intricately carved Roman numeral XII towards heaven above, the smaller denoted VII. This was not a nervous clock passing mere seconds in the shortened hysteria of functionality, but a clock as solid as tradition passed down from his great-grandmother's living room. It reminded him he was back in its eternal routine of his days. Every passing minute now ticked like a miniature axe chopping down the forest of time. Framed photographs in shadow were their family mausoleum. He went to his room and squeezed his eyes shut so tight it felt like a migraine, but the Indian sun would not burn again in his retina. He looked out his window. A blind man in outer space was very cold and lonely indeed. Its silence would be inescapable. The white walls of his room felt as bland and unimaginative as the classrooms sterilizing his days.

Freshman year he had ritualistically boxed up his trophies, his model airplanes, and all the other accumulated knick-knacks of childhood. He had torn his posters and pennants from the wall. He had sold his baseball card collection to the beady-eyed man bartering with all the frenzy of the stock market exchange. He had chastised himself, pussy, pussy, pussy, for his difficulty as he stood at the dumpster with one last toy. Pussy, pussy, pussy, he had mumbled as he pulled it from his jacket, warmth from his body bestowed upon it as the life it had absorbed from his imagination. Pussy, pussy, pussy, he had uttered until he had finally been able to launch his stuffed animal lion into the dumpster. He had tried to convince himself it was just lifeless pillow stuffing that sat on top of the rotting fruit and eggshells absorbing trash juice. He had peddled away so fast that the shameful tears had blown off his face to sprinkle the concrete.

The only decorations, a framed art print depicting Chicago and a family portrait, were there at his mother's insistence so his room didn't look like a prison cell. The only other adornment was a full-length mirror. He took out his books and studied trying to ignore the dull ache of what he might be missing out on. But it did not work so he turned on the television to let pale light and sound fill his room.

And for a while nothing happened.

The soft tinkle of laughter and his mother's keys dropping on the countertop made him aware that he had been squeezing and releasing himself. Now self-disgust accumulated with the blood. He tucked his shame into his jeans and covered it with a blanket as his mother skipped up the stairs. Channels flashed as he searched for a sitcom. She opened the door without knocking.

"Hello honey."

He did not look at her as the laugh track heehawed in a respectable undertone of hilarity.

"How was your day?"

"Good."

She got up and paced.

"God am I glad to be home."

She passed the television.

"I am starving honey. What do you want for dinner? I was thinking burgers. How does that sound?"

Every time she blocked his view of the stupid show he was annoyed that he had to pretend like she was interrupting his amusement as the laugh tracks hee-hawed. He stared at the screen unable move for fear of exposing himself; surprise mom, your little boy has become a man.

"Maybe some french-fries," she joked with enthusiasm.

He gave no outward response to her optimism but still she insisted upon taking her good humor out on him.

"Are you ok Isaiah?"

He jumped away in revulsion from the soft touch of the back of her hand testing the temperature of his forehead.

"I'm fine."

She sat down on the edge of his bed. He willed innocence to shrink back.

"You look sad."

"I'm just tired."

"Has my poor little baby been working too hard at school?"

She tickled the bottom of his feet. He yanked them away.

"Mom I'm watching TV."

She got up again to pace and purr out words Isaiah ignored. He pretended to follow the plot. He missed the punch line preceding the riotous laugh track. She stopped in an animated pose, partially blocking his view of the screen, to force his attention upon her. Her business suit was wrinkled at the edges from the haste she had unbuttoned and un-tucked it with.

"Mom, couldn't you talk to me during the commercials?"

She decided to protect her good mood by keeping it to herself, and contented herself with grinning unfocused at the television.

"Sure. Grumpy butt. I was starting to wonder if you actually were a teenager. Finally here are those moody tantrums Modern Parenting warned me about. Dinner will be ready in about thirty minutes if you are hungry."

She playfully tossed the pillow at him and it accidentally landed on his crotch.

"Grow up."

At the commercial break he felt guilty and tried to smile as he looked up to talk to her. He hadn't noticed her leave. He flicked his unruliness like smacking himself with a ruler, and the pain went straight to his testicles.

"Mom," he yelled a few minutes later. "Mom."

"What Isaiah?"

"Can you come here?"

She trudged up the stairs muttering, "Oh so now you want to talk to me."

Her black mascara had run around her pale blue eyes, but her cheerful smile made it seem the world's traces would rinse away, the slight puffs and droops would lose their tired marking of age. She had changed into girlish pink sweat pants and t-shirt that refreshed her practical prettiness with renewed vitality.

"What darling?"

He gave his most piteous expression.

"Can you call me off school tomorrow?"

She looked at him not understanding.

"But what about your perfect attendance?"

He didn't have to fake the exhaustion; he didn't have to explain what he also saw in her eyes.

"Honestly I could care less."

"Isaiah you are so close."

"What does a stupid certificate mean? I have already got scholarships for college."

"I don't understand."

"Please just call for me."

"I guess you are almost an adult. Let's go talk to your father."

That was what he had dreaded. It was hard to force himself up and trudge behind her down the steps to face his father. He was glad the television news muffled the bored scrapes of his father's fork on his plate.

"Hello son. Your mother says you are not feeling well. Is everything ok?"

His tone also was upbeat in contrast to how his body and skin drooped in weariness. The sacks underneath his bloodshot eyes made them seem to bulge out of his head towards the television, as if when he had loosened his tie and the top button of his dress shirt the tension and frustration had escaped and rushed to his head, seeping out his eyes and pushing them forward in exhaustion.

"Isaiah asked me if he could call off sick tomorrow."

He looked at him chewing.

"Only if I can call off too."

The heartiness of his dad's laughter belied his exhaustion, and he shared a look with Isaiah, his eyes crinkling in amusement. He straightened up like a warrior come home from the daily battles of common sense, fighting the hordes of barbarians of irrationality, and laughing at the constant conquering routine of the day. Isaiah couldn't help but chuckle along at the insignificance of his own world-weariness.

"Take tomorrow off. You know your sister is going to hold it over on you though. And son."

"Yes."

"We are both very proud of you."

"Thanks dad." Isaiah tried to smile.

THE INNOCENT ANUS

Isaiah's weight caused a dip at the edge of the trampoline. His sister and Maggie chattered between giggles like strange birds beak to beak, their flittering transferred through the trampoline in waves he tried to negate. He cupped his eyes to block the boiling glow from their living room door as he gazed up into the cloudless sky to stare the stars just a million miles out of sight into existence. It was a massaging contrast for his cramped eyes.

"I don't how to explain it, Matt is made of softer lines, harder angles," Rachel said.

"Ok?" Maggie responded.

"He wears so much jewelry I thought he was gay at first. He is in a band."

The dismissive laughter Isaiah expected didn't follow her statement. Rachel had changed. A car sped out of the subdued backbeat of nature, hitting a crescendo at the opening of their long driveway before fading back into the night. His fingertips scraped back and forth across the tight black mesh of the trampoline. He occasionally checked to see if black rubber accumulated beneath his fingernails. But the filed tips remained as translucent as the clipping removed from the waning moon.

"Oh no Rachel. Don't tell me you're becoming a groupie," Maggie said.

"No. If you saw him you would know that isn't true. If I was a groupie it would be the bass player."

The trampoline shifted as Rachel faced him and the wobbling brought him closer to them in the center. She did not shift her veil of prettiness to share their impish smile, instead the green eyed stare from underneath locks of dark hair cascading out of her State baseball cap studied him like he was the dullest of textbooks. A misplaced flake betrayed the thickness of the paint on her face that needed none of the pomp and vanity of makeup. Her summer freckles were still dark but now with a neon orange tint. She was an abstraction of herself.

"You would love it. Campus is lovely. The architecture inspires thought, like old sturdy poetry. You can see it reflected in people's eyes when they walk."

She had already said this rehearsed line at dinner for their parents' approval. He strained his vision up again into the stars. The wobbling from her sharp movements as she waited for him to respond ended well before he even blinked. Pressure built within him. It caused him to shift and face away from them. Maggie finally spoke out of the silence.

"So what is the name of his band?"

The pressure was an irresistible force, its opposite and equal reaction an ingrained law of the universe. He harvested it.

"Pixie dust," Rachel said.

He released the pressure. It was a masterpiece of power and beauty, a loud animal sound wet and forceful, smacking his butt cheeks together in a sloppy rhythm.

"Eww."

They clawed their way to the edge of the trampoline, bouncing him to the center.

"Sprinkle some pixie dust on that."

Rachel may have gone beyond hope. Maggie's rich feminine laughter was always an extension of Rachel, like a hug or a shared mockery of the self-serious world. As a boy at Rachel's sleepovers he would dance in a wig, make kissy faces in red lipstick, whirl in a hula skirt, do anything for Maggie's infections laugh, so Rachel would allow him to hang out a few minutes more. But Rachel was an ice queen now as they laughed, as if in retrospect she had become like the other high school girls in their alien ill humor, the girls who would stare at his euphoria until it sputtered, before changing the subject.

Finally Rachel started to shake, unable to keep it in, and the enchantment faded as amusement took over with violent coughs preceding her laughter. Merriment brought them close together in the center of the trampoline. In the afterglow he was pressed against the meaty femininity of Maggie's leg. She did not pull away. With no one from school there to see he was not embarrassed. Her summers spent in a one-piece bathing suit, she had always looked envious at Rachel in a bikini, but her layer of fat had insulated her adorableness from the cruelties of growing up. Night softened her double chin, and the gentle illumination of porch lights complimented the childlike cuteness of her small upturned nose, and soft mouth puckering out of her chubby cheeks. Her warmth spread into him. Her clean perfume was on the breeze that he breathed deep to cleanse his cilia of the foul scent built up from Goldenwood. On the other side of Maggie, Rachel's movement transferred through the trampoline gave him the sensation of being connected to them both through Maggie's touch, in a private cocoon that protected them from the freeze of outer space and made the starry sky a vast carousel.

He cupped his eyes and strained them anew. More stars became visible, some so dim they disappeared when the film of saline got too thick over his eyes. He blinked them back into existence. He played connect the dots, tracing invisible lines.

"What are you doing dork?" Rachel asked.

He waved his hands back and forth as if conjuring the weightless tone evolved from their many childhood nights.

"Conceiving constellations."

"We are all in the gutter, but some of us are looking up at the stars," Rachel said with a longing stare.

"Quoting your boyfriend?" Isaiah scoffed.

"Oscar Wilde. His favorite writer."

"You're such an English major, just like mom. I hate Mrs. Dronomine's English class. I am going to study the essence of the universe, my mind nuclear exploding with physics, to burn down the cathedrals of academia, all the ceremonial fluff floating down like pillow filling."

"Oh goodness, here you guys go," Maggie said.

"By observing it we make the universe beautiful."

He did not need to see the quizzical look in her eyes to know she was beyond the stars as she thought about some stranger named Matt. If Isaiah played guitar he would sing songs of a brimful of stars. If he were a poet he would speak timeless poetry in a pulsating rhythm, quantum creation of language to mark its beauty. Instead he pointed up at the sky in rebuttal.

"Those stars, they form a rounded hump, and with those stars there they form a buffalo."

"Um, ok," Maggie said.

"See those three stars, part of what some call Orion's belt? They are now the fingers of O'Dorkimus Maximus pointing at the stars," Rachel said.

"And see that cluster right there of four pulsating stars? That is butt-holus maximus discharging a gas cloud."

He turned his butt towards them and let out another monstrous fart.

Like an unwelcome thought a car squealed into their driveway with loose metal rattling from the bass of the radio. It shut off abrupt and the car door slammed closed. The doorbell rang twice in short succession. Moments later their glass door ground open and Barrett bounded towards them.

"Hello, hello, hello."

His earthquake landing on the trampoline bounced Isaiah towards the edge. His poorly concealed stare made Isaiah aware of Rachel's fertile parts. He resented that Barrett made him conscious of the animal conception of their shared biology.

"Hey hot stuff."

Maggie and Isaiah scooted apart.

"Are you drunk?" Maggie asked.

He stared at Rachel proud. "Not really," He lied sheepishly.

"You reek of alcohol Barrett," Rachel said.

He could feel Barrett's lust pumping through the trampoline, and he scooted his genitals away from the tickling vibration of his twitching. His face pressed against the soft mesh of the trampoline where thousands of dirty feet had bounced, and he noticed a hint of dog crap. Barrett's feet near his head made him think of the cesspool accumulation in the restroom at school. He jerked away so his face hung off the edge between two springs. He breathed the lawn's aroma and dangled his hand through the gap to rest his hand on the cool grass. He pressed his fingers down to feel the mammalian comfort of the solidity of the earth. Rachel and he were born out of laughter, conceived in jokes their father told their mother.

"Your brother is getting even weirder since you left Rach'. All he does is study."

"Better than driving around drunk. Really Barrett? You drove over here? Are you an idiot?"

Isaiah grunted and concentrated on weaving three blades of grass.

"Whatever. There is this party. We should stop by for a drink," Barrett's pitch rose as the trampoline lifted Isaiah with his suspended animation. "Everyone wants to know what Rachel Templeton, Goldenwood's untouchable princess, is up to in college."

"Tempting," Rachel said dryly.

"Introducing the bastard child of television's false revolutions," Isaiah said in the loud voice of a boxing announcer.

"See what I am talking about? Weird. Come on. You would be a refreshing presence amongst the skeezy whores."

The trampoline shook with Barrett's yearning.

"Isaiah I have this friend you need to meet when you come to visit me," Rachel said.

Barrett hopped down with another quake and thumped on the ground.

"You are missing out. Come on Isaiah."

Isaiah did not look up.

"Come on, you have nothing better to do."

"Naah I'm cool."

"Bye ladies," Barrett said.

"Don't kill yourself," Rachel said.

Isaiah could almost hear the plastic wrap crinkle as they entered the stately doors of Our Father's House. The festival of formality celebrating his sisters' visit continued Sunday morning with dress up that itched his neck; the Templetons attended church for the first time together since Easter. Rachel walked down the aisle wearing a light blue flower dress. Purplish light refracted through stained glass windows high up in reverent ceilings. The thick wooden beams matched Jesus' cross. Their suburban church was accessorized in mood holiness from a commercial developer's line of pious architecture. God commodified in elegant Tupperware containers, God ten minutes a day for better abs, God to be stored under the bed when not in use.

Jokes about the cult of the mortgage payment were silenced in his throat though. Pastor Joe waited calmly for them to reposition their sanctity forward to eternity, his large nose quivering with his nostrils expanding as if sniffing the mood of his congregation. A smile intensified out of his kind countenance for Rachel. She did not blush as people watched her walk down the aisle in calm elegance. Barrett ignored Isaiah's nod as he stared rigid from between the pleasant looks of his mother and aunts. They all looked at her as a manifestation of the sanctity of the church, a fruition of the virgin vitality the suburban air itself advertised as it blew the rebirth of an Indian summer.

She smiled broader than even that impish smile she shared with him and he stopped scrutinizing her face for signs of insincerity. A delicate mix of their parent's features, their dad's expressive forehead and eyebrows, their mom's delicate skin surrounding her pale green eyes, shone with her own intelligence. He was mesmerized along with the other churchgoers from the wooden pews that lent the prescribed discomfort for somberness.

"Welcome," Pastor Joe said as if he had been waiting for their family.

He started his sermon with a loud voice performing his role with lightheartedness as he read passages from the New Testament. He did not judge the Sunday forgiven their false uncertain allegiances. All irony cut short as an affront in Our Father's House. They were what mockery ridiculed the world for not being. Stares came from the best part of people's imaginations in churchly good behavior, even those sinners pointedly not noticing Rachel could not ignore her. Just as they shared noses and bone structure, he also felt her wholesomeness was mirrored in him for the onlookers. He was aware of Emily's glances. Pastor Joe had the right intensity of fire and brimstone for his suburban flock, smiting the devil boogeyman back to his closet. At his climax Rachel listened with her back stiff.

Pastor Joe stood casually at the bottom of the steps after the service. The sun shone on the church to show off God's bounty. In divine brotherhood his eyes twinkled and his voice had its most fervor as he greeted each family. He shook his father's hand with enthusiasm. Rachel took his hand confidently in the same manner he took hers. He took Isaiah's hand without the vise grip many men used. Last he took his mother's hand.

"How beautiful your daughter has become."

"Thank you."

Rachel joined Emily and Maggie in their flower dresses as three bushes in a Christian garden, and their laughter was as pure as the cold water of their morning routine, nothing like the gravelly mirth of Carrie Ann's brothel girls.

The decorative red brown brick wall at the entrance of their neighborhood welcomed them to Golden Acres. The sun shone on the Promised Land of their manicured neighborhood. Lawnmowers were out in force to combat the sprouting dandelions. There was one aberration, David's house on the corner with a yard full of dandelions. Mr. McCormick's defiance of the civic association incited a riot of conformity. It had caused even the most rebellious purple haired kids of the neighborhood to spray paint 'redneks' on the garage door instead of burning the American flag. The unkempt house may have been forgiven if not for the wilderness of vegetation in the yard. A burst of dandelions was interspersed throughout the thigh-high grasses and weeds. They had reached back to their Paleolithic roots, adapting from low overnight blooming dandelions to dinosaur dandelions rising above the brown tips of the swaying grass. Most were bright yellow in a galaxy of conceptualized sunlight, some were fragile with wispy white seeds, and a few others were just skeletal remains on withered stalks.

SCIENCE EXPERIMENT

He felt no emotion enacting this ritual of youth. There was no melodrama. The control subject was more curious why the chemicals didn't tempt him, even as his friends moaned Fridays leaving school, "I'm going to get fucked up tonight."

Sitting upon his deck the ceiling of clouds made Isaiah's backyard an extension of his house. His parents were exploring Rachel's campus with her. Left to boredom he had thought of this science experiment. He ripped the plastic wrap off the neat little box as innocent as a pack of gum, the surgeon general's warning just a polite suggestion. He pulled a neat little white cylinder out, examining it from tobacco tip to butt. He let the cigarette rest between his lips and stared off into the distance like performance art.

As a child he watched his mom pollute her lungs in horror, imagining them blackening as her vibrant body withered with premature age. He would obsess over the thickness of the blue web of veins spreading across her hands and leading up her arm like ivy slowly strangling her mortality. He had enacted ad campaigns to guilt her into quitting. He had implored his father until he would emotionally plead, 'Claire, don't Claire, we need you.' She had relented to only smoke occasionally for stress relief. But now he was testing the immortality of youth.

His fireplace lighter's large flickering flame was more inspiring than the cigarette he brought it to. After three methodical sucks he tasted the noxious smoke. He didn't take it into his lungs, but still it overwhelmed him as he blew it out. The cloud surrounded him and he blinked away tears. The man who first took flaming leaves and breathed their toxic fumes into his chest should have been lost to evolution. He set the cigarette down. He opened a lukewarm Natural Light with a crack to sniff aluminum and bitter bread bubbles. He brought it to his mouth and took a large gulp, watery and reminding him of a faint whiff of urine. A second gulp he swished around. It tingled. He swallowed and tried to shake off the aftertaste. Smoke rose steadily next to him. He held his breath and poured the rest of the beer directly into his stomach. His whole body convulsed with the fumes and he burped.

He puffed the cigarette to watch the cherry flare, then allowed a little into his lungs. It was like breathing deep too close to a campfire and he was proud to not cough. As the paper browned he imagined himself smoking as a philosophical debate with himself. Each inhalation was mood manifested with an exclamation point of gray ash. Except it hit his lungs like he had sucked down a flamethrowers blast. Wet sloppy coughing brought burnt phlegm up and the smoke he couldn't cough up felt like it was trapped in his stomach. He tried to clear his throat of the taste but the acrid tobacco smoke stuck to his tongue as he spit. He crushed it and pushed the butt down a crack in his deck. His equilibrium shifted with queasiness back and forth. Foggy cataracts muted the sky as he laid back. The light tingling would be almost pleasant if it wasn't for his stomach's unrest.

Tears of discomfort rolled down his face.

He forced himself to sit up even though he wanted to stop before the side effects got more negative. After three more beers he finally got rid of the burning in his throat. He was at least becoming accustomed to the taste. He was not intoxicated, just a little off balance, senses just dulled. Underneath the discomfort warmth spread throughout his body. He wondered if this was his hypothesis. He finished the six-pack and for a while didn't think as he puffed to watch tracers as if they condensed in the clouds.

He swatted violently at a tickle on his neck. On his hand was a faint line of black juice. On the cold wood of the deck a ladybug spun with one wing twitching at the wrong angle, trying to right its crushed body. Guilty, he turned away from its death throes. He flicked the cigarette butt down and stomped out its glow. He used the same foot to twist the ladybug out of its misery. Finally he felt something. In that intensity of feeling he finally may have found the theorem of his youth.

LYING WAS THE EASY PART

Normal was just a slight manipulation of the truth. Even the weather had given up its pleasant manipulation to show its fleeting transcendence. Violent thunderstorms last night overthrew the Indian summer to allow autumn with wet vengeance to again take its rightful hold on October. Sporadic raindrops splat on his windshield to streak in a momentary pattern, erased with each measured swipe of his windshield wipers.

"Does my shirt look ok?" Isaiah asked.

The weather made Barrett more ill tempered than usual at the morning's imposition on the autonomous blur of his mood.

"It looks fine."

"You didn't even look at me. Does it look a little too short and faded from one too many times in the dryer?"

Barrett looked at him angrily.

"You look fine my lady. And by the way if you pull that shit and disappear again like Friday, making me hitch a ride in Simpson's pizza box hatchback, fucking Dominoes sign on the roof, I'm going to kick your ass."

Isaiah did not answer. A man standing in the median startled him. He stood drenched on the grass near the edge of the curb, only soaked jeans and a t-shirt protecting him. As they approached he spread his arms wide and stared at the heavens with a hallelujah pose. Isaiah didn't notice the puddle until it was too late to avoid, sending a sheet of water over him. The filthy water couldn't make him any dirtier but it re-flattened his hair and clothes. He did not move as it streamed down him. In the rearview mirror

Isaiah saw him drop his arms and slump. When another set of headlights approached he again straightened to raise his arms and stare worshipfully at the heavens. A spray of water again drenched him. The car passed and he dropped his arms.

"Did you sneak off to the library you tool?"

Barrett's mockery was a reaffirmation of the dawning distinctions he saw outside his window.

"Did you see that craziness?" Isaiah asked.

"See what asshole?"

The man had disappeared into the mist.

"Nevermind."

Barrett was lost in the well-lit strip mall and the advertisement colored world of CreviceXYouth. Barrett insisted the girls smiled wider for him than the surges of daytime shoppers, all those creepy haired old men and crotchety old ladies perfumed like rotting flowers, nagging about the latest displays of kitsch as their tongues shot out to taste the glow in wage stretched cheeks. But Barrett insisted for him they parted lips glossed in the same day-glow shades as their California vista panties, showing teeth as white as aspirin.

"Want to hear a funny story?" Isaiah asked.

"Can't you see it's the beginning of miserable? The first Monday minutes I hate the most before I am thankfully mind-numbed. I don't get my swell from fitting it tightly in notebook coils, so keep your asphyxia hard on for the library."

The magnitude of Barrett's animosity was ridiculous. Isaiah welcomed the change in the weather, for absent was the pressure of missing out. The first forceful thunderclaps of the cold front had carried the humidity of his moods away. Pleasant again would be his quaint routine. The sky was a giant comforter of clouds to keep his toes warm. They filtered the sunlight in soft illumination, allowing more contrast in the gray sky to outline the fall foliage, the remaining green emanating from the trees in the essence of life, the buildings' concrete had flecks that were the remainders of large mountain stones, and even the dirty leaves rotting in the gutters had brown undertones the eventual color of dirt.

Quivering birds bent along with the vegetation in the face of increasing cold winds. As he drove past a flock took flight from telephone poles.

"So you want to hear a funny story?" Isaiah asked.

"No."

The birds wildly swirled with the wind, dancing in alternating directions in unity, almost crashing inwards before pulsing out to alight on telephone poles.

"So you want to hear a funny story?"

Barrett didn't respond.

"Why I really had to leave class early Friday? It's embarrassing though so don't tell anyone."

Barrett lost focus outside of the window.

"Warm chocolate running down my thighs."

"What?"

"I tried to let out a silent but deadly and instead sharted my pants."

Barrett was unable to suppress a few chuckles.

"You can't tell anyone though. I could barely shuffle down the hallway, to keep any more poop juice from squirting out into my pants."

Barrett started laughing wholeheartedly. "Don't worry," affection returned from the habits of their smoldering friendship, "I don't want anyone to know I hang out with the shit stained superstar."

In the parking lot Barrett stared into cars as he bobbed his head in case anyone was looking.

"Let me out."

Barrett hopped out before Isaiah had completely stopped and jogged in the rain to smokers' corner. Isaiah parked and walked to class under a yellow umbrella bloom, rainwater streaming off the metal spokes to drip on shades that came to close out of the murk. Without umbrellas they splashed puddles to soak themselves in their desperation to reach the refuge of Goldenwood. For a moment he wondered if the man still was making his hallelujah pose on the median then dismissed him as insane. The sheen of the imitation gold spelling Goldenwood High School grew in sight as he walked towards the building, straining his neck for one last view of the sky before it was blocked out. Like a herd of wet rats students stomped and slipped inside the doorway as he closed his aristocratic umbrella, shaking off the excess water and wiping his feet on the royal purple and gold carpets.

In his locker mirror he checked himself out, patting his hair and smoothing wrinkles in his shirt. Getting rid of his contented expression proved more difficult. As he walked he concentrated on a melancholy expression. Failing he mimicked David's expression so it would show—

—like the counselor's bad suit as he smiled with practiced professional sympathy when the receptionist admitted Isaiah into his office.

"How are you doing today?"

It was easy to assume a man with a perfectly groomed goatee and thick gold chains shining around his neck was faking his sympathy. But this was the man who could pardon his lapse in reason, so he did the unnatural thing and returned his soft stare, sharing an intimacy he normally wouldn't with a stranger. Lying was the easy part.

"I'm ok."

His office was a growth of the building, the bookshelves coming out of the wall like outcroppings, the diplomas, the plush chair the adjunct perched upon behind his desk, even his bland expression a further extension. He would trade lie for lie with this institution without feeling a tinge upon his conscience.

"Isaiah, if kids were ok I'd be out of business," his laugh was well formed with perfect annunciation of each ha ha. "So tell me what brings you here today?"

The only thing that seemed to have intelligent life was the tentacle tipped in ink that snaked around the top form of the thick stack on his clipboard.

"Well. I've been sad lately. You know, I've been thinking about Chris with the anniversary and all."

The pen stopped, cocked in place.

"Isaiah, you have to trust me. I can help you better if you give me specific thoughts and feelings. I understand, and I can help you."

If there had ever been a bulge of stress surrounding this man's eyes it had long ago flattened, an anomaly of sincerity that had left flaccid sacks underneath. His dry voice was created by mechanisms with all the characteristics of human parts. Upon closer examination you could see the marbles that were his eyes holding color in the iris.

"I have been having a hard time concentrating in class."

The pen did not budge. He knew he needed to make it move. But the practiced lies had disappeared. He racked the truth for the right lies to tell. But how could he explain to this strange clinical man that he had skipped lunch to sit in a bathroom stall for forty-five minutes neither pooping, jerking off (opinion Dr. Freud?) or doing something else normal like drugs, and that the stink did not bother him, but that during the rest of the day his senses were in a constant state of irritation by less odiferous smells, sounds, the puke yellow light. How could he explain that he had skipped out on class to save a yellow jacket, he had caressed and spoke to vegetation, in a final desperation to feel something, anything, he had walked outside in the full moon's light naked to feel cool air cleansing the pits and cavities of his body.

"I don't know. There is this sadness inside of me. Yesterday I couldn't stop picturing him in the coffin."

The circulated air had its own rustling sound in his office. It blew across Isaiah like all the stagnant smells were stirred up and sucked into the administrative center of the building. He hadn't anticipated actually feeling vulnerable, but the repressed mood again rose in a black bilge. It responded from its dense core inside him to fill the bland vacuum this man was enthroned in. He wanted to release it in a torrent of angry discourse to roll his marbles and see if they moved like a real person's. Like a bomb it would explode in these catacombs to butcher the tentacle appendage of the pen off the bone, a sixth digit rattling as the hand was left naked in clutching judgment, his marbles rolling like broken toys.

"Worms eating his flesh in the ground, seeping into the dirt."

His pen moved now. Isaiah tried to regain his composure, uncertain if this had been enough. But Mr. Myosis nodded enthusiastically for him to continue. Isaiah could not resist the laugh that came unabated as if he was really in an emotional state, and he tried to cover his smile with a false grimace.

"Death just entropy."

"Entropy?"

"The end of the universe."

The resulting chicken scratch did not seem to admire his depth.

"Have you ever been told Isaiah," again he said his name in the businessman's tone of creating false intimacies. "That there are levels of grief, and the anniversary may have temporarily put you back to the first level. Do you remember how you dealt with the grief?"

"I went to the funeral."

The counselor laughed off his frustration.

"Yes. But Isaiah, we need to explore how you felt, and how you dealt with those emotions."

He had been able to squeeze out a few tears. He had sat with his parents in the communal sadness in the back of the church studying Chris. He had the same peaceful look in the coffin as when he disappeared into the background. He looked as if once buried he would open the coffin door and walk right into heaven. Isaiah had been annoyed at David McCormick weeping uncontrollably. David hadn't cried at his own mother's funeral in middle school. He had invited Isaiah over the very next weekend. Isaiah had gone over with dread, certain his hallmark sentiments would be exposed, expecting darkness, the trashcan overflowing, Mr. McCormick gaunt, unshaven, and tearful with hallowed eyes, mourning at his wife's shrine between swigs from a bottle of whiskey. But Mr. McCormick had greeted him as usual with reserved politeness and a gruff how are you doing. The absence of Mrs. McCormick's rasping laugh that sometimes led to a couple of muffled coughs could have been explained as if she had just stepped out to the grocery. David had come down the stairs football in hand and they had gone out to play. For months afterwards he had expected him to break down, with small feminine sobs at first, but it had never come: Until Chris's funeral.

"I broke down."

He described David's act as if it were his own, the uncontrollable sobs that filled the church, the wails to God, everyone watching as he lost control in a torrent of tears, the things that Isaiah had watched in discomfort.

"I felt so confused."

As he finished a parallel torrent of words filled the clipboard. He emphatically dotted a period and looked back up contented.

"Isaiah, things have no reasons sometimes. Isaiah, what Chris did, it is impossible for us to understand the reasons why. All we can do is work on how it makes you feel," he cooed.

Isaiah looked at the framed diplomas on the wall, at the books on the shelves, anywhere but in the eyes of this man who designated truths for both of them out of their combined phoniness, lest his irritation disrupt his sad façade.

"Do you feel guilt?"

"What?"

"Do you feel guilt?"

He knew what the silence was doing to Chris. He had often seen him trapped in a bout of social awkwardness. Isaiah had seen him close off until it seemed he might suffocate, pale faced, his whole body shaking as he tried to stammer out the words. He had seen him try to avoid unforgiving eyes reminding him that he was a freak, reminding him of his constant painful communication with the world. Isaiah knew this was how he looked now on the other side of the phone receiver, still he let his self-consciousness intensify. He heard his discomfort grow with every breath undulating through the line. Isaiah paged through his football offensive playbook with the phone held in place by his chin. The silence grew as heavy as eternity.

Chris finally stammered out a broken attempt to continue.

"Well...Well...I...I, I um."

Isaiah's pulling away was deliberate, just a part of the natural way of the world as they grew toward high school. David had gotten the point from Isaiah avoiding and ignoring them in the hallway until each passing was an uncomfortable moment. Now he had to ignore Chris's quavering voice begging him to end the torturous moment, brutal enough to sever the ties of friendship. He remained silent.

"I was just wondering if you wanted to hang out," he said all at once in a sudden burst of courage, still his SOS was quiet and hard to understand.

Isaiah paused to parenthesize his comments in the unease.

"Ah man, I wish I could," he had been having trouble achieving the detached monotone of his new group's superiority of boredom, but Chris was the yin to the yang of his confidence, and he perfected a detached baritone as he continued. "But I am so busy, you know how it goes, with football practice and honor classes, but I'll call you guys sometime soon when I have some free time."

If Chris's eyes had opened in the coffin they would not be looking through demure long lashes at Isaiah with joy. Contempt would sear thought the fog of his shyness like the noon sun at the equator. To bring a doe eyed creature beyond fear and make it contemptuous you had to do more than hunt it, you had to trap it and make target practice out of its hope of freedom.

"No. He slit his own wrists, bled to death."

Mr. Myosis's goatee widened with the tips of his smile. His pen flourished large hurried letters across his page.

"Good, good, one of the steps is anger. Have you ever considered suicide Isaiah?"

"No."

"It is ok to be honest with me about things like this."

"Yes honestly," Isaiah couldn't help his derision. "I'm happy. I have good grades, I have my pick of colleges, I have lots of friends, and I love my family. Life is good. That is why it makes me so sad for Chris."

"Good. Good. Well Isaiah I have another student I need to speak to. I want to set up an appointment to see you again in the next week so we can talk further and I can help you with the grief. See the receptionist to set up a time."

"There is one more thing."

"Yes."

"Could I get an excuse?"

"Of course, of course, I have already written out the form for you."

"Thanks. But…well, this is kind of embarrassing, but Friday for a few periods I just couldn't take it, and I spent the last few periods in the bathroom crying. I was wondering if you could write me an excuse."

"Of course, of course, but next time you feel that way I want you to come see me immediately. I am here to help you Isaiah."

As Isaiah waited for Mr. Myosis to sign the excuse for him he could not help a residual chaos. He had achieved his pardon but still who amongst them had been sick in a room like this with real tears? How many more had suffered endlessly in these hallways unwilling to be anesthetized, how many had finally crashed into this room with the emotion a maelstrom sending them into the anarchy of their own minds. At night they sat alone in their bedrooms as the television stations switched ever faster in madness. Mr. Myosis had read about it some casual evening. Who signed off on that?

"Like I said, if kids were ok I'd be out of business."

Isaiah was able to fake a chuckle until he was in the hallway. He looked forward to the boredom of class as he walked back with his pardon towards normalcy.

SOBER AS THE LIVING ROOM FURNITURE

What was wrong with him? No wonder his friends hadn't thought to pass Isaiah the flask as they had huddled together and drew warmth. The cold had seeped into him from the metal bleachers. He had planned a nonchalant swig but Barrett had never offered the flask. The football had went up into the lights end over end, white spots in his eyes as he followed the trajectory, and at some point when it landed he hadn't found himself roaring along with the crowd. Instead like a stranger he had scanned the faces pink and red in the cold, gloved hands holding hot dogs and hot chocolate, their breath steaming like the tops of the Styrofoam cups. He missed those long green yards between the shining white lines, and he had desired to run under the lights.

He had commiserated with Willow Valley's meek outnumbered fans. Their team's scuffed silver helmets had not shined as bright under the lights. And when the Goldenwood side had grown silent he had known there was something wrong with him for inwardly rooting along as the opposing bleachers started to rumble, until their cheering had increased and seemed to push their team down the field. Offensive lineman had collided into Lumpy, and he had leaned into them exhausted with his upper body as they drove him backwards and onto his ass. After every play he had gotten up slow, breathing hard, his hands on his sides. Isaiah had hidden the abomination of joy he shared with these enemy strangers as they erupted with their conquering touchdown. He was unpatriotic. He had pretended to hang his head with his dejected peers, but he had secretly savored the solemnity of their faces. As they had walked out disappointed he felt the strongest bond he had in devotion to them. There had been honesty in their unhappiness. The cheerleaders had been in glumness prettier than they ever had been doing their rehearsed butt wiggles with big fake smiles.

That was why he sat here now as sober as the living room furniture, not as significant as the muted MTV, with no choice but to overhear the dueling tittie jokes in the other room. As if they could sense his betrayal, no one had offered him a beer.

Barrett stumbled around the corner with Carrie Ann's load on one arm, Stephanie on the other. The clear vodka swished in the plastic as he showed off with a gulp. He tried to hide the grimace as it went down, then wiped his mouth off and forced out a burp as he leaned down close to Isaiah.

"How you doing buddy?"

Isaiah shied away from the rubbing alcohol smell. Still if he offered the bottle Isaiah would take a swallow for the shock it would cause Barrett. But he passed it to Carrie Ann's chest instead.

"Isaiah here is sober as a nun at an orgy. He is straight edge as a robot's dildo."

Carrie Ann's breasts lost their power when she laughed mouth agape in a chemical sheen of contentment. The alcohol brought out the fullness of the mockery she did not try to hide, but it also exposed in its red blush the zits she concealed with her makeup. Barrett was a loudspeaker constantly announcing how drunk he was.

"Let us escape this sad scene and get schloppy," Barrett said.

Like an idiot Barrett's voice warbled without the ability to control his volume. Still he had saved them from the mundane. He spun the laughing girls back into the other room to leave Isaiah sitting in this bored domestic scene alone with the television. No matter how dumb they looked to him, no matter how moronic Wadsworth's laughter sounded, their drunken euphoria distracted them from the bored frustration of Goldenwood. They no longer complained about the game they lost. Lumpy had stopped his repeated complaints about the refs not calling holding, pulling at his sweater so hard it stretched his collar. Gone was Aaron's somber sarcasm.

"Keep your heads up boys."

Their laughter filled the room with sickly sweet fumes. The scene on the muted television was not much different. He felt the cold judgment of a camera lens marking him irrelevant in the corner.

"Oh I love this show."

"Isaiah! You heard the slut. Make yourself useful and turn the music up.

Barrett put that fucking cigarette out," Lumpy yelled.

"Quit the rebellious act. Everyone knows your parents don't care as long as the house is clean when they get back."

On the spring break television show the camera focused on a girl's bosom. A shirtless man with no rhythm danced like a chimpanzee fantasizing and defiling himself in training for propagation of the species. Commercials were indistinguishable. Stimulate, repeat, exotic waterfalls streaming down the soft weight popping out of a bikini. Stimulate, repeat, even his loins lost their enthusiasm. In the dining room the noise intensified. Joke. Laugh. Brag. Sarcasm. On the television the girls, girls, girls, danced with gravity and each other, bounce, girls, girls, girls, they came in from the dining room to dance amped up on alcohol and MTV, girls, girls, girls. Even without their cheerleading uniforms Crystal and Tammy were all enthusiasm, and their thin lip smiles alternated with pouts of puffed up pink. Angela led in the nicotine queens, sophomore girls showing flesh as their invitation to the party, dancing around the television as they chain smoked. The noxious cloud would have made him leave if it wasn't for Angela. He pretended to watch the television as her athletic hips rolled the curves of her waist. She dipped her shoulders, and pressed her petite chest out.

At the end of the song she impulsively sat down next to him in a cloud. Unlike her friends the taboo cloud surrounding her was seductive. Isaiah remembered his science experiment, and almost had the courage to ask her for a cigarette. But instead he looked at the pictures on the wall. He was poaching memories he wasn't invited to. Her perfume was stronger in the flush of sweat, mixing with the alcohol on her breath, and the exhaled smoke that he breathed in when she leaned in to speak to him.

"Hello."

"Hello," He mumbled like a braying donkey.

She stuck her cigarette in her mouth and offered her small hand. Her skin was delicate. Her mouth pursed like a woman's when she sucked, the cherry flaring up precise.

"I'm Angela," As if every boy in Goldenwood didn't know her seductive laugh.

"I'm Isaiah."

She scooted closer and took her hand back to hold the cigarette between two fingers. Her hands were the only part of her that betrayed her age, the cigarette looked unnatural in her small fingers with chipped polish on her long nails. The beer looked like it would slip through her childlike hand.

"Nice to meet you Isaiah."

She put a hand on his shoulder and giggled fresh beer breath. Her shorts rode up her inner thigh.

"Nice to meet you."

Globs of kindness saturated him from her eyes that were not those of a sinner.

"Having fun?" She asked.

He scooted closer.

"Yeah. It is…"

Her gaze pulled him towards her. But his wit had nothing to excite her laughter. So he just stared back at her.

"Angela, get your snatch in here to play asshole," Lumpy yelled.

She stood up. Her hand ran up Isaiah's neck, small fingertips brushing the side of his face to pinch his earlobe. Then she exhaled a kiss and turned. He wished her supple dancers body would lose its choreographing and crash back down onto him. Instead she stumbled into the dining room. She laughed with her beer raised and stared at the ceiling as she gulped. Then again she lurched around the room bumping from one boy to another, rubbing her hands up jeans and grinding against the fabric as if the boys underneath were just props. When she stopped she shared a smile with Isaiah's longing.

Lumpy put his wax colored arm around her and sat her down next to him. His shirt rode up to show his pale armpit sickly in contrast with the healthy flush of her face, a clump of deodorant in his wiry black armpit hair attached one of her shiny brown locks. The card game Asshole started with cursing cadence. Lumpy counted on his fingers as he made Angela chug her beer. Not even Angela noticed Isaiah walk into the dining room, into the brightness like a movie scene where he didn't exist. The confidence of their loud drunkenness was intimidating even in its stupidity. Barrett's face was flushed and his goofy grin still aimed at Carrie Ann's bounty. Wadsworth swayed to stare intently at his cards, then straightened up and leaned forward as they started to chant.

Isaiah walked outside. He inhaled hard to chase away the smoky residue. The music and laugher was muffled, and he watched through the window as they hunched over clenched beers. They looked small and scared, youth masquerading in their insecurities as they huddled towards each other afraid of the outside world. Past Lumpy's full driveway the streetlights became further dots beckoning the more alluring charms of the evening. When he looked up at the sky he muttered.

"Fucking awesome."

He stood up astonished. He walked down the porch, out into Lumpy's front yard so his trees would block the light of the house, staring up at the sky. Around the moon there was a luminescent ring of light. There was night sky in between it and the moon but even where it dimmed it was still a little brighter than the surrounding skies. Dumbfounded, he said fucking awesome again like his words were being stenographed. What a sheltered existence he led that upon seeing this all he could do was curse. He had never seen anything like it, did not know its explanation. The ring looked like the end of a giant tunnel through space that opened in the sky above him, the ethereal light leading into the distance of space until it reached the moon. He remembered his dream, and for a while he waited to be transposed.

Eventually he walked back inside. Filled with new confidence, he looked for Angela, ready to be the confident older guy, ready to take control and drag her outside to smoke a cigarette staring at this phenomenon surrounding moon.

"Has anyone seen Barrett?"

English sat alone smoking at the table covered with scattered clouds. Small groups were dispersed around the house talking. He shrugged his shoulders and took a swallow from his flask. Contentment had filled the lifelessness in his bloodshot eyes.

"I think he went upstairs."

Isaiah walked upstairs.

"Barrett?"

He heard something from Lumpy's parent's bedroom door. He knocked.

"Can we have some fucking privacy?" Lumpy's voice came from the muffled noises of the bedroom.

He left without Barrett and drove home staring up at the tunnel in the sky.

QUANTUM IRRITANT

Mr. Quinn spread his arms out wide. It was not a call to attention. Just showing he had something to say silenced their side contemplations and laughter. His honor physics class was full of students tucked in from their socks to the parts of their hair, ponytails, or Kurt's perfectly measured afro.

"I could write it down like this."

He took the chalk and scribbled the beginnings of an equation on the chalkboard. Isaiah copied along as if each desperate symbol created equilibrium. Then Mr. Quinn stopped halfway and pulled his beard like a gnome.

"But I already put this equation on your ditto. Let me show you something."

With a wide grin he pulled down on a spring that he had set up on a hook stand on his desk. He puckered his mouth into a fattened circle in his wizard beard and raised his eyebrows.

"Boing."

He let go of the spring as he made the humorous sound.

"Oscillation."

He pulled it down again.

"Boing."

His lab partner Tim laughed with the quiet hum of the spring. It was a slight sound that slowed down with the vibrations. Tim's head lulled like Pluto in ellipses of gravitational force. The pattern on his shirt was proof that his mind worked on a different frequency, garbed in logic and angles.

Mr. Quinn was pleased with their laughter.

"Just releasing some kinetic energy."

Class was almost over but Isaiah did not want to leave this other dimension. Their clusters of thought comforted him with each measuring heartbeat.

"Last, as always, I offer you one thing to ponder this evening."

Mr. Quinn paused as he looked out at them.

"Well actually why don't you guys tell me something we can ponder."

Isaiah raised his hand before he thought of anything to say.

"Yes Isaiah."

"Vibration."

Tim, the smartest kid he knew, looked at him with clear eyes that had algorithms in the odd green confluence. Isaiah looked at Mr. Quinn. He wanted to impress them.

"Like the spring, vibrating, I was thinking about wormholes vibrating. You know, like wrinkles in time. Where do they intersect?"

Tim looked at him as they all waited for him to explain.

"What I mean, isn't the past, those who died before their time in this dimension, those ghosts in our memories, aren't they real in more than a philosophical sense in other potential realities. In a sense aren't we all immortal?"

He watched Mr. Quinn hoping for magic. He hadn't meant to speak of Chris in this untold dimension. He didn't know where the words had come from. He looked to Tim's blank expression, desperate to see pondering materialize in their faces. If they could answer, these misappropriated days would shimmer, Chris's face would materialize in Isaiah's memories, and they would look out together upon a new horizon with wonder.

"Goodness son, I wish I had an answer for that. I really do."

Mr. Quinn spoke with empathy, but what touched Isaiah was the thoughtful expression he gave to his questions. The bell rang and he pulled his beard in consternation.

"Sorry for the rude interruption Isaiah. That is a tough one. Is it a thing that science can even answer? Where do we intersect?"

The quantum irritant continued its monotone as they gathered their things to leave. In the hallway Isaiah muttered to himself.

"Entropy is life slowly dripping out a fifteen year old's veins."

SWALLOWING SCORPIONS

Isaiah swallowed another scorpion. Holding his breath, the vodka slithered down his throat long past when he thought it should be gone. He clenched his stomach as the fumes racked his body to keep from retching the poison back up. He raised his head and howled as the burn filled him.

"OoooooooooooouuuU."

"Yee haw!"

Barrett tipped the cap of his cowboy hat at Isaiah. Its curves made his face more angular over his red bandana. The symbolic first crack of aluminum had been lost in the euphoria of the party. He had clutched his beer and drank with them at the beginning of every sentence, but only when he howled after taking the second shot had they finally noticed him drinking. Barrett wrapped his arm around his shoulders.

"Holy shit."

"Holy shit," Isaiah responded.

Barrett bicep, bared in his sleeveless flannel vest, pulled Isaiah's head into the crook of his armpit. The can of Copenhagen bulged in the front pocket of his jeans like a hockey puck and dug into Isaiah.

"Yee fucking haw partner."

Weekends would all now be like holidays in their longed for contrast. He celebrated Halloween's anomaly with childlike excitement, meticulously made up like a werewolf with fake hair sprouting from his face and chest. Tonight the typical masquerade had transformed, ghouls, devils, and demons screamed curse words and drank with animal sneers as if their inner ugliness finally had a chance to leap out with rage.

"OoooooouuuuuuuuuUeeE."

He paced amongst them the big bad wolf all snout, sniffing at angels, witches, she-devils, cats; perfume aromatized the bloom of flesh. The pleasant tingle in went all the way to his hungry palate, desiring a lick straight from the base of his loins. Carrie Ann's outfit of course stood out, her body wrapped in a red sheen of material like cellophane, her bosom pressed out like cream filling. But never before had he noticed Stephanie's breasts were even larger. Her identical haircut and makeup hid fewer blemishes. Maybe because the angles of her square face didn't elicit the same progression down, or that her waist and thighs were thicker, were the reasons she wasn't obsessed over like her friend; but at the moment nothing mattered but the way she arched her back towards him as she stared from underneath her nurse's mask.

"Ready for another one Greggy?"

Isaiah turned to the king of the damned. Fog narrowed his scope of vision. Lumpy leered at him from behind his plastic Tommy gun in a three-piece gangster suit, surrounded by bottles in a makeshift bar at the end of his dining room table. Isaiah poured them shots without averting his eyes, expressionless as a mirror so Lumpy's inhospitality would reflect. He swished the vodka around in the water glass. This wellspring was no longer unknown to him.

"Such a wonderful year my dear Lumps."

Isaiah was a charming gentleman with brilliance unimpeded. He put his nose to the rim of the glass and pretended to sniff.

"Just drink, drunken ass," Lumpy said.

Isaiah raised his glass high. Lumpy's pupils became turds squeezed between suspicious ass cheek eyelids.

"To mother Russia," Isaiah said.

He tensed his abs when it hit.

"Oooooooouuuuuuuuu!"

Lumpy pulled Angela away from her sophomore date.

"Enough of this mano-e-gayo bonding. Let's get these sluts drunk."

Isaiah sipped beer to settle his stomach. He turned around, using Barrett's shoulder to steady himself.

"Isaiah, you better not puke in my bathroom," Lumpy said.

He was concentrating too much on his balance, swerving with every Frankenstein step, to respond. He made it to the bathroom and closed the door. He anchored himself and managed to pee mostly in the toilet. He turned the water on, and with an effort to not fall in to the sink, he brought his heavy head down to put his face underneath the flow. He gulped, trying to force the liquor down. When he could drink no more he let the water run over his tongue. Those pud-pinchers were not going to make him puke. When he stood the liquid swished like he had a fish bowl in his stomach. Blemishes looked theatrically large where the makeup had washed off his chin. His red lined reflection had a film over his swollen eyes and his features were inelegant. He blended makeup from the rest of his face back on his chin. It was easier to walk straight as he went back to a corner to stand contented. Small sips of beer wet his mouth. Voices came in snippets of conversation.

"Stop… cold empty days… she gave me a B… sideburns, preppy cut, so hot…. stop."

The dining room seemed larger. He didn't recall all these people being here. Underneath the jumble of costumes their flushed faces had an abnormal transparency. He was captivated especially by Barrett's rare expression. The well-known tip of his bold nose was the only thing not prostrate, as the rest of him plead for gentleness from Carrie Ann's devilish grin.

"Stop…take another shot…annoying dude…I'm drunk…stop."

He grabbed a chair and sat down beside them. The discomfort caused by Carrie Ann's stare was delayed until he had already transfixed her with pet hate.

"Carrie, Carrie, carry me away to hell you hot little devil."

He took advantage of Barrett's uncertainty and felt him stiffen as he put his arm around him.

"Didn't mean to interrupt you kids." He was a wild creature confident and following instinct. "Stephanie. How are you sexy?"

Stephanie's surgical mask left all the surprise in her eyes and she looked away.

"Have we ever even had a conversation?"

She giggled.

"You would think I'm intimidated by your or something."

She giggled.

"You are in Karen's class with me weren't you?"

She giggled.

"Who would ever think you would grow up to be such a hot nurse."

She giggled. But over the surgical mask she no longer feigned shyness. Carrie Ann's forceful grab pulled Stephanie up by the arm and dragger her towards the kitchen.

"Follow me boys."

They followed her into the kitchen.

"Wait right here."

They went up the stairs. Left alone Barrett and he sought goodwill through the wobble of their heads.

"This is awesome. I'm glad you finally got cool."

"Screw being a teetotaler," Isaiah said with mock solemnity.

Carrie Ann's footsteps interrupted their laughter. Out of her purse she pulled a bottle of Aftershock.

"Ok ladies, time to drink like real women," she said.

She poured four shots into glasses and handed them out. Stephanie took her mask off.

"Cheers."

He had become numb to the fumes but the syrupy sweetness hit his stomach like a sludge of rotten fruit. Carrie and Barrett shared their first dance, she squealed and waved her hands, and he imitated her. She ended up in his arms leaning on his chest. Stephanie scowled at the half shot left in her glass then forced herself to finish it.

"I mean come on, Lumpy, if you want to get sluts drunk, you use Popov only if you are trying to take advantage of little girls."

Carrie Ann's spectators laughed and for once Isaiah didn't hesitate to join in. Stephanie looked at Carrie Ann's hand making mock masturbation movements, then the blender, a wooden spoon, and refrigerator magnets, anything but Isaiah. He moved closer and lost his balance as his vision shifted. It forced him to put his arm around her sooner than he had planned. She stiffened. But he couldn't pull away from the uncomfortable embrace. Only when he regained his balance did he sway the other direction to lean against the refrigerator to keep from falling. Barrett was staring deep into Carrie Ann's nipples as she talked so neither one of them had noticed.

"Carrie, I need to use the bathroom."

Stephanie took Carrie Ann's hand and pulled her away from Barrett towards the bathroom.

"Hurry back ladies."

Isaiah walked back into the dining room.

"Stop…Casper the dog…is everything a song lyric to you…stop."

"Do it you slut," a girl he didn't recognize under her makeup screeched at her friend. Her friend took the shot.

"Would you think I was funny if you were sober?" Someone asked.

Lumpy handed him a shot.

"Hoss get that bitch off your lap and drink with us," Lumpy said.

"You guys are crazy," Hoss answered.

He laughed his booming baritone but the flash of his eyes had no amusement. He resumed very politely staring into the mouth of a witch on his lap.

"Barrett get over here. It's twelve," Lumpy screamed

Isaiah put his arm around Barrett thankful for the help standing.

English started singing. "Happy birthday dear devil, happy birthday to you, happy birthday dear—" The crowd slurred their screams. "Fagot. Pussy. Shitface. Cocksucker. Daddy." English finished. "Devil. Happy birthday to you."

Howling laughter filled the house then quieted as they drank. The shot roused the poison already digesting and convulsions shook Isaiah in a dance. He felt connected to them all linked together. He wasn't sure what he laughed at. He laughed harder. He laughed at nothing. Then he pulled away to stand erect.

"I'm wasted."

He stared at the maudlin flesh surrounding him.

"Boobies."

He laughed at that for a long time. He no longer could stand. He laughed as he lurched to the living room. He laughed as he stumbled and hugged Aaron's back. He laughed at Aaron's inability to hide the red glow on his face that ruined his blank condescension. He laughed as he sat heavy on the lazy boy.

His equilibrium spun like a compass tip drove mad by a magnetic storm. Soon everything spun as if he were the fixed point of the universe. He eyed the remote control and for a moment had faith. Then he cursed the heavens, for although the laws of gravity seemed to be shifting, his drunkenness had not blessed him with Jedi mind powers. He closed his eyes to harness the power of the spinning universe and tried to will the remote to his hand, but it was bound by the gravity of the spinning orb. Softly pulled down he was tempted to disappear easy into the blackness. With great effort he kept his eyes open. He wiped the drool from his face and strained to heave unbalanced on one leg and grab the remote. He fell back and had to fight off the fumes again. When they dissipated he pressed the power button with a sense of accomplishment.

Screams in the living room disrupted him. The door slammed open and he saw through the window Wadsworth's skinny butt wobbling as he ran squealing naked around Lumpy's house. His head bobbed on his skinny neck as his bird legs pumped. His pale white butt was the last thing to be lost in the darkness.

The chair creaked and he looked up confused at the apparition of Stephanie sitting on the arm.

"Mind if I sit with you?"

"No."

"Do you have a smoke?"

He didn't think to light her cigarette for her until they were already smoking.

She repositioned to his lap and put the ashtray on her lap. They smoked as on the television a tentative gazelle leaned towards a river and stuck its tongue out. There was an unappealing nicotine stain in between Stephanie's two front teeth. He put his cigarette out prematurely. She leaned over him to put her cigarette out in the ashtray on the coffee table. Her breasts didn't give rise to his earlier stimulation. Instead he assessed how the fat felt underneath her bra. With curiosity he noticed the pink edge of her nipple as large as a CD.

Then her lips were on his. His mouth was closed to the shock at first, but her tongue forced its way in. He felt only slobbery wetness as her tongue sought his. Acid from the burnt tobacco and beer were in her saliva. He tried to follow her tongue's pattern but it kept changing. He was unable to appreciate her pillowed against him as he concentrated on avoiding her teeth. The chair leg snapped up as her tongue went deeper and she spread slobber on his face. The alcohol in his blood responded to her arms around him as she pressed against him. He could taste the metabolized alcohol boiling in the back of her throat.

"Holy virgin balls. Guys, check this out!"

At first he thought the voice was coming from the television. He was lost in the animal mechanics until she pulled away.

"Virgin boy is getting some ass."

Lumpy leered over them. She got up and pushed past him out of the room.

"Way to go pimp!"

Barrett jumped on his lap with disregard for his erection.

MAGGIE'S HUMILIATION

Lumpy smiled in the full glory of his wickedness.

"By the way, have I mentioned you sir are the most foul human being I have ever met?" Barrett said.

"You really peed in her mouth?" Aaron asked.

Lumpy laughed in satisfaction at their incredulous stares around the lunch table. His chin pressed down into his fat gobble neck.

"She is so dumb she thought I was cumming for the first few seconds."

"Until she threw up," Wadsworth said.

"You are a sick bastard," Hoss said.

"Whatever. She was so drunk she won't even remember."

"Why waste a perfectly good blowjob?" Wadsworth asked.

"I really had to pee. She's so dumb she'll do it again. And it felt amazing releasing it. How many guys can say they've actually pissed in a girl's mouth?"

Isaiah hid his disgust and tried to change the subject.

"So what do you think the neighbors thought seeing Wadsworth's white ass freak show running squealing around Lumpy's house?"

"Lumpy your cruelty sometimes doesn't even make any sense," Aaron continued, ignoring Isaiah.

"Aaron, your face still looks red from the vodka," Isaiah said.

"So does your pussy," Aaron said.

"Virgin boy is getting cocky now that he actually kissed a girl," Wadsworth said.

Isaiah wanted to hang him upside down and play tetherball with his head spinning around on his stringy neck.

"Right, like any girl wants you."

Lumpy raised his hand like a father silencing quarrelling children.

"Speaking of girls wanting someone. I have to tell you guys about this shit," Lumpy's eager maw exposed yellowed teeth. "Maggie Monroe right? She put a fucking love letter in my locker this morning."

Isaiah cringed at the thought of Maggie having nervous little heartbeats for Lumpy.

"Maggie? I thought she had a crush on you Isaiah," Barrett said.

"Like she has a chance."

"Shut the fuck up and listen."

Lumpy took the note out from his pocket. It was smudged and dirty at the corners. He unfolded it and showed them the big bubble letters with hearts dotting every *i* before starting to read.

"Dear Greg. I know you probably don't know who I am, but I am in your English class. I would have never had the guts to write this letter, but I lost a bet with my friends, so I just wanted to tell you I have a crush on you," Lumpy paused to chuckle. "I think you're hot," he wheezed. "I would love to hang out sometime. I know you probably don't, but if you do, that would be awesome. If not please discard this and forget about it, please don't tell anyone. Maggie Monroe. 5th period. She even," he could hardly contain his laughter. "Wrote little hearts," his laughter erupted. "All around her name."

"What the hell was she thinking? She couldn't have picked a bigger group of pricks," Barrett said.

"Frank, she has been trying to pretend she isn't looking at me all lunch period from over in that back corner."

Frank, like a good little henchman, went over to Maggie's table and after a minute of discussion came back with Maggie meekly following. Her chubby cheeks blushed with cuteness, but her potbelly pressed out well beyond the two small breasts so she looked like a stretched out eighth grader. She waved at Isaiah then looked away as she stood awkwardly.

"Hey Maggie. How are you?" Lumpy's voice reeked of kindness.

Her makeup was like a ridiculous baby doll and her designer jeans fit like a teacher's, strangling a fat roll above her waist so it puffed out around her zipper. With a nervous smile she stared pleadingly a little below Lumpy's eyes.

"Hello."

"Dickhead, offer the lady a seat," Lumpy said.

She flinched as Frank grabbed an empty chair and slid it to her with a loud grind. She hesitantly sat on its edge. Frank scooted behind her. Lumpy leaned towards her.

"Did you start our paper yet?"

"Yeah, I have written one draft."

"Really? I haven't even started yet. Do you want to write it for me?"

Her face paled and Isaiah hoped she was going to get up and walk away. He willed her to look at him, walk away, walk away, and read the warning in his eyes. But she giggled as if she was in on the joke.

"I can help you if you want."

"Naah. I just want you to write it for me."

She continued giggling. He leaned in even closer.

"No, I'm serious. Will you write it for me?"

"We could get in trouble."

"Don't be a wimp. Guys don't like wimpy girls."

Gently he rested his hand on her shoulder. She did not cringe, but instead sat up straight in a posture of feigned confidence that caught Lumpy off guard. But if anything it would just make him humiliate her even more viscously. Tenderly he continued.

"I'm just joking babe. Since you won't write my paper for me I have another question."

Lumpy pretended to be nervous, looking away as if gathering the courage to ask something. Maggie waited trapped.

"Do you," he looked around the table and his lumps rose. "Maggie, do you," he held it, pretending shyness, held it longer, then burst out, "do you believe in douching?"

Her smile faded.

"Do you douche? You know, wash your vagina?"

Lumpy brought his face close enough to whisper in her ear. "Because when I'm eating pussy it has to be clean. And fat girls especially have to watch the smell," he finished loud enough for the tables around them to turn to stare.

She sat rigid. Lumpy did not laugh, not when Frank started to wail laughter behind her, when Bean and Wadsworth pointed at her, or when Barrett shook his head and laughed incredulously. Hoss hid his face with his hands then stared at Lumpy.

"Wow you are a monster."

Lumpy kept his face close to her ear like a gargoyle. Barrett looked at Isaiah uncomfortable as he chuckled. Betrayed by a genetic pack instinct, or cowardice, brain synapses fired pleasure to reward Isaiah's survival instinct. And that was when Maggie looked at him again. She calmly stood and pushed her chair in. She quivered but surprised Isaiah by being strong enough to hold her sobs in as she squeezed around Frank behind her laughing hysterically. But of course she tripped and almost fell. Finally Lumpy roared out laughter. Sprinting past her table into the woman's restroom she startled her friends who were pretending not to watch. Emily turned towards them with blonde hair shaping pretty disgust aimed directly at Isaiah. He could not repress his smile quick enough as her eyes caught his unflinchingly. She got up and followed Maggie into the bathroom.

"I am changing my bet to Maggie Pooch Pouch Monroe," Aaron said.

SANCTUARY DEFILED

His sanctuary was defiled. Isaiah had hidden in the bathroom stall today because after yesterday's humiliation of Maggie he could not bear being at his lunch table. But shuffling footsteps had invaded the quiet of the isolated hallway as if a fruition of the dark mood. Now heavy panting invaded his sanctuary and echoed like added layers thickening upon the cement blocks around him. Every swish of the pants seemed to stir up the eau de toilette to overwhelm the bleach masking it. The stench filled his fear sharpened nose with every wide nostril inhalation. The cheap leather shoes sown together in meaty slabs visible underneath the stall could only belong to a teacher. If he had been doing something more normal like drugs he would have walked out with a hint of a sneer. But he was humiliated hiding here on the toilet. Normalcy was a hard illusion to keep when you had just spent thirty minutes in a bathroom stall with your pants around your ankles. An imagined eye peered at him through the crack. He shielded himself with his physics book. He read the new scribbles were on the stall wall.

Freak. Wierdo. Your mom gives the best bone'n'moan this side of the whorehouse.

With no hall pass he could only outwait the teacher. Every creaking movement and elbow bump was audible. He wanted to poop, but he couldn't even force out a fart, only a feeble splash of urine. The teacher huffed in his need for physical relief, inhale, exhale, marking the time with every gasp, puff. His animal need amplified into a fury of discomfort. Isaiah's flaccid, blinded Cyclops mound of flesh seemed to wink from its eyeless socket.

You are a very bad boy.

He lifted his shirt over his nose and concentrated on his breathing, slow counting, one-one thousand, two-one thousand, inhaling his cologne and deodorant.

You bounce on a shiny red dildo toy.

Sharp squeaks from shoes being forcefully ground into the tiles kept cadence with the rasping. He pulled his shirt up over his ears.

You suck with joy.

He lifted his shirt over his eyes and pressed his hands against his ears. He concentrated on the blood coursing in a crashing ocean of sound. Finally the teacher issued a gruff harrumph and stomped out. The footsteps faded.

From room to room
hall to hall
can I write my way out of this hell
if I start at the bathroom stall?

Water sluiced snot and saliva in the sink as he hurriedly washed his hands without looking at his reflection. Coming out he flinched at the figure walking towards him. But it was just David, also flinching as he passed. He hurried into the bathroom and the stall door slammed. Isaiah stood listening for crying. David had been unable to suppress the flush of humiliation on his face when he had seen Isaiah. He was embarrassed to be caught with desolation in his eyes that betrayed his far-off expression.

The bell rang its longed for diversion and Isaiah turned quickly to reenter the forgetful routine. Ugly brown shoes were the first thing he saw as Mr. Stigler rushed past him.

"Get to class."

With a bulrush he opened the bathroom door and came face to face to with David. He planted his ugly brown shoes and blocked the way. David was herded back and tottered in mid step, almost falling to avoid splashing the cesspool accumulation under the urinals. Mr. Stigler held the door open with a thick arm.

"I should have figured it was you. Look at me."

His voice filled the bathroom and echoed out into the hallway.

"David McCormick, I said look at me. Where is your hall pass?"

Isaiah was the only one in the hallway and he inched towards escape.

"I said where is your hall pass? Are you deaf boy?"

The dense hair on his forearm prickled as he grabbed David by the elbow and pulled him close. His heavy breathing rasped with a hungry purr. He grinned like an amused conquistador as David shrank away. This forced intimacy was a violation of the treaty of sterility the institution had made with them long ago, cooing to them after naptimes, in between playgrounds, so they would unreservedly accept its restraints. The effort of his hostility caused a growling cough, and his smile disappeared with discomfort as he inhaled hard.

"Answer me."

David started his rebellion by meekly pulling his elbow away. He marched towards the arm barring the way without stopping. Mr. Stigler would either have to let him pass or David would learn the true grip of the establishment around his neck with tickling hairs torturing his chin. Mr. Stigler pulled his arm away but bumped the weight of his gut against him. He sniffed the air and spoke in a mock nasal voice.

"Damn son did you learn a gerbil up your ass?"

Isaiah turned and hurried down the hallway so David's vacant eyes couldn't stare him into non-existence. The water fountain clunked as Mr. Stigler sucked and gulped. Isaiah immersed himself in the bustling flow of the main hallway. But people laughed too loud in the puke yellow light. Lockers slammed like lightning clasps, jolting his senses with humiliation. As Isaiah was at his locker David walked past, calm as if nothing had happened. Isaiah wanted to say something. But David's gaze didn't swivel in the slightest as Isaiah came up beside him, and he wove past him through the hallway avoiding shoulder jostling with the grinding crowd. He disappeared into the laughter.

Isaiah felt an uncomfortable tingling in his anus. Unintentionally he imagined a dead gerbil inside of him. The carcass became a mound of rotting flesh. The rot spread through his body cavity. Discomfort intensified as the vision spread. His body cringed until non-existent nerves were clenching. He was decomposing from the inside out, through his ribs, pale skin yellowing and oozing fluid, pain still shrieking and his mind conscious of dead and dying cells as the rot spread towards his heart.

SEDUCTION

He sniffed the burnt tobacco smoke on his fingertips then went back to playing with his sideburn.

"Don't you guys see?" Karen again asked.

In the responding silence she looked at Isaiah entreating.

"Nothing? Come on guys. Well then take out your notebooks. Let me try to explain it to you again."

He held his pencil but did not take notes. The torn skin around his fingernail beds had healed over. The cramped hand holding his pencil had dissecting eons in the crisscrossing lines of his palm. What did they do this for?

The industrial weight of the pencil made him think of the wrinkles of his father's nightly exhaustion. Underneath the crisscrossing eons on his palm faint blue lines led down to the thick veins of his wrist. He did nothing as the class took notes. David was tranquil in that far off place of the book he hid from the class. Isaiah set his pencil down.

Why?

Mouth agape he followed the scuffed tiles of the floor that led from classroom to classroom through the entire school. Absent of thought he was left to the tedious rhythm of the chalk.

"Salinger is inferring…"

Karen was conscious of keeping her distance from the green expanse of the chalkboard so as not to get any chalk dust on her outfit. If only dumb he could watch her move, it he only was deaf to her dull tone.

"…I think he has broken our thoughts down to their elemental forms."

He tried to force synapses to fire, to stare into existence an alternate state of mind. But he found himself watching the clock spin through the uniform spaces of time waiting for class to be over. Nothing made an impression. Not her words. Not the whitewashed walls. Every desk was filled with apparitions, every notebook overflowed to disappear in a large heap compressed by the trash compacter arms of the clock. How did David manage to escape this space-time into a book?

"What are you doing?"

Isaiah hadn't noticed Karen's silence. He hadn't been aware of her walking down the aisle until she blocked his view of David. It was Isaiah's fault she now looked down on David outraged. She would have never noticed him if not for his attention upon David. Isaiah was horrified as the whole class watched. David was trapped in the limbo between two worlds. She grabbed the book and snapped it closed. She held it up and waved it around to the classroom.

"What is this garbage you are reading? *Grandeur of Illusions*? When we are discussing great literature?"

David was trapped underneath the humiliation. But despite a red blush, and the steady sadness suddenly exposed in his slumped body, he quickly managed a blank expression as he looked up at Mrs. Dronomine.

"What do you have to say for yourself?"

"Nothing."

The class giggled to hide the fear of their secret childhood realms being brought into violent collision with the world. She dropped the book at David's feet with a loud smack.

"This goes for all of you. You need to pay more attention. The drivel most of you turned in for the first draft of your paper shows you barely even pay attention to me. I try to be nice, but you won't like it if I have to get strict."

She went to her desk and grabbed a stack of papers. She grabbed an empty chair and dragged it out into the hallway.

"I am going to go over these with each of you one-on-one."

She admonished them with the stack of papers.

"Most of you should be embarrassed. Isaiah, at least I can count on you to turn in something halfway decent. Bring your chair out here."

Usually politeness would have caused him to shift his eyes from hers but his periphery was heavy with nothingness and as he sat in front of her in the hallway he stared back unflinching as if drunk.

"I'll be honest with you Isaiah, your paper already is an A, it was technically the best, grammatically concise, but I know you can do better. There was no feeling."

He couldn't remember much more about his paper than hitting spell check when he was finished.

Her blue business suit was comic book tight. It was easy to picture her nipples as dark shadows as she returned his stare with her lips parted. For a moment they forget their roles. Then she blushed and averted his eyes to his paper. Their age difference disappeared as manhood coursed through him. Fornicating her would be to lay down the whole building, ripping biology dissecting its insides until the cafeteria beat with the urge of his life.

"How are you Isaiah?"

But she had regained control when she looked back up at him. He wasn't prepared for the power of her coquettish smile. It conquered him. She was more skilled at this art. She tilted her head playfully and the smooth skin of her neck besieged his imagination. He looked back up from her body. Soft down marked her upper lip, and he dare not look again beyond the almond tips of her eyes underneath her long eyelashes.

"Good."

"Isaiah, Isaiah, Isaiah. What am I going to do with you?"

Her crossed legs confused him. She held her pen like a witch's wand.

"I still have an A don't I?"

"That's not what I mean. Lately in class I feel like I am losing you, and I want to know what I can do to engage you."

She leaned closer and grasped his shoulder, then slid to momentarily trace his collarbone before putting her warm hand on top of his. Her upper lip was completely upturned. He looked around the empty hallway. He focused on the stains on the ground.

"Are you afraid to look at me?"

Her perfumed smell was no different than the girls at school. But in close proximity he was aware of her ripeness on the chair-desk top advertising the nectar below her thin waist. Her fingernails pressed into his knuckles.

"I don't want to lose you. I have a lot to offer. I know you are going to brilliant. I need you to tell me how I can make things more interesting, how

I can reach you?"

Her fingertips bent the stubble on his chin as she lifted his head to look into his eyes. Like a spurned adolescent her bottom lip stuck out.

"You're not like David. He doesn't care. And he is barely passing my class. Did you know he didn't even bother to turn in his last paper at all?"

She shivered with disdain. She slid his paper to him.

"But you, Isaiah, I want so badly to motivate you."

She took his hand in both of hers.

"Do you understand?"

A strong smell came from her crotch. Her blue eyes washed over him and focused on his mouth.

"Do you understand me?"

She took his hand and placed it upon her crotch. Even through the thick fabric he could feel the wet sliding underneath. He knew this hunger, the overwhelming lust to feel something, anything. But all he felt now was confusion. He looked at the blonde fuzz on her upper lip uncomprehending. She thought it was fear as she savored his innocence with a shudder of perversion. But he was not naïve of the stirring of his loins. It was the only thing he felt when she lectured in the front of the classroom. Even in this innocent age he knew things, had seen then on his computer screen. His finger twitched like tapping the button on a mouse. She gasped with surprise, and clasped his hand as she put it back on his desk.

"Could you tell David to come out?"

She was the one who could not look at him as he got up. She was the one trembling as she dismissed him. The tiresome haughtiness of red ink on his paper held no interest for either of them. Still tingling from her breath against the side of his face, wet-willy cool in his ear, and her smell still in his nostrils, he summoned David to go see her. She had regained a stern composure as she stared at David's paper and stabbed it with her finger repeatedly before David had even closed the door behind him.

THE MAN IN BLACK

Isaiah opened the front door to a stranger with sunken in eyes, intelligent insane eyes, his lips perfectly horizontal. He was certain he had never met him before yet his expression was familiar. The man offered him his hand. He said hello and asked his name. It was not an introduction. Isaiah wasn't mistaken into believing it was a greeting. It was a handshake for a new business partner, a welcoming into a new age of prosperous co-existence.

"Isaiah, may you be consecrated by our meeting. I am a recruiter. But not just a recruiter, or just a believer, but I am also the president."

Isaiah shook his hand out of common courtesy. The man started speaking as if he expected this and that was why he was here. Isaiah's hand felt like it was rotting enclosed in his hot sweaty grip. As he spoke he wanted to offer him gum, but does a man in all black (or white, Isaiah would never remember the color even as this odd experience was passing) hooded robes chew gum? He did not hear what he was saying as he dwelled on whether to offer him gum or not. His rotting breath stank like it was opening seeping wounds in his nostrils.

The man must have sensed his obliviousness, because his voice expanded. It didn't change one decibel, but still it expanded. His house vibrated with it, blades of grass in his yard bent with it, oil stains in the driveway bubbled with it, until the fire and brimstone in his imagination glowed. Evoked in his mind was an orgy of cold chowder murders, faces of death in a puritan wrath. He was not sure whom the punishment was for, but afraid what the neighbors would think he invited him in. The man walked in as if he had already invited himself.

Sitting at their kitchen table he was silent until the burn of his echoing voice retreated into all Isaiah's guilty silences. He looked Isaiah deep in the eyes until he felt discomfort. Isaiah couldn't turn away even though this was the way he imagined a lover, or father, would stare at him in a Hollywood motion picture, not this stranger in a robe.

"My friend, I don't mean to criticize your manners, but where I am from it is customary to offer a visitor something to drink upon entering your home."

Admonished, Isaiah apologized and asked him what of his humble household he would be kind enough to accept.

"My friend, no apologies needed. I would only like a simple glass of water. Please. One does get a thirst spreading the word."

In all his pores Isaiah wanted to trust him.

"A change is needed, a drastic change. My brother, let me speak to you as one to another, the world is dying, do you want to die with it? A change for our souls is needed; the time for zealots is upon us. In this world's insanity the heavens are imploring us to become zealots, willing us to die, willing us to get our hands dirty, to do whatever is necessary in the name of the almighty, so that we may join him. The world is dying, but we do not have to die with it. Humanity will die, but I will endure, and I want you to endure with me. Our civilizations, our worldly dreams can mean nothing in the immortal glory of the afterlife. Death is but a chess piece, but a piece in the game we play to win our immortal souls."

As he continued to speak Isaiah's stomach quivered. He talked and talked until Isaiah was numb, until his voice was all that existed, his words the parameters of the universe. Isaiah imagined his rotting DNA splitting him open and leaving candy colored blood on his hands.

Finally the man was ready to move on. He offered Isaiah "A business, no the ultimate business card." His chuckle did not touch eyes still intensely focused on him. Isaiah walked him out as quickly as possible while trying not to seem hurried, and he sent him out the front door with what he hoped was a permanent goodbye.

An airplane was roaring overhead, leaving a trail of condensation behind. Isaiah imagined it as a slow motion bullet, splitting the sky and leaving two halves rotting on the ground.

PRESCRIBED NUMBNESS

Muffled memories of the night before held nothing of how Isaiah had ended up in bed. The first drink had been because Tuesdays were the worst. The weekend's afterglow faded into Monday's routine and by Tuesday seemed like distant scenes from long since watched comedies. His body was stiff and his teeth slimy with a film of pollution. When he turned on the bathroom light he saw brown chunks and a pink stain of dried vomit down the side of his face and shirt. He took it off and balled it up to throw in his trashcan. Brushing his teeth he spit out mouthfuls of bloody toothpaste. Drained of all emotion he felt neither horror nor curiosity. He showered and let the spray hit his face, opening his mouth and letting the warm water dribble down his body. He made his bed and took the soiled linens to tiptoe through his silent house to put them in the wash. He ate his cereal like a cow chewing cud.

Streetlights glowed under the melancholy skies, illuminating perfect the orange of smashed pumpkins littering his street. The sun would rise soon aglow in a pleasant fall shine, azure skies with clouds meandering across the spontaneous foam of his subconscious. He wanted to fall into piles of leaves like he was ten years old again. He examined red blossoms on bushes surrounding the pine tree in his front yard wondering at their blooming in early November. The diesel engine of a school bus accelerated down his street and he returned the looks from the windows. They already had deadened senses. Today was not to experience the world. This fleeting freedom didn't create an overbearing happiness but a tinge to the numbness he would also see the world through.

The prickling desire was his only concern, and he finally lit his cigarette after picking Barrett up. Sweet unquestioning world, the smoke replaced the taste he hadn't been able to brush away. He sighed in his relief from the twitchiness that sent long tendrils in his nervous system.

"Whoa fiend, your parents are going to freak if they smell smoke in your car," Barrett said.

"I don't care. It's too cold for smoker's corner. I'll just blame you anyways."

Barrett laughed and lit up a cigarette.

"You didn't even ask me about Carrie Ann's vagina."

"How was Carrie Ann's vagina?"

Barrett punched him in the arm.

"She let me get on top of her like a Marine and called me daddy as I did pushups. My best friend is supposed to ask me about things like that."

"Congrats man."

"I did it. I banged the hottest girl in school."

"Good job man."

He couldn't envision it. He was not sure what it meant. Except that he was allowed to share Barrett's euphoria as they bounced into the building. They nodded at each other when they passed girls, a rite of manhood to be throttled with bare will and conquered by long stabbing. They separated and he walked past the counselor's offices. He pictured Mr. Myosis every morning adjusting his gold jewelry and stroking his goatee in his reflection on the door under his name in thick letters. He respectfully averted his eyes from the small blond girl crying hysterically in his office. He wondered what melodrama she played at. Like the afterbirth of all of the recent weirdness he could discard his false vulnerability and leave the crypt of melodrama to the pale faced gothic kids in black makeup.

The door slammed open behind him and her hysterical voice accosted him.

"You bastard. You did it. You bastards did it. She tried to kill herself."

He looked back dumbfounded, trying to figure out what she was raving about.

"Huh?"

He did not flinch to defend himself as she rushed to press her face inches from his.

"Maggie, Maggie Monroe you asshole. The girl you and your ogre friends humiliated."

Her face was so distorted with emotion, puffed eyes blurred with tears, that he hadn't recognized Emily until now. He had forgotten about Maggie's humiliation. He had not thought once about the intensity of hatred in Emily's glare in the days that had followed, sitting behind her while enjoying the lines of her body. He remembered her disdain again now that she was so close he could smell her salty tears. The wetness aromatized her fruity lip-gloss and mixed with the sweet metabolizing of her breath so he could taste her emotion when he breathed. It would be but a slight lean down to kiss her.

"Emily," Mr. Myosis started to pull her away. "Calm down."

She let herself be pulled back into the office but screamed back at him.

"You humiliated her. She took twenty Xanex, she had to get her stomach pumped, and she is in a psych ward right now."

Mr. Myosis pulled her back in the room. Isaiah needed to hear her sniffles fill the hallway. So inept did he feel upon hearing about Maggie's empty suicide attempt that he needed Emily to pound its reality into his chest. Her wet emotion was raw in his senses and he couldn't help the voyeur desire to follow her into the room to feel the humanity he wasn't invited to. But Mr. Myosis came back out, too close to him, gorging on the smorgasbord of her emotions with life given to those rolling marbles in his head. He spoke in between licking his lips.

"She is just emotional."

Isaiah needed to silence this ghoul but instead he whispered back companionably.

"I know. I know. Her irrational—"

"I know what I am doing. Why don't you come and see me later today. Ok?"

He shut the door behind him. Isaiah stared into the office of despair. But the receptionist's eyes were upon him. He walked away purposeless down the apathetic hallways.

When he got home Rachel's car was in the driveway. Upon the counter was her key chain with the small photograph of their family on a roller coaster. They shared an expression of buoyancy. Only Rachel's eyes were not scrunched, sitting next to him with their outside hands gripping the coaster car and their inside hands clasping each other's, her eyes were open wide with a large grin. A pounding beat came from her room, and he was tentative to go upstairs and face her. He looked around at the potted plants, the ceramic cats, the colorful carpets, how he had disregarded these graceful touches of beauty in his domestic comfort. Maggie had always giggled in their house with his sister and mother. They had accepted his mother's hands in their smooth skin without the slightest pause at her age spots and thick blue veins as they joked. These memories gave him nerve. Rachel would understand that it was not his fault. He went upstairs and opened his sister's bedroom door.

"Rach' I had nothing to do with it. Will you tell Emily I am not like that? I had nothing to do with what they did to Maggie, you have to believe me."

The confused image of naked flesh registered too quickly. Before he could close the door he saw a hairy buttock between his sister's spread thighs, a civil war of contrasting expression upon Rachel's face.

He drove to the library. It would be as clean and disinfected as a doctor's office. He lit a cigarette and smoked with his windows open. Still he could not dissipate the animal scent akin to armpit in his nostrils. It lodged in his senses with the familiar flowery fragrance of her room. The image of her conflicted emotion was a hologram that appeared everywhere he looked. He wondered what lies he would have to tell Mr. Myosis to get a prescription to maintain his numbness.

PARTY AT THE END OF THE WORLD

This was a celebration of disappearing. Nothing else mattered at the party at the end of the world. It was the dawning of the new millennium. Every shot had more meaning when Isaiah pretended it was his last. It made him want to enjoy every swallow of beer, every euphoric moment of new creation racing through his bloodstream.

"Damn man, you don't have to smoke the whole bushel. How did you even remember how to get here?" Barrett joked with English.

English looked back at him out of exaggerated slits as they stood on Stephanie's porch smoking cigarettes.

"I didn't, and that is why every day is an adventure to me."

On the porch more than the normal party crowd smoked cigarettes. Dusty had even foregone his trench coat for a leather jacket. All were invited to the celebration of a dying world, and there was misappropriated camaraderie. On good behavior, even the subtlest of cruelties were ignored in their interactions, somehow the threat of an angry God raining fire and brimstone on them bonded them together in ways the normal routine of life never had. Barrett had shared his good will towards all men by making a joke with Dusty about liking his jacket.

"It is going to be happening soon, Y2K changing everything," Wadsworth said excited.

"I can't wait for it," English said.

Fat snowflakes sprinkled into cold puddles on the driveway. It was full of cars. Stephanie's parents were on vacation, so she had thrown this party at her large house out in the country.

"Yeah, I can't wait for the end of the world either," Aaron said.

Even tonight, when there was no reason for his logic to disallow him partaking in a cigarette, Aaron exhaled his smoke sarcastic of his own act.

"Computers, banks, governments, school, crashing. I think that would be awesome. Survival of the fittest."

Barrett smiled fiercely and crumpled his beer after a long swallow.

"It's not like there are going to be comets come with fiery death from the skies. There will be no tidal waves. Just an excused absence from society," English said.

Barrett used a mock stoner voice. "Maybe the curse of the Goldenwood Millennium class will take us all this time. It will be the end of the world. Armageddon is soon."

"That would be pretty cool too."

"No school on Monday," Isaiah said.

"You guys know nothing is going to happen, right?" Aaron said as he flicked his cigarette butt.

"There will be no Hollywood special effects. The world will end in a progression of dull moments stretching out in an eternal classroom listening to lectures drawn out for eons until nothing exists but the stretched out moment," Isaiah said.

"How much did you let him smoke English?" Barrett asked.

They laughed. Angst flared up with his cigarette and vented out from underneath the porch into the winter night. He followed Barrett inside. In the living room the strobe light flashed in constant timelessness. Celebratory hats shifted their comical perches as if controlled by the shimmers from their untamed streamers. Glitter was captured like whiffs of musty perfume. Girls danced in flotsam moments. Each flash bulb impression was disconnected from the passing of another year like a warped memory from histories bloated brain. They were too drunk for gluttony, too lonely for greed, and they danced lustful in each disconnected moment to the frozen world. The beat pounded out and he joined the dance in unfettered weightlessness.

He didn't tire of this, nor did he will it to end, but instead in one of the lost moments he shifted out of the dance and into the fluorescent margins of the dining room. The blinking was behind him like eternities shadow. His body was flushed with sweat, and he stood against the wall. Stephanie sat at the table in the fixed joviality of a drinking game, and he waited for her to notice the spontaneity of his appearance. Carrie Ann's voice called out to him.

"Help us get this girl wasted."

She pulled Stephanie up forcefully and pushed her against him.

"Like this you little slut."

She took his arm and wrapped one around her and one around Stephanie.

"Have you noticed we're trying to play a game here?" Lumpy said.

But his bullying had no sway on this festive night. Isaiah swayed with the girls for a song then went to open a bottle of Bud Light and go back towards the dance.

"Where are you going buddy?"

"…drink, drink, drink…"

Isaiah snapped the bottle cap with perfect trajectory through the reflection of the strobe light and it disappeared and reappeared to smack Barrett in the neck.

"I'm going to get you back for that fagot."

Isaiah danced laughing back into the strobe lit depths of the music. The tingle was just a good mood. In a flash Angela was in front of him, almost completely turning with every hips rotation to the beat. Her ass receded until it pressed her crack against his crotch. She did not turn to find out whom she danced against. Absent judgment he enjoyed the feel of her against him in each lost flash. He gave up trying to follow her rhythm and instead kept contact by pressing his body hard against hers. Her shoulder leaned against his chest as she nuzzled her cheek up against his shoulder. She bent down until he could feel the fissure between her firm cheeks tighten and loosen. In two blinks she was facing him with her legs around one of his and her skirt riding up until the small bulge of her panties sprang against him. She grabbed him and darted her tongue in his mouth. Just as sudden she twirled off into the mass of people, dancing alone to the music.

He walked back into the dining room and Carrie Ann's stare caused him to wink at her as he walked past. In a progression down the hallway the jubilation grew more subdued. The front room was strewn with a jumble of bodies underneath blankets lit only by a big screen television set to Times Square, counting down fifteen minutes till the end of the millennium.

He walked outside to reckon time in the slower rhythm of his breaths in the winter cold. From the front room the television glowed with fleeting energy disseminating from the bulbous mass of New York City counting down in frantic ticks. He walked into the yard to consider the time machine vision of the stars measuring time only in their pulsations. He saw no impending doom. The moon was still neighborly large in the sky. Once he had seen a giant ring around it like the entrance to a tunnel to another world. Up, that tunnel of light had led, up. As the clock counted down to the New Year, that was when it would come all the way to the ground before him, offering escape as the first comets and balefire lit up the sky. He would escape gravity as it imploded into the frantic screaming crowd at Times Square. He would float upwards like in the dreams he had, his family with him in the line of souls as the earth boiled behind them with the explosions. Chris would be with him, and David, who was not here to celebrate, and they would not have to forgive him because good intentions would meld with their ethereal forms. He lit a cigarette and watched the skies as he waited.

"Isaiah?" Barrett screamed from the front door. "Get your ass in here. Stephanie is looking for your ball to drop."

Barrett shepherded him in the front door.

"What the fuck were you doing out there?"

"Waiting for Armageddon."

"How drunk are you man?"

Barrett stopped him in the hallway.

"You need to get your game face on. We're going to get laid man."

Isaiah nodded with a smile. He felt fondness for Barrett, his back taut with excitement as he pushed through the crowd congregated in front of the TV. He sat him down next to Stephanie and Isaiah yielded to her closeness with an arm around her. Carrie Ann's mischievous grin was upon him as Barrett put his arm around her. Stephanie did not look at him as she clung excitedly against him. Wadsworth enviously looked at him. He was glad for her silence as they listened to the babble of voices blending in with the television. Then the Times Square crowd of faces extended outwards into them in a hushed expectation of the countdown.

"10!" Barrett and Carrie Ann's voice. "9!" Stephanie perked up as she screamed out with the rest of them. "8!" Aaron in unison with the crowd. "7!" Voices he didn't recognize. "6!" The computer in the other room blinked expectant. "5!" Was David alone with a book in his room? Where was Chris, a vengeful ghost waiting for them to join him? "4!" He pictured his parents hand in hand with a bottle of wine between them. "3!" He pictured Rachel in a room in the arms of a stranger. "2!" Voices with no reason to forgive or be forgiven. "1!" His face acquiesced to Stephanie's incessant pull and he kissed her as he waited. "Happy New Year!" Then the world turned dark as he expected.

There was silence.

He waited.

Time had stopped.

He waited.

He was part of something that he did not quite understand.

He waited.

He became aware of someone screaming.

He waited.

Then Lumpy laughed loud. Isaiah opened his eyes and they adjusted to the dim light coming from outside. Stephanie's heaving fear beat against his chest. With a rush of power the lights came back on and the celebration popped back up on the television. The world had not ended. No brimstone rained from the timeless heavens. God hadn't unfastened their belts, pulled down to their mortal coils, exposing the naughty parts of their pale souls to punish them. The computer beeped on oblivious of Y2K as it reloaded. Stephanie kissed him with a fervor that had noticed neither darkness nor light. He stared at her impassive as his lips continued the mechanics. Lumpy's voice made her stop.

"We really got you guys good."

He patted Frank and Bean on the back.

"That was hilarious."

"Lumpy. You asshole!" Carrie Ann's scream came out of her nervous laughter.

"That was a letdown," English said to Dusty.

Lumpy wheezed and hit play on the computer. In immediate irreverence the princes of the new millennium sang with a chorus about past parties like 1999.

"Welcome to the new millennium you paranoid fuckers. We got you fucking good. Classic," Lumpy screamed at the top of his lungs. "The world didn't end, so nothing left to do but get wasted like its 2099!"

Aaron's sarcastic laugh wailed into the celebration spilling out of the television from Times Square. Government, banks, Goldenwood, everything would go on as normal.

David was alone reading in his basement.

Isaiah swallowed a shot like the end of the world. He wasn't even there as he was numb to the shudders. Stephanie didn't understand his disappointment. Her attention no longer excited his hormones. Angela was a lifeless rag doll next to Lumpy.

He snuck up the stairwell. Stephanie's family portraits led him down the hallway in their comforting recesses. He welcomed the spinning. He shut the bathroom door on the sound of the party. He no longer held back the boiling acid as his throat burnt and the smell splashed in the toilet to replace the artificial flowery smell of feminine products. He took a pink hand towel and wiped his hand and face, then cleaned off the remaining chunks from the toilet and tossed the messy wet ball into the corner hidden behind the toilet. His heart pounded heavily into the tranquility. He hadn't really thought the world was going to end but had been seduced by the idea of change anyways. He opened the door to the intoxicated burst of voices from downstairs.

"Isaiah?"

He steadied himself as Stephanie looked at him from the top of the steps.

"Are you ok?"

"Yeah. I may need to lie down for a second."

She grabbed his hand and brought him into her bedroom. He gave in to the apathy as he lied down to hide in her blankets.

"Isaiah?" She whispered. "Do you mind if I join you?"

He lifted the blankets to make room for her. She clicked the door lock. The bed shook as she took her dress off over her head. Then she snuggled in beside him. They did not move for a long time. Then in a rush she was on him and he could feel the naked skin surrounding her bra and underwear. He passionate kiss stirred up the drunken fumes. She grabbed his hand to rub it against her crotch. The function of it was practical, when his hand felt for the weight underneath her bra she sat up to un-strap it and pull it over her arm with her elbow digging into his ribs, methodically she balled up her panties, then took his shirt off, his collar catching his nose before she yanked it off. He barely caught a glimpse of her breasts before their flesh was against his bare chest. He toyed with his belt, and she quickly took control and unbuttoned his pants to take them off with his boxers in one movement, tugging violently at his feet until they came off. He was curious of the slick part of a woman's body that he had never examined before. Her hand manipulated his disassociated body into excitement with workmanlike aggressiveness. He caught a whiff of sweat and dead fish protein that he knew was different from other girl's scents because of his sister. But this did not stop him. He had no will but that which the act required. Her keys tinkled in her purse as she took the condom out and opened it quickly. She pulled him on top of her and rolled it on. Like a thing outside him the desire and lust built as he yielded to her insistent tugging. He could barely tell the difference from her hand in the transition.

He was doing it.

Oh melodramatic moment! Where was God? Where was Satan? Where were the choirboys, dry humping the air in a chorus of 'way to go'?

He was a virgin no longer.

He moved in a slow dance of repeated movements but it seemed to suffice as she moved with him. The heat consumed his body and started to control his rhythm. He could feel her skin and he moved quicker, breaking through the hymen of dogma to enact the ritual of American manhood, all the pushups finally made sense as his arms flexed holding himself on top of her.

But his sensations lost momentum. His excitement became little more than a twinge not even as strong as that when watching a naughty video on his computer. He tried to regain momentum by staring at her breasts. He tried to remember if he had seen any in real life not of his relatives. But she was not responsive anymore. He became numb as he went through the motions. After a few more thrusts she lied limp and he felt like he was doing something wrong. He slowed.

"Don't stop," She moaned.

Faster again, detached, as if he was above watching himself. He felt alone on top of her lifeless body. He closed his eyes to try and make his body rise in animal fury, thrusting as he tried to regain the feeling of being connected to her. She gasped and he slowed.

"Don't stop."

Faster again, her nails dug painfully into his back as her body tensed to life.

"Don't stop."

He concentrated on the base of his genitals, the warmth of her inanimate body, because he had lost sensation to the condom with its latex smell. There was so much sweat in the friction that he couldn't feel anything but the slick resistance of her hips. Reef escaped his mouth from the effort. She moaned curse words about her genitals, and asked if he liked the way she felt, and he might have laughed if he wasn't so detached. Their silhouettes became deliberations in his head.

And then suddenly, just as she had gone so silent that he thought she might really be dead, her hips blasted into him with a spasm, and she squealed out high-pitched cries like gasps of pain.

They both were now limp. His cumbersome weight pressed down on her. The stick of their movements as their sweat dried irritated his skin. Her elbow dug into his ribs. He was uncertain how to escape off of her as flaccidity returned uncomfortably in the wetness of the latex.

She giggled and pushed him off of her with her forearm. She rested her hand upon his chest for a few measured heartbeats then stood. He knew he should feel something seeing her naked body, he should absorb her lines and memorize the taboo brown hair and the pink shade of her nipples, he should make this moment the culmination of thousands of playboy moments, but he only felt drained. She took tissues from her nightstand and bent over to wipe herself and threw them in the trash. She put her balled up thong back on. She lied back down and he stared at the ceiling waiting for her to say something. She mumbled as she brushed against the drooping condom in an embarrassing bunch of latex still attached to him.

"Oh. You might want to take that off."

Soon she was snoring. He got up and found his clothes on the floor. She was sprawled out with a sheet only covering only her lower half. He tried to be inspired by the image of her breasts. Then he went into the bathroom.

"You don't have to leave," She mumbled.

He closed the door. He flushed the condom without looking. He stared at his naked reflection in the mirror. This is what people did in movies when something had changed inside of them. But there was nothing different in the conquistador face that stared back at him. He turned to examine the claw marks on his back. The smell of her on him was faintly metallic. Then he noticed the light switch was covered in blood. His hand had thick coagulated blood upon it, and there were flakes and goops in his pubic hair. He put his clothes back on.

Back downstairs people still partied at the dining room table. Lumpy was loud as usual in his drunkenness. Isaiah reached his hand down his pants into the gummy wetness and pulled it out.

"Smell my finger."

He slid his fingers underneath Lumpy's nose and slid lines of blood across his chin and the wetness of his lips.

"What the fuck?"

He walked towards the door to a smattering of laughter and gasps of disgust.

"What the fuck did you put on my face?"

"That is my sacrifice to royalty."

Isaiah averted his mad charge and used his momentum to push him crashing into the wall. He landed on top of Lumpy and was able to pin him in his drunken incoordination. He struggled as Isaiah smeared his hand all over his face. Barrett pulled him off and Hoss held Lumpy back as Barrett opened the front door for him.

"You better get out of here."

"I am going to kill you," Lumpy screamed.

He slammed the door behind him. The alcohol warmed his veins like the answer to his desperate prayers to feel God within. Was that nothing more than his body heat like a planet's core, the dying sun bestowing comfort upon a summer day, in the end nothing but a minute fraction of a degree in the breeze blowing his bone dust across the desolate earth? Was this warmth, this glow, the end of the universe?

ETERNITY

He welcomed eternity with his first real hangover, as if his liver had stored all the toxicity of the previous millennium and was expelling it to start the new one fresh. He had awoken that morning with a start, pleasantly surprised at the world's moderate continuance. His parents had insisted he join them for church. All through the service past abstractions had putrefied until his abstemious head throbbed with every Herculean effort to clear away the carcasses of thought.

He was a passive vessel as they stood on the steps of the church in an impromptu discussion group. His mother endured the brutal cold with an apologetic bout of shivers as she huddled closer to his father and continued to listen to Mrs. Lumpinsky. Every foggy breath was a talisman of the holy life thick within them. Only Pastor Joe seemed untouched, either because of the thickness of his robes or the heat still flowing in his veins from the work of his sermon.

"It is such a shame. Is there anything I can do to help the poor girl?" Greg Lumpinsky's mother asked with concern pinching her plump face.

"When a soul goes through something like that, sometimes we have to put our faith in God. Be supportive, speak with her, and let her know we are there for her and praying for her, and God willing he will show us what more we can do."

Pastor Joe chose his words carefully. Isaiah could tell he was uncomfortable coming to any definite conclusions as he looked at him with honest concern. His inattention to her caused Mrs. Lumpinsky's round frame swell in the wind as the tassels of her beanie whipped around, sturdier than a weather balloon she looked to the other woman's sympathy to answer her own question.

"We need to make sure our children understand this is the best time of their lives."

"What a troubled generation," Mrs. Crowmartie said without feeling.

Isaiah somberly looked at them, ready to explain his generation, pondering every word as Pastor Joe had. But Mrs. Lumpinsky turned to Pastor Joe seeking approval.

"Yes. Definitely. How did they get so lost?"

"Remember, the Good Shepherd finds his stray sheep, for as in Matthew 18:12-14, if a shepherd has a hundred sheep, and one of them has gone astray, does he not leave the ninety-nine on the mountains and go in search of the one that went astray? And if he finds it, truly I tell you, he rejoices over it more than over the ninety-nine that never went astray. So it is not the will of your Father in heaven that one of these little ones should be lost," Pastor Joe said.

They all nodded in agreement. But Isaiah could not repress a stab of cynicism. She didn't understand. And Lumpy, the grotesque disembowelment from Mrs. Lumpinsky's womb, was not lost and bleating. It was difficult to continue his benevolent smile for Pastor Joe.

Mrs. Crowmartie's effort over time to keep her jaw rigid had caused her the habit of pressing the lower mandible out in an underbite when she spoke. "It is all by God's plan. We all must accept his will."

Her jaw regained its normal position with a disbeliever's smile. Before Pastor Joe responded she started her first shuffling steps down the stairs and into her certainty.

"Thank you for the wonderful sermon. We'll see you next week."

"Indeed. We must put our faith in him." There was sadness in Pastor Joe's smile.

As soon as their car heater hit him Isaiah knew a fever was coming. The delirium flushed up his neck and face with a sudden hot fury, the ache reverberating back down through his muscles. The effort to make conversation was painful and he snuck away from his parents to fall into bed.

He was not sure how long his penance was for, but in the misery of his fever he knew he deserved to be punished for his sins. It was as if providence had brought the topic up outside the church. He clutched his blankets and prayed it wasn't eternal damnation, for this delirium was a shadowy state that seemed to claim the whole of existence. Faces were guilt, memories were admonitions, and time bunched up in knots that he could only see from this disassociation. With a cold sweat he shivered out prayers for forgiveness, for deliverance. Clutching, he prayed. He remembered his Grandmother Alice when she had been alive comforting him in this same room when he had been sick as a child. The same bible she had been reading with smoke trailing from her ashtray was now on his bookshelf.

"Hush, hush, Isaiah, it was just a nightmare."

She had held him against her and continued to repeat. "Sshhhh, sshhhh, sshhhh."

Eventually he had felt serene. She had gotten down on her knees at the foot of his bed, her joyous expression of grandmotherhood replaced by solemnity.

"It's going to be ok."

Her face close in unfamiliar seriousness had scared him more than his nightmare had. But the conviction of her stare had let him release even that fear. That peace neither her wrinkles nor the pink in her eyes could diminish. He did not shrink away from the web of wrinkles scrunching up her face as a smile had returned with the same intensity.

"You want to see something really scary."

She had laughed her familiar cackle and removed her false teeth, nicotine and coffee stains on them, and held them high. He had giggled as she had chased him across his bed.

"Mother," his mother had said.

In the same tone his grandmother had answered.

"My child."

He awoke blanketed in a kinder delirium and laid in the quiet of answered prayers. His cool sweat was a sign the fever had broken, and he pulled his comforter down from his damp forehead. His grandmother's voice still echoed in the aftermath of the fever. Outside snow lay in a virgin tract. Vaguely he remembered his mom coming in to tell him that school had been cancelled as he had slept all day. The shirt covered with vomit that he had thrown away was folded on top of his sheets in the clothesbasket where his mother had brought organization to even this little bit of disorder. From his neat desk the cursor blinked expectant. His television was a monolith from a dead civilization. Most of the finely bound books on his bookshelf his grandmother had given him as gifts. Of them he had read only Tolkien and C.S. Lewis in that summer of fantasy. School left little time for idolatry. The thick leather bound Bible was the largest book, as if the rest of the thick volumes were mere addendums to its mass. He pulled it out and the two bordering books fell to form a teepee. The texture of its wrinkled leather was like Grandma Alice's hands. She had caressed it when she read like holding his grandfather's hand. Isaiah had only seen his grandfather in photographs, the robust sturdiness of middle age unbeknownst that eternal rest was soon upon him. He remembered the wisdom in her eyes. He had believed it was okay even as she lay dead in her coffin, upset at the makeup covering her wrinkles making it harder to imagine her smiling. He had been honored that it was him she had left it to, and he had always pictured himself reading it like clasping something he had lost. Now he held it like something found. It could calm the tremors of his tantrums, as her look pierced through the window, the potential movements of the protons in the air, the blank monolithic screen, to again comfort his terrors. Like their laughter at the illusionary nature of the world he smiled and opened the bible.

The man and his wife were both naked, and they felt no shame.

He set the bible upon his nightstand. He liked seeing it next to his alarm clock. Misplaced from routine today was a blessing. He was thankful for the frigid wind that gusted against his window with snow in random flakes. With the bible there he could read the sins scribbled haphazardly in his notebook. Smote he reread the names he had scribbled, and then again. He wrote Maggie's name down. He was tired of pondering black holes, and every little end of the world, for every death was just as unique, Chris, he had already seen one universe end, every boy and girl could end the universe if they were curious. As his grandmother looked upon him he formed the names on his lips. Even as he had wrote the names the letters became illegible. As he prayed for them universes collided in untold dimensions in his head, untangling knots of script into a string of eternity. With the worst of intentions the bitter scientists still unwittingly prayed.

His sin was not knowing it was a joke; he should have laughed like his grandmother had when reading the bible.

UNECESSARY MISSIONARY

I guess you won't be signing my yearbook."

Isaiah spoke calmly to Barrett's back in the parking lot. He had expected Barrett to ignore him since he had received the message from his parents that he wouldn't need a ride to school.

Like a missionary he pulled a cigarette out as he approached the trench coat mafia. Andy stood with Dusty as pillars guarding the weaker misfits in the group that included Joe and Howard. Isaiah repeated the names as he had read them aloud from his notebook the other night, Andy who had hissed at them, Joe the mothball, and stinky Howard. Their heavy combat boots stomped for warmth. Faces that disdained hygiene came out of the cadaver folds underneath the billowing trench coats hiding the rot of their bodies. Howard wore a dingy cap, and their large leader Dusty's blonde hair flowed in the air, Howard had salon died black hair, but the rest of their exposed heads had hair like grease icicles. They laughed, bone saws of the past in the back of their throats. For a moment he hesitated and looked back to the light of Goldenwood. It held comforting warmth for the winter days, instead of standing thick headed underneath the harsh winter sky in the predawn darkness with exposed red ears losing the warmth of their caveman existence. The frost air sent a bite into the depths of his lungs where they healed from the flu and burn of cigarette smoke. Then with resolve he stepped in their circle and held his cigarette out like a peace pipe.

"Sorry to interrupt fellas, can I bum a light?"

Their laughter stopped. He sought youth in their eyes that had not been subjugated to the lazy troll existence of their folds. Joe and Dusty gave him cold looks with the genetic tracers of a berserker past. Howard looked away as his thin lips grimaced to expose large teeth jutting out of his gums. Andy tried to look as intruded upon as the rest but could not help a slight smile. He hadn't noticed Cat nestled beside Dusty, his Nordic boned gothic queen, and the stare from her black lined eyes was the hardest. Isaiah submitted to her wide lidded delving, awaiting her witch's decree. They were not curious, but outnumbering him they stared him down with Viking resentment, as if he were a missionary claiming answers they did not want from the monasteries of the civilized world.

"How are you guys doing?" Isaiah said.

Dusty reached into his pocket to hand him his heavy Zippo. His eyes were Stonehenge measuring tools above his jabberwocky jaws. Isaiah lit his cigarette and his hard drag seared pain into his healing lungs.

"Thanks."

They were silent as Cat stared at him waiting for him to leave.

"How are you doing Cat?"

"I am PAGAN. Do you know what that is?"

He had overheard her brag about the Wikken religion in her bloodline before, but was unsure what that had to do with him.

"No."

"People against God and nature."

Her proud bloodlust would rival any of the most time-formalized religious leaders arguing the ultimate truth of their denomination.

"That is cool. Man it is cold out here. Only the true smokers are brave enough today."

They did not shift to let him in their fjord against the barren cold, leaving him in the outskirts of their necromancer circle.

"What is funnier than a dead baby?" Dusty asked.

Isaiah shrugged his shoulders.

"A dead baby in a clown costume."

Their shoulders turned against him. Cat looked at him unblinking.

"You do not belong here."

He shrugged his shoulders. But somehow her stoic statement had humiliated him.

"Yeah. Ok. Thanks for the light guys."

He flicked his half smoked cigarette and walked toward Goldenwood.

They did not need his prayers. They would perform their rituals in the dank cellars of their blacklight stains. Among feces they would worship and make love, surviving in a Wal-Mart display the trench coats would reproduce and rear their fat zitted children eating candy corn from a paper plate. He hurried into the building.

Mr. Quinn set upon them the awkward ritual of selecting new lab partners. Isaiah was disappointed at losing Tim as his partner until it dawned upon him the opportunity chance had bestowed upon him. Fate was a full time trickstress, disguising her relationship with free will. Ramona looked at Isaiah hopefully from underneath her square cut bangs. In the confusion Stanley was resigned to not even search for a new partner. Even in this class of dorks this process was especially humiliating for him. Isaiah walked over to him, ignoring his heavy doses of halitosis.

"Want to be partners?"

Stanley Steamer, he repeated in his head. It took Stanley a couple exhalations burdened with the deep chemistry of his sloppy metabolism to answer.

"Sure."

"Cool."

Mr. Quinn noted their new groupings with a smile.

"Another successful social experiment. You guys can go ahead and start the lab."

He pitied Ramona being stuck with Ronald, he domineered her immediately with orders trying to impress her. He thought his name also, but his obnoxious expression was not open to any kindness at this time. Stanley stared down at the ditto.

"I can get the supplies," Stanley said.

"Ok. Cool."

Stanley stood quickly, and by the time he returned from the front of the classroom he was out of breath. They started the experiment as he breathed with painful awareness, like an old woman sighing he heaved with the exertion of existence. Other than discussing the experiment Isaiah did not know what to say to him. Finally he tried to start a conversation.

"I love these experiments. They make the world seem as big as the one I imagined as a kid. Remember how endless the backyards seemed to spread out to a gigantic world?"

Stanley huffed out uncertainly. "Yeah."

"Did you stare up at the sky and ponder outer space as a kid?"

"Yeah."

"What did you imagine?"

He answered with a slow stink puff. "Asteroids."

"Like the asteroid belt?"

Isaiah was either getting acclimated to the acrid smell of his breath, or it had become shallower with comfort. He looked up, hesitant to trust Isaiah's benevolence.

"Yeah. But I imaged a giant one when I saw a shooting star. Like a giant boulder in outer space speeding towards us."

He held his breath as he waited for Isaiah's reaction.

"Spinning. Yeah. Like a rogue planet, with these cavernous holes in its misshapen form, in our solar system, colliding in a pinball game aimed directly at earth."

"Yeah."

"That would be quite an end of the world."

He grunted and his laugh wheezed out with a wet muffled sound. Isaiah resisted cringing away from the steam entering his nostrils.

"Have you ever played the videogame Armageddon?"

"No." Isaiah didn't mean to be short but he didn't know what else to say.

"Oh."

"Is it cool?"

He huffed out embarrassed. "It's ok."

Stanley dared not look up again as they finished the experiment.

When Dixie Winn appeared in the hallway before Isaiah he followed expectant. Dixie, ah, who gave her the idea to wear that skirt, a habit learned from older cousins from the eighties that she had not quit. He wondered how she could even fit her high fructose deposits of cellulite into the bright spandex. Ann Crust listened to her talk, happy just to have a friend, contentment underneath her frizzle frazzle patch of thinning hair.

"I am a third generation Goldenwood student. My father and grandfather helped build this new school. It makes me proud. Grandpa always says that the lessons they learned here from the ruler are the same lessons he used to build these walls."

Blood red spots of putty in her cheeks were rich with nutrients. She waddled whole milk strong in her skirt and spandex leg warmers. The building too needed sacrifices, for Isaiah saw the carper roll up readying for pray, to soak her rich Winn blood into the white porous bricks. She tripped with a teeter, then tottered forward unable to untangle her arms from her precious books as she fell towards the concrete with nothing but her putty cheeks to break her fall. In a rush of adrenaline he had started towards her before she started falling, but still it took an endeavor of strength greater than any he had performed on the football field to catch her. As he helped steady her he realized the blubber roll in his hand had a sausage nipple poking out between his fingers.

"Oh, sorry."

"Thank you so much Isaiah."

The spots on her cheeks gushed rich red nutrients down her neck. She leaned into him as she giggled and rubbed the folds of her sweater, spending most of her attention on the area where the sausage tip had found his hand.

"Dixie Winn," he whispered after he had managed to pull away.

He made it a point to give Doris the lunch lady his best smile. Lumpy's hatred could now be unveiled. He did not look up from his tray as he danced around kids to the outskirts of the cafeteria.

"Teacher's snooty ass-monkey isn't even smart enough to know the difference between a slut's period blood and hymen blood," Wadsworth said.

Behind him at his crowded lunchroom table they snickered like thrashing fish in a net. He could break Wadsworth at will but this was only his world for 107 more trivial days.

David McCormick, he said the name with more amusement than the others. David sat alone as always. He was a non-threatening transcendentalist in his misfit clothes, the tight Notre Dame jacket over a t-shirt hanging in extra fabric that extended his bottom roll over his tight faded jeans. Dorkscapes furrowed his forehead as he curved in affection towards his novel. His double chin massed in suppleness as he delved into the next page. Unchanged, untainted, all David's awkward glory from middle school unappreciated by those who shared the same time and space.

He flinched at the chair scraping against the floor. Mats of hair shot out in shelves but the disorder did not reach his gaze. Isaiah would have turned from that gaze if he hadn't already started to sit. In it there was not a hint of the past liveliness of their friendship.

"Mind if I sit?"

With a limp shrug he went back to reading. Isaiah took out his things to study as he joined him grasping french-fries and chicken nuggets to eat silent. David was expressionless for a long while before Isaiah caught a slight turn of his head and flit of his eyes. Isaiah tried to catch a glimpse of where his other world juxtaposed with this one. But it was just a brief blip of distraction in his reading. Isaiah regretted the discomfort he was causing. Isaiah heard Lumpy's voice from out of the babble and he looked around, fearful he had brought him upon David. But his voice was just carrying from their table oblivious of Isaiah. He remembered what Pastor Joe had said about waiting for God to give him the sign to act, so he didn't try to force conversation. For now his proximity was enough. David could not always be far away. Isaiah would wait until his mouth pert of its own grim resolution would stretch and plump in its full range of expression to share what he found off in the distance.

PSYCH WARD

From the hospital bed Maggie looked at Isaiah. She was calm in recent wakefulness.

"Isaiah?"

"Hey Magpie."

Her difference surprised him. He searched for the remnants of her comforting chubbiness, but it had been sucked from her cheekbones, gone was the double chin, remnants only in her plump lips and her healthy pink glow. Girlishness had been drained like the baby fat from her face. Without makeup her hallowed eye sockets accentuated her defeated look. The heroin chic seemed straight out of a magazine.

"Why are you here?"

He was self conscious as never before around her. It was strange to feel this surge of attraction when looking at her. As the last tendrils of sleep passed her confusion was replaced with anger.

"I am glad you are ok."

He smiled at her.

"I was worried about you."

She lacked her previous feminine exuberance as she daintily picked up a skim milk container. She touched it to her lips for a brief taste, and then carefully set it down, all the while staring at him.

"And I just wanted to apologize for what Lumpy did. I am really sorry. You have to believe I had nothing to do with it."

He faltered as he looked at the medical machinery around her bed.

"We've been friends for a long time and I never would do something like that."

She seemed to relax. He took this as a sign of forgiveness and sat at the edge of her bed. Her detached face seemed to connect at the neck to the white folds of the sheets, nothing left underneath but more tubes and machinery reconciling the act that had put her here. The emaciated stare revealed some remaining vitality when she sipped her skim milk hungrily and ran her tongue around her soft lips. He wanted to clasp her until the softness came back into her.

"I mean come on you can do so much better than a monster like Lumpy anyways. You're too cute for him."

She turned away from him to stare at the plain white wall. He caught an unpleasant whiff. It was not shit, but the process of proteins deconstructing nutrients of which shit was a refined product. He noticed now the bag filling with thin gruel streaming down the thick clear plastic.

"Your life is ahead of you. This is insignificant in the grand scheme of things."

"What?"

"There is beauty in life. When I feel depressed, I contemplate the depth of the universe inside me. It is like ."

He trailed off at the anger in her eyes.

"What are you talking about?"

"God," he said, tentative as if asking a question.

"Is this another joke?"

He was desperate to make her feel better but he didn't know what to say.

"No. I miss hanging out with you. When you get better we have to do that more."

"I get it," she screeched. "I realize it. I made a grand mistake thinking that even a lard ass like Lumpy would like me. I don't need any more of your cruel jokes. I've accepted my place, the fat girl, for Christ sake I get it, I am the fat girl, and now I'm the fat girl who shits her fucking pants, a disgusting unlovable waste of humanity."

He moved backwards as she ranted.

"They said you're going to make a full recovery."

A nurse came into the room.

"What is going on?"

"I was just trying to help her, trying to help."

He backed out of the door. He could now picture how her body had heaved unable to throw up the poison. Her parents had found her unconscious, had watched as doctors pumped the sludge of digestion from her stomach. When she woke with a long tube down her throat did she wonder what had happened? Did she remember what she had done with a rush of murky emotion in the bright light of her hospital room, which previously could have been imagined the bright light of heaven? No sound but the hum and beeps of the machinery, lying like an animal as thoughtless as when they had found her? It was hard to imagine Maggie growing the nerve to take the pills. Even if it was just for attention, how lonely must you be to need attention that bad? And if she had accidentally succeeded, would she have awakened in the afterlife punished with an eternity of hateful ogres standing over her and humiliating her?

HAPPY BIRTHDAY

An uncoming of age was upon him. He had spent the afternoon of his 18th birthday trying to dissipate all childish thoughts.

"Happy birthday!"

His father got up and put his arm around Isaiah in rare intimacy as he brought him to his liquor cabinet. The lowball glasses and stainless steel ice container had already been prepared. With matching stainless steel tongs he dropped ice cubes into their glasses and poured amber scotch from the decanter, adding water to hand the drink to Isaiah ceremoniously. He took his first sip pretending to be hesitant. The scotch had a different heat than the vodka he was used to, syrupy fumes filled his olfactory with rich warmth that dabbled down his throat. His father tapped his glass. His mother set her glass of wine down and walked over to hug him.

"Happy birthday. I can't believe my baby is all grown up. We love you son."

His father sat on his chair while they sat on the couch like any other evening. Quick this day had dawned and quick the short ceremony of daylight had faded back into dusk. This ritual was one already past, but he pretended to be immersed in a new experience as he drank.

"So how does it feel to be all grown up?" His mom said.

"Like another day."

At least now he could buy his own cigarettes. He was happy to see the alcohol smooth away some of their day's exhaustion, grateful that they had a reason to turn off the television and smile at each other.

"Ready for college?" His mom said.

"I'm ready for high school to be over. There is this one teacher, Mrs. Dronomine, her lectures are like mental water torture, drip, drip, drip."

"Sounds like someone has that disease we call senioritis."

She giggled.

"Wait. Isn't that the teacher Barrett thinks is so attractive?" His dad said.

"Henry."

His mother slapped his arm.

"What? I'm just saying that doesn't sound all that bad."

"Where is Barrett? You could have invited your friends over for dinner."

"He was busy."

"Do you want to do anything special tonight?" His mother asked.

He shifted the glass, the clinks like iceberg clippings in the small amber sea.

"Just going to do some studying I have to finish."

"That is my son, always practical," His father said. "I know it hurts your mother to think of it, but if your friends want to take you out you don't have to hang out with your boring old mom and pops all night. If you promise to be safe and make it to class tomorrow I'll even waive your curfew for the night."

They laughed at that for they had never had to instill a curfew for him.

"May I have another?"

His father raised an eyebrow but motioned over to the liquor cabinet.

"So eighteen. Welcome to the good life my son. Go pour us another one."

"Henry."

"Mother, my son turns eighteen once, and if he wants to have another drink with his father then he'll have another drink with me."

He often sat quiet with a scotch as he watched television in the evening. But now with flushed vitality he watched Isaiah pour the drinks in the manner he had, pondering a thought with youthful delight as Isaiah handed him his.

"I miss the old college days."

His father took personal sips as if the scotch was nothing more than a prop. Isaiah mimicked this way of drinking, and barely acknowledging the act at no particular pace gave it an air of sophistication, even more than the expensive decanter of scotch shifting amber light at its edges.

"Enjoy every moment. Don't take it for granted. It was the best 4 years of my life."

"You didn't meet me until your senior year honey."

"And you were the grand finale baby."

His father winked at him.

"You will meet some interesting ladies."

"Maybe you also will meet your future wife there." His mother said.

She smiled pointedly at his father and Isaiah laughed. She always understood, even if she allowed his father to pretend to share some secret of manhood with Isaiah.

"I will tell you one thing, I am over this high school bullshit."

"Language. Your mother is here."

He apologized but they weren't really angry. They enjoyed being like teenagers again in his confessional.

"I am still disappointed midterms kept Rachel from coming home for your birthday. But I am so excited you two will be in college together. Even if both my babies will be gone," His mother said.

"It is not all fun though; you are going to have to work hard to be an engineer."

"Yes."

He grunted as they pondered the family photos, Rachel's senior portrait next to his, his mother's sadness was not just about him, but the progression of their family. He felt a pang looking at his picture that displayed nothing of the heavy gap between his life and the exploits they imagined. His mother took a deep breath and smiled again at him. They remained silent as they drank for things they did not want to take for granted. He was immobile long after their glasses were empty and his parent's got up to clean the kitchen. They laughed as the dishes rattled. The domestic sound soothed him. When they stopped laughing to look at each other seriously he wished they would continue. They were unaware of him watching. There was a slight rasp in his father's reassuring baritone.

"That is just the way things are Laura."

Serious lines creased her face.

"I know Ernest, but it is sad."

Her voice had named him, had whispered it full-throated with hopefulness at her swollen belly, Isaiah. His father had liked the sound of it on her lips. He watched the people he was conceived from, the bend in their supple spines as they hugged, and wondered where flesh touched, where souls touched, thinking of his sister hundreds of miles away. He snuck up to his room.

Life wasn't always so boring. He had read of its potential. He stared out his window. The winter murk allowed no ethereal light from heavenly bodies, all he could see was his closest neighbors' houses insulated in a warm glow. Friday night, but he had no excuses to go out in the cold, so he turned on the television. He watched a movie about a sullen boy who did not once laugh, or tell a joke, or even smirk at his demons as he drank from the bottle, till the melodramatic squeal of tires and smack of metal made everyone sober. The only smiles were left for the Hallmark commercials. He switched it to the news station his father was watching downstairs. He turned his radio on and wished he knew the name of the band. His computer was another glowing portal to the world. When he turned it on a box immediately popped up.

PRINCESS69: Hey what ya doin'?

He typed comedy into the search bar.

Isaiah82: Nothing

On the television a news segment came on, and he was jealous of the open walls in a clip of a slum. At least the inhabitants were starved into hungry movements of insane existence.

PRINCESS69: Not fun. LOL. I wish I was there ;)~

On his computer large swollen Japanese breasts lactated streams of thick creamy sustenance.

PRINCESS69: Oh my god, I'm so bored. When I'm bored I get horny.

On the television was a storm surge, then footage of a tornado, at the end of a horror story bodies piled up in mounds of anticlimactic flesh.

PRINCESS69: Hello? U there hottie? Lol.

The newscaster's voice swelled into the blaring chaos that filled the screen, intensifying as protesters were mauled by armed men in dirt roads. The camera panned to a boy sitting with hands covering his face, blood flowing around his fingers. It zoomed in on his dazed and defeated brown eyes, blood flowing down his tear tracks.

PRINCESS69: Are we ever going to meet? ;-p

He persuaded himself there indeed were things outside his four walls. But with the television on, the radio playing, the computer open up to various streams, still through all these boxes the scope remained only virtual in his imagination.

Isaiah 82: Are you always virtually laughing at the riotous loneliness?

PRINCESS69: Huh?

Isaiah82: Gotta go. Ttyl.

He turned everything off. In the silence he eyed his bible.

He was comatose with lethargy when he answered the unknown number on his phone, so resigned that he did not even pause in surprise at the world presenting itself with Stephanie's voice.

"Want to come over and watch a movie?"

"Sure."

"Great. See you in a bit."

"Bye."

His excitement was for a motive taking him from his room. The harsh sky tapped his windshield with a mix of frozen rain and snow, and he slid on roads in a world that seemed his alone. He slammed his brakes to feel the panic of his inept steering wheel as his car slid before a jerk of friction stopped him sideways in an intersection. He walked through the winter wonderland of her yard covered with snow. It melted on his uncapped head. The missing moon and stars were exotic in his imagination as he approached the glow of her house. His ice-cold fingers were like bones knocking on her front door. But no elf answered. Stephanie was thick in her jeans, casually covered so he could see her bra through her white t-shirt.

"Hi. Follow me."

She pranced into the dining room. The drunken charade of New Years seemed sinful in contrast now to the bright room with its wide chandelier, the homely warmth rebuffed the iciness smacking against the window.

"Mom, this is my friend Isaiah," She said casually.

"Nice to meet you."

She read a magazine with a glass of wine, her fine sweater of middle-aged comfort made him think of his mother, and her unthreatening welcome inspired his best church smile. Her jewelry was thick in curves that softened the severity of her jaw even more square than her daughters.

"Were going to watch a movie."

"Ok. Have fun."

With a moist hand she pulled him to the living room couch where drunken with eventuality he had watched Times Square on the same television blend into the eternity of the new millennium.

"I got American Tart for Christmas."

Her tone was that of a girl taking orders at a fast food restaurant.

"Cool."

"Vodka?"

She handed a full water bottle to him.

"Popcorn?"

She set the warm bowl where their thighs pressed together. Sin's already committed, he shared the vodka and leaned against her, supple and expectant as they watched previews. The butter mixed with the alcohol on her breath. At the second laugh her hand was upon his thigh. She put the bowl on the table. The butter was thick on his hand she held. A few more laughs and her hand was on his crotch.

"What about your mom?"

"Didn't you hear her go to bed silly? She won't come back down."

She unbuttoned his pants and thankfully the butter caused lubrication as she yanked like she was trying to give him an Indian burn. His tongue cleaned kernels from his teeth, running over his budding wisdom teeth, unable to completely remove the starch from the recesses.

"Softer."

"Sorry."

She leaned in but instead of kissing him she stuck her head under the blanket. Her mouth was wet and buttery in a first shock of new pleasure. He flexed his calves, afraid of being rude he moaned out his laughter at the movie. She came from under the blanked and quickly their pants came off. He knew there was pressure built up, and this time he took control on top like an athlete letting his hormones take control. Powerfully this time it built within him, and to prove himself he pounded out the feeling, neither of them making a noise. Then it was over. It happened too fast for him to completely examine the pleasure. Limp he tried to hold on to the intensity. With a soft grunt she pushed him off of her. She put her panties and jeans on and handed him his. He dressed with her in the shadows of the movie. The scenes were sad and disconnected now.

"Let's smoke."

They put their shoes on and he followed her outside. She lit two

Marlboro Lights and handed him one. He absorbed nicotine like the habitual fix of ancient sin. Spent, he shivered and tried to interpret her anew in the evening light. Her young skin was pretty in the shadows, her earthy swells swayed underneath the cold, but there was nothing fragile in the angles of her expression, and her eyes looked off to nothing but the tip of her cigarette.

"That's a really funny movie huh?" He finally said.

"Yeah. My grandma got it for me. Isn't that hilarious?"

"Yeah. I can't even imagine a little old grandma watching something like that."

"She didn't. I told her to get it."

"It is funny to imagine a grandma watching it though."

"I suppose."

She turned at the door when he tried to follow her in.

"I think I'm going to go to bed now. I'm tired. Thanks for watching the movie with me."

She kissed him and their warm saliva ran down to cool on his face. She stopped as abruptly as she had started.

"Can we keep this secret? Don't tell anyone from school please?"

"Ok."

"Good, we may have to do this again sometime."

Her mischievous smile displayed the most emotion he had seen all night. "Sure."

She closed the door. They hadn't even finished watching the movie.

Back home he picked up his bible, choosing a place where the gold edge of the pages was most worn away. With a poetic cadence he read aloud to leach the evil. The scratch marks from Stephanie itched on his back. In the eternity of his youth these words had seemed unnecessary. But now he understood the sacrifices of flesh and bone, and he offered himself for forgiveness. Alone in his room he gave penance. Forgotten like the day he wasn't born.

STRANDED SYMBOLS

What did David see off there? He still managed to escape Karen's class even without the books forbade him.

They had been watching a documentary before the AV had malfunctioned. Now the video repeated the same short clip. Karen stomped her foot. The class didn't look away from the screen as she fooled around with the AV equipment. Behind the narrator on the video a room full of adults stared blankly outwards, mirroring the class watching the video repeat. It seemed as if they were superimposed in the future staring back as a warning. The ill-omen settled upon Isaiah as the image repeated, and he imagined Rachel in her college classrooms, his parents exhausted at work, sharing the same bored stare. He looked around at his classmates. What unhappiness had he missed in these hours barely acknowledged? What misery had been behind the shark smile leading to the fin of Tony's nose? Josh had been more than the clean-cut boy he remembered from memorial photographs. He had witnessed the callousness that had sunk in Maggie's cherub cheeks. And Chris. Oh Chris. What run on thoughts had occupied his mind, what unimagined worlds were left undiscovered underneath those long lashes.

But David sat in the corner oblivious to every flash and repeat. Where did his angst hide? Where was the wretchedness he had glimpsed before the aversion of David's downcast eyes? Even at lunch his disregard for Isaiah was impersonal, briefly focusing with a polite hello before withdrawing again. Every day in the bored silence his pupils narrowed in slow migration across his bandit literature, a never-ending supply of thick books bound like sheaves of tissue paper. It was impossible he could totally escape this place. Isaiah awaited a glimpse of his unhappiness, resolved to comfort him, but he was never given the chance.

"I guess we won't watch the rest of this today. Go ahead and study quietly."

Karen unplugged the AV machine. Amiably she sat back at her desk to continue grading paperwork. Their reflection still stared back from the blank television screen. The posters on the wall bled into the whitewashed bricks in a blur as his eyes strained to reconnect. He was reminded of New Years Eve when time had seemed to end. But the clock measuring forward could not dispel the eternity of the forewarning.

A stranded symbol, the small pine in David's front yard remained lit with Christmas lights. Isaiah pondered the remnant holiness in the hush of winter. During the holidays the plump old-fashioned bulbs, strewn haphazard in red, blue, green and orange, had been whitewashed by the neighbor's department stores worth of white light attempting to outshine the stars. But now there was reverence in the pine. The stars could never be imagined insignificant pricks of light. The few clouds floating regal in the upper atmosphere scattered snowflakes in isolated descent. Snowflakes sparkled with the color of the bulbs as they neared the tree. The neighbor's now observed the season with despondency settling upon their shudders and drawn curtains.

David pulled his book bag from the trunk of his hatchback and his coat lifted to expose the pale flab of his love handle. Isaiah watched him walk in his house unobserved from his car parked on the street a few houses down. As Isaiah walked up the steps he remembered the light taps of his plastic tennis shoes as a kid. The mulch bed, now covered with snow, had overflowed with flowers in the summers when Mrs. McCormick had been alive. Now only weeds ever ripped the plastic liner. When David answered his knock Isaiah was face to face with the awkward eons that had passed since middle school.

"Hey. I know this is odd, but I was just wondering if I could maybe borrow a book?"

David managed to stay expressionless without a hint of surprise.

"Oh. Yeah. Come in."

He led Isaiah in with minimal hand gestures like a malfunctioning turn signal. The house was in an advanced battle of clutter and order. The hallway carpet was clean but the metal trim had a screw popping out. The kitchen's faded linoleum was shiny but had chips where the panels met. On the dining room table was a toolbox labeled and ordered, next to a pile of mail and papers scattered, and on the counter once decorated by Mrs. McCormick's potted flowers were records stacked next to a pile of keys in an ill fitting puzzle of metal. Mr. McCormick was not there. Isaiah imagined wherever he was, the serene smile on his face as he had joked with Isaiah as a boy was now gone, and now the disorder was also rising in stubble on his rough face.

Down the stairwell David led him into the basement. The familiar dimensions of their boyhood den made it seem like Isaiah was entering the past structures of David's mind. David glanced at Isaiah like he was humoring a memory. But down here he actually focused on the things surrounding them. In contrast Isaiah's familiarity felt vulgar. There was the loveseat Chris had sat upon. On that couch they had told stories and traded baseball cards, underneath the posters of large cats and dragons that remained. Isaiah tried to ignore the ceramic wolfs David's mother had made for him. He was spying on a past he had betrayed. The new things that decorated his basement were the passing life in between. Books had multiplied on the shelves, like Poe and dark birds poetry books perched aflutter to join the science fiction and fantasy novels. Their generation's revolution of posters that was in full rebellion in David's basement Isaiah had missed. Unlike the even placement of posters in school here they covered every possible space on the walls. Like a succession of band t-shirts in the hallway they hung, Bob Marley, Pearl Jam, Ohio Cemetery Records, Pink Floyd, St. Augustine's Hope, Led Zeppelin. CD covers were pinned up like a play list, Alice in Chains, The Red Hot Chilli Peppers, Soundgarden, The Cult, The Who, Nirvana. Around his computer were stickers, Radiohead, Built to Spill, The Counting Crows, Modest Mouse, Jane's Addiction. Isaiah tried to remember the names, Tori Amos, Braying Donkey, The Pixies, The Beatles, Tall Elk, like battle flags they were displayed all over the boxed in horizons.

"Wow this is different," Isaiah said.

A Fender acoustic guitar was on a stand in the corner. It was hard to imagine David's clumsy hands gripping it and those fingers that turned pages instead strumming it. The strings were stained with the brown rust of blood and the wood and fret board had absorbed a layer of dust. Eventually Isaiah could look nowhere but the ground as he waited for judgment.

"See anything you like?"

David's far off distances were recalibrated with affection as he scanned his bookshelves. Isaiah followed his gaze trying to gain the wellspring of David's calm, but the basement held nothing for him but despair. The habit of small talk came in an uncomfortable mumble from Isaiah.

"Um. I dunno. Something to escape the boredom. Like. What did we read that summer? Anything like that. Maybe one of the books you read during lunch?"

David took a book out of his book bag and handed it to him.

"*Grandeur of Illusions.*"

David serenely met his eyes expecting ridicule.

"Perfect," Isaiah bowed his head and read the back aloud. "Sometimes discordant, like our rarely touching lives, still out of this chaos, as if allowing our minds to see the world through immeasurable pixels of words, forms a breathtaking adventure."

He looked up with gratitude he did not deserve.

"You know what the worst part of school is? It is the smell. It is not just that the building stinks. That would be bearable."

David looked away as he zipped his book bag. Isaiah stepped closer to block his retreat back into himself.

"But a new smell comes to my senses after lunch. It is faint, like a whiff of butt crack mixed with dirt. Desensitized to the reek of Goldenwood, I always wonder why I again notice a new stink."

He was rewarded with a slight smile in his chubby cheeks.

"And the thing is it follows me. It gets stronger as the day goes on, and I sniff at it trying to decipher its source. I have come to the conclusion it may indeed come from me. It is like my butt crack secretes some kind of skunk like defense mechanism."

Isaiah could not bear David's boyish expression as he laughed. Ashamed of the past Isaiah was now the one that felt the discomfort in the following silence. Finally he muttered.

"Well I should be going. Thanks a lot man."

He forced himself to stop at the stairs. He hadn't known he was desperate for this kindness until it had overwhelmed him, and he wanted to return it somehow to the boy he had cursed.

"Hey, do you want me to pick you up for school tomorrow?"

Whether David's pleasant tone was faked or not it was more than he deserved.

"Yeah. Sure."

ABERCROMBIE NATION

Is he cool?

The question lingered. The inquisition he expected had finally come in the kitchen of the apartment. A college kid with a Jim Morrison t-shirt and piercings filling the cartilage of his ears leered at him.

"Phil Pfizer?" Isaiah asked.

His sneer increased. It had taken Isaiah a moment to recognize the insolent expression underneath brows not as dark as the dyed black hair at his shoulders. Phil had been a sophomore in a Chicago Bulls jersey and basketball shoes when Isaiah was a freshman. As a junior he had been a skater zit faced and happy in hip and baggy. He had even been a young republican as a senior, wearing button down oxfords and khakis following in the footsteps of his father the superintendent. That loathsome expression had remained his only constant.

"Welcome to my apartment. Hit this."

Phil eyed him through an exhalation of smoke doubtfully. Isaiah took the glass pipe swirled with colors from fingers full of gothic silver rings leading to a thumb-ring with a yin-yang. The thumb handing him the lighter bore a cross and bones. Isaiah nonchalantly put the pipe full of marijuana to his lips but hesitated.

"Here let me help you."

English had nonchalantly invited him to this party in the hallway earlier that day, and Isaiah had only accepted as a respite from another bored Friday night. Now he saved him from looking like an idiot by holding the pipe in place as his other scrawny arm applied the flame.

"Suck," he purred.

Grateful like a drowning man saved Isaiah inhaled. The flame disappeared as the nugget flared. Pungent spice filled his sinuses. English lifted his finger from the hole at the base of the pipe.

"Keep sucking."

If his first hit of a cigarette was like sucking down a flamethrowers blast, then this was taking a sun flare into the depths of his lungs. He tried to exhale the heat slowly but could not suppress a curt cough. That first cough began an avalanche of coughs spewing from his depths. It felt as if it was coming from his stomach. English patted him on the back as he frothed and coughed up his previous state of mind.

"Open up those virgin air sacks."

English took the pipe from him and his delicate face scrunched as he inhaled like an alien in another atmosphere. His feminine good looks could have been straight out of an Abercrombie catalogue, with the pressed candle on his t-shirt matched with designer jeans. He looked at Isaiah as if trying to decide if he was really there, and removed his finger from the hole, sucking long and hard to puff his cheeks out meditatively. He sucked again fast twice. Then he blew two thick smoke rings that rose slow before he exhaled a translucent stream to disperse them.

English passed the pipe to a dirt rocker with oily strands of hair covering his face and hanging down his back. He smoked without once looking at Isaiah. He passed the pipe to an intimidating looking man with a NIN t-shirt. Isaiah looked down to the half eaten bowl of Ramen noodles that juxtaposed the drug paraphernalia on the kitchen table, avoiding the man's stare on him like the grave dug, with his shovel forehead above a face like the remaining dirt. The small bead polyps on his nose flexed as he blew out through the ring in his snout. He set the pipe on the counter and took an orange from the fat mesh sack to add more peels to the pile in front of him.

"Dude your dad is fucking hilarious. What did he say when he dropped off your groceries? I can smell the marijuana dumb ass. The incense you cover it up with just makes your apartment smell like some poor hicks covering up the stink of their dog vomit existence," the intimidating man said.

Phil snorted.

"I would have never thought so in school, but your dad is super chill," the dirt rocker said, re-greasing his hair as he brushed it from his face.

"And daddy brought me my crazy pills. I get my best drugs legal and cheap. Want to buy some of these too boys? It is the good stuff."

Phil rattled a pill bottle at them.

"I already have a prescription," English chuckled.

"I still can't help but think of the rabbit when I look at that microwave. That was awesome," the intimidating man said.

"What are you guys laughing about?"

English's drooped lids dampened his curiosity.

"Needless to say don't tell my cum-dumpster this story," Phil said. He stared at Isaiah with ruthless mirth. "I better not find out you are a rat."

But it was the man's look above the thick brown patch of fur on his chin that caused Isaiah to stare at the pack of cigarettes in his shirt pocket like a badge in discomfort. The intimidating man set the orange down and lit a cigarette, checking the other room to make sure the party continued unobservant before he started to speak.

"Phil was sitting here sneezing and complaining about Mr. Wiggles when I had this wonderful idea."

He ran his hand, wet from the orange, through his buzz cut.

"My sweet Jenny, bless her heart, she just cannot resist a pet store, and despite my allergies, while looking at the lovelies she decided we needed a pet. So she bought this rabbit, cheap, because, you know, they fuck like rabbits. I went along so she would shut her mouth and open her legs. Her soft spot was overjoyed with the idea I had a soft spot for God's little creatures," Phil said.

"I mean the thing was scared and shitting all over the place and having a heart attack every time we came near it, so how could we not fuck with it?"

The intimidating man chortled.

"And let me tell you, that fucking annoys you after a while," Phil said.

Isaiah hid his disgust as he tried to decipher whether they were just trying to scare him. The intimidating man's smile chilled his heart, his bright eyes were alight with resolve to find the face of God and spit in it.

"So I had this great idea, and I said to Phil, you know how a frog or cricket, supposedly when you microwave it will explode?"

"You guys are sick fuckers," English laughed.

"The first time I turned it off after five seconds," Phil said.

"Pussy," The intimidating man scoffed.

"I fucked with it. I opened the door and gave it a chance for freedom, but it was so scared it stayed there petrified. Stupid rabbit would rather die than move. A shivering Easter bunny, you wouldn't believe how big its eyes were. So I said screw it, I closed the door, to see what would happen when we made the motherfucker fry. And I turned the microwave on full blast."

The intimidating man started to unpeel the orange again.

"We watched the fair creature freak out while it cooked. I looked in its eyes the whole time. You wouldn't believe how its pupils expanded in a life before death orgasm of intensity. And then boom!"

The intimidating man jumped forward and ripped the orange segments open as he peered at Isaiah from the blood red clefts underneath his heavy eyelids.

"I wish. It wasn't really that awesome. It was singed and cooked, its face melted, with little fissures of juice and blood leaving gooey chunks in my microwave. The thing made my whole house smell like cooked rabbit meat. And I had to go buy another rabbit for my sweet Jenny, dumb slut didn't notice anything."

Isaiah allowed a cough for their grim consideration. He took the pack of cigarettes out. He waited for the joke to be over. Phil got up and walked into the other room still laughing and wrapped up petite Jenny in a hug. Isaiah followed and sat down beside English.

"Need a light?"

Amused, English lit the cigarette Isaiah had forgotten between his lips. He opened a Bud Light and handed it to him.

"Ultra slims? I didn't know anyone but housewives and grandmas smoked those anymore," Phil said.

"How does Rachel like State?" Jenny asked.

She held the exoticness Isaiah had sought here. But Phil's arm around her brown blouse, his hand hanging between her sweet hippie buds, his other hand on her long hemp skirt, tainted it. Still he imagined she shirked from Phil as her pale green eyes touched him with kindness.

"She makes it sound like the Promised Land."

She giggled and leaned away from Phil to offer her hand. It was larger and rougher than Isaiah. expected, her jewelry cool in contrast with the warmth of her skin. He gave her the same smile he shared with his sister.

"Jenny Young. She was always a cool chick. Tell her I said hi."

He regretted letting her hand go as Phil pulled her back towards him.

"Cool. Cold. Frigid," Phil interrupted.

"Shut up Phil."

Isaiah was disappointed that she giggled and gave Phil the same warm look.

"She was a little stuck up Jenny."

This puffy faced girl had answered the door and turned her back on Isaiah so quickly that her blonde dreadlocks had whipped him. She seemed to have vice grips pressing her cheeks together as she smoked and squinted at him. With an offhanded gesture she handed Isaiah the pipe. He lit it methodically and managed not to cough. He passed it to English. The audience feigned inattention as they passed the pipe in a solemn procession of exhibitionist smoking. Things slowed down and the edges blurred in the haze. Posters glowed under the blacklight and lava lamps blobbed red and blue light. The red bars on the stereo mixed the music with the slow mammalian hum of conversation. Strange faces stared out. Phish t-shirt scrunched his bearded lips like a rotting peach, CounterCulture t-shirt exhaled wide mouthed as he rolled up his sleeves to show off severe lined tattoos on pale biceps, McDonald's Beef t-shirt exhaled from where he was sprawled on the floor barefoot, Dave Matthews Band t-shirt let her potbelly fill the sack of her shirt and fingered the hemp necklace around her plump face. The intimidating man sucked with the force of a gale. Phil stared at the pipe underneath his big nose, and blew the smoke out in a dragon's blast turned towards Isaiah. Jenny's lower jaw jutted out with the dull look of livestock as all of her attention concentrated on the pipe. After a moment lost within, life glowed again in her eyes.

"Ooh. Isaiah you haven't met Mr. Wiggles yet."

She hurried down the hall. She came back delicately holding the twitching rabbit.

"That thing better not shit on the carpet again," Phil said.

"Shut up."

She sat down on Isaiah's knee. With the same quick nervous movements as the rabbit he looked to see Phil's reaction. He seemed oblivious to them. She leaned back against him and he hand brushed over his as they pet the rabbit. He caressed her and the soft fur.

"Aw I think he likes you."

She rested the rabbit in his lap and picked up the pipe. Isaiah held the rabbit tenderly as it shivered in his hands, its heart beating fast against his palms. The pipe flared with Jenny's eyes staring into his, then she blew the smoke in the rabbits face. It blinked and twitched its nose in a quivering ball.

"Is that good stuff baby?"

Her fingertips did ballet on the fur and tickled elation across Isaiah's knuckles down his tendons to his wrist. The rabbit calmed. Enchanted Isaiah wanted her to caress his face in the same way. Phil grabbed her arm.

"Pack another pipe slut. Isaiah looks like he knows how to stroke things right."

She stood and took the rabbit from Isaiah's lap. She carried it back shielding it protectively from Phil.

"Let's go back to bed honey. I know, I know, mommy's sorry."

She sat back down next to Phil and packed the pipe. When she smoked again her face smoothed in troglodyte contentment that altered her prettiness into a homely plain of pallid skin. With her hand on Phil's lap her underbite stayed exposed, her lips waving a cigarette as she scrunched her brow. Isaiah looked off in the hallway at the clothes hamper with dirty laundry hanging by a pant leg out of the shadow into an unkempt pile of clothes on the floor.

"You are a bisexual. A frumpy grumpy pot princess," the intimidating man said to the puffy faced girl.

The dank living room shrank inwards from the posters to a cataract globe surrounding him. His swaying leg chimed a set of keys to the music. It contained what he had come here for. He listened to it shift from guitar to bass like a knob was turned. Down into the deeper spaces between the shag of carpet fibers he imagined atoms disconnected in tangled snakes of wavelengths. He made an effort to alleviate years of bad posture but straightening his spine made his chest stick out like a steel rod was stuck up his butt.

Phil madly bit the air towards him. Then he drank from a bottle of Jack Daniels and handed it to English.

"Welcome to the haze. Illusion becoming psychedelic reality," English said.

"You came to the right place, for here we have the finest assortments of poisons," Phil said

"This one here," English put the bottle softly to his puckered lips. "Can control your mood swings for a lifetime before engulfing your liver and causing blood to spurt out your rectum."

"Tee hee hee," merriment wheezed out of the intimidating man's throat. "Tee hee hee."

"Drink up my sweet one."

English brushed Isaiah's hair affectionately and handed him the bottle. Isaiah pressed the wet opening to his lips and let it wash over the acidic cotton fields in his mouth.

"Wow, you don't have a virgin liver," Jenny said.

"You're so sweet."

Phil's pink tongue stretched out of his mouth like a sea creature, fattening as he licked the side of Jenny's face. English lit his cigarette.

"With this one here, you can breathe your own neurosis; common kin of those who can already taste the blood coughing up from their lungs. Smoke up my sweet one."

Isaiah smacked his flattened cigarette pack against his inner thigh in a quick twitching movement.

"Oh we've got weeds and we've got suds, fermented and cooked with thick gloves, and that puppy over there, if you dare prepare, is the quickest and sweetest hallucination to leave your family your corpse's vacant stare," English sang.

Phil darted his pink tongue again at Jenny. Isaiah exhaled ever-rising swirls, the chemical cloud stratified towards the ceiling his only connection to them. The hallucinogenic smoke layers of white, red, blue, black light exposed their evil caricatures lurking underneath. Phil scooted to the middle of them.

"This is the greatest band ever. Isaiah doesn't even know who it is. You and the rest of the Abercrombie nation don't understand. He knows our pain. You can hear it in his voice, suicide, suicide. I understand his pain. Look what our parents have done to us. The world can hurt so much sometimes."

He accentuated every word with a jut of his nose and actually ended with a controlled sob.

"The curse of Goldenwood. But we have the last laugh, because suicide is punishment for our parents."

His congregation listened rapt with the tie-dyed light glistening on their eyes.

"Punishment for living this husk of a nazi dream. Punishment for conspiring with a government spreading aids to kill off brown people. Punishment for forsaking their very own children to the man," his rings charmed as his hands sped up. "The Gods of Karma are punishing them, man, and taking us for their own," impassioned tears formed in his eyes. "We will be in the arms of Buddha, we will be sipping tea with Christ, and the demons won't touch us anymore."

They were captivated.

"He looks so sad, and you just know that someone has done something horrible to him," The puffy faced girl said.

"Stop. You're going to make me cry," Jenny said.

English lifted his heavy lids with fiendish intensity.

"I have demons, trying to take control, I've thought about suicide."

They were silent. Isaiah hung on for his next words.

"But when I have, I realized that no matter what they do to me, I can still get motherfucking high!"

He flourished double devil horns. Jenny's hand was higher upon Phil's inner thigh.

"There are so many children suffering in this world. Only if we could join together and do something."

She looked at Phil in dumb rapture. Isaiah didn't know how to break her trance.

"No one gets lonely in a tribe," McHippie let his greasy hair fall in front of his face as he nodded along to the music. Before his sentence was even finished they were slow nodding at each other.

"But for the super man, we got our chronic kryptonite," English said.

"I once met this old hippie. He looked at me with wisdom lost in years, and he said, God put it here for his flock, so pass that shit on," McHippie said.

"I think it is time for Barry," Phil said.

He grabbed the three-foot cylinder, like a giant beaker with a little basket attached to the side. They gathered around it. Isaiah was trapped in the circle. The McHippie banged his appendages out of time. The intimidating man stomped his foot and banged his head much too fast. Isaiah felt a slight claustrophobic pressure on his nostrils.

"The devil's fucking music," Phil said.

Ache spread thick through channels the drugs had paved.

"I have to go," Isaiah said.

Their faces were no longer masks. Phil looked at him scornfully with demon madness in his eyes.

"Don't be a pussy. Give Barry a kiss so we know you're cool."

There was unfriendliness in their bloodshot eyes. The intimidating man ate an orange with large bites ignoring the sections. Gooey juices squirted and formed a syrupy mess in his patch of chin hair. He burped and wiped the juices on his shirt. Even English, who did not think Isaiah saw, pretended to smoke an imaginary joint and then rolled his finger around his ear to denote craziness.

"Fine, you are dismissed," Phil waved his hand. "Take this pussy home English."

His heart pumped much too fast like the rabbit's had in his hands. He said goodbye so Jenny knew he left.

A pack of Zigzag rolling papers landed in Isaiah's lap.

"I always knew you were cool senator. And now I am going to teach you how to roll a joint. Don't forget to legalize it."

English ripped open the plastic on his pack of Zigzags with his teeth, pursing feminine lips faintly mustached to blow the plastic towards Isaiah.

"Your parents will never smell it if you use toilet paper rolls and blow the smoke through a dryer sheet out your window."

As Isaiah watched he folded the paper in half with thin delicate fingers. Then he took marijuana out of the plastic baggie and with his mouth slightly askew concentrated on evening it out.

"Like this. This sack is a little light, but don't worry about it. Phil always does that the first time he sells to someone. He will be fair in the future. You can pay me tomorrow."

He rolled it with quick deft movements and pinched the ends. He parted his lips and his tongue came out as he put the joint in his mouth and pulled it out. Saliva soaked it and glistened on his lips. His fine brown mustache looked like it didn't need to be shaved yet.

"An amateur move is to Cheech and Chong up a monster joint, wasting precious weed with poor craftsmanship and an uneven burn. Walla, got it?"

He leaned towards Isaiah to put the joint in one hand and the plastic baggie in the other. Isaiah tried to avoid the wetness of his saliva as he cradled the joint in his fingertips. The hunger he had seen in Stephanie surprised him now in English.

"I can head your FDA."

English moved quickly and Isaiah didn't have time to react before a shock of wetness was on his mouth. English forced his tongue in. The smell was wrong, pungent saliva and rotten cashews, and his mustache tickled above his spongy lips. Isaiah yanked away. He awaited nausea, anger, but English was unaffected as he leaned over his lap to open the passenger door.

"See you Monday senator."

He winked at him and drove away. Isaiah should have put his hands around his neck and squeezed that smug look off of his face, made him wheeze for oxygen, desperate under Isaiah's control for that sweeter substance for his lungs. But in his shock Isaiah was numb. Life was changing and Isaiah could not keep up with it. He walked down the sidewalk in swaying observation, escaping the orb of electric light from his house that exposed his humiliation. He eyed the darker shadows of dry underbrush under the pine trees on the side of his house that was Rachel and his secret world as children. But he could not hide there with this haze that tainted his connection with home. His legs were heavy, his head heavier, pulling his balance forward as he fought to keep from staggering. A car turned on his street and wind resistance increased with the phwap of its air pocket. The engine hum filled his ears as it neared. In a time warp the crescendo seemed to slow beside him. His paranoia peeked as the tires screeched and the car swerved. He jumped into the grass and saw inhuman faces inside. The ghouls cramped in the windows were not in costume, but were warped in evil as they stared back at him enlarged in the drawn-out moment. When the car finally passed he turned back towards home. Spared, he stumbled as he ran. He just wanted to be safe from the night in the soft glow coming from his windows. He did not try to sneak in. He did not care if his parents saw he was high. He was disappointed they were in bed, the lights left on for him. If hell opened up over his head tonight, a future archeologist sifting through buckets of ashes from the ruins of his home would ignore the familiar things he now took comfort in, dishware drying on the counter, the soda stains in the pillows on their couch, a pen that had run out of ink keeping his mother's place in the magazine she was reading because the brilliant young scientist made her think of Isaiah, and only a bored child in a classroom would understand the love signified by the things found. He could not hide the joint in his Bible, would not put the plastic baggie in between the pages. He put it in *Leaves of Grass* instead. But he couldn't chuckle at the humor in this. It could easily have been a bag of oregano, but he couldn't pretend innocence remembering the process of attaining it. He turned his light off and made it to the familiar bosom of his bed.

He did not believe in the devil.

But a red glow filled his room. He could discern red eyes staring.

He did not believe in the devil.

The red glow filled his mind even under his covers. He prayed the chemicals in his veins would wear off. But there was nothing but the red glow, to know thy devil, and panic paralyzed him. Finally mad with it he threw off the blankets determined to face whatever was there. It was just the red glow from his alarm clock telling him it was 12:37.

FOREIGN LANDS

It was a matter of small talk. David was not some foreign exchange student yet, yes, no, maybe so, was how he answered Isaiah's attempts at conversation as he stared out Isaiah's car window. He had regressed back into silence as he read at lunch.

As Isaiah tried to study a girl's voice invaded his concentration with squeals of insincere emotion. He attempted to ignore her, but she brought the rest of the lunchroom babble in behind. With a twitch he could no longer help but look up with scorn at her two tables away.

"Can you believe it?"

Her thick makeup didn't conceal her cuteness when she kept her industrial mouth closed. But she did so only to look with disdain around at her table full of sophomore girls.

"What an idiot."

She was well on her way, when she lost the metal from her teeth and learned to accentuate the swell of her breasts, she would find calculation in her mockery and become another self-righteous hussy. She talked so much that he could see the mush of french-fries in her braces. The smell of catsup on his tray was now repugnant and he got up to get rid of it.

"What was he thinking?"

"I mean, where did he even get the idea in the first place?"

"Is he some kind of weirdo?"

"Is he from another planet?"

This budding princess of derision had never stopped talking. He could hear her from the trashcan and on his way back he stopped beside her.

"Could you shut up? Your driving me crazy with your Goldenwood tabloid headlines, oh my gosh, oh my gosh, oh my gosh, do you ever stop?"

Her open mouth had red bands that closed with the hinges of her mechanical jaw. Shut her chin was delicate crystal underneath her dimpled frown. In the silence his toxicity went inwards. She fought tears in front of her fearful friends. She had not yet formed completely her defense mechanisms, and she had no quip to fire back; her meanness had been a question for her friends.

"Sorry. I'm just trying to study and I can't hear myself think you are so loud."

His kindness could not eliminate the edge of irritation in his voice. As he sat David hid again in his book but Isaiah had caught him watching even if he couldn't decipher his thoughts. Braces girl's jaw, hot and oiled with chattering, now remained inert. Upon his conscious she was another victim. He could not go back to studying. He started to doodle on his notebook. He wrote 'Metaphysical Mood Swinger' large on the top. He drew a disco ball, and a horn section and a dance floor with rudimentary bones scattered. Then he drew a protagonist, big time, no minor-league-tagonist, but a professional bone man with a fat gut existence. The legs were quick disjointed lines, bones underneath baggy shorts, and a tight Skeletor t-shirt, like skin holding the organ lard to his skeleton body. His neck was all spinal cord, attached to a head with one swollen eye, inquisitive, the other half-sized with stoner-lidded resignation balancing it out. Finger bones rose in his dance. He drew part of the sun in the corner with just a few rays peeking through.

"I'm bored."

He could not stand to be repressed by the silence any longer. He held the drawing up to David.

"Cool man."

He wanted David's dorkiness to link him to more innocent days. But David's double chins again nodded back into his book. Brown fungus shelves came out of his unruly mass of hair with curling sideburns. His chubby cheeks sprouted soft wiry stubble. His faded jeans exposed white socks contrasting stained tennis shoes. He truly was somewhere else in his misfit autonomy.

Isaiah opened *Grandeur of Illusions* self-consciously. The cover was made from tree bark, the pages held the pulp of residual photosynthesis, and he imagined a snow-capped forest. He fingered the cold lingering in the metal ring of his notebook, its elemental force was also in telephone poles strung along barren mountain passes. Was this what David saw? It was winter and there were stories to be told. He imagined them in a cabin transfixed by the fire as they read the books in their laps.

Like a disconnection the first words of *Grandeur of Illusions* struck. There was simply a boy named Caldrid in a field with some thoughts. There was nothing extraordinary in the first few pages. Sure there were hints of an alternate universe at the edges of the innocent acres, you could sense the insects were a little too benevolent, the world was slightly too tuned to the uncontaminated light of the first sunset of that world. Probably there was nothing in the first few pages to make him see differently. But he did.

At the end of the first chapter he closed the book with his forefinger keeping his place. Braces girl was still silent as if she would never speak again. He wished he could he could make her giggle again. For he had felt a slight sudden shift while reading, and he looked at David with new good humor, for he had glimpsed the fantasy that kept David enraptured through the torment of boredom in between.

"Boing."

Isaiah wasn't sure why he made the noise. David's eyelashes flickered. Before he could retreat back into his book Isaiah made his mouth into a big circle.

"Boing."

David looked up at him puzzled. Isaiah tried to share the oscillations of laughter he had felt in physics.

"Sorry."

Isaiah could only get this one word out to try and explain that some sort of joke wasn't being played on him.

"Sorry."

He did not want David to think there was cruelty in his laughter. He remembered how cruel his laughter had sounded after Barrett had kicked him in the butt. He did not want those eyes to penetrate him and illuminate the cruelty he hid within.

"Sorry."

He laughed as he looked down at the notebook that contained David's name as a curse.

"Sorry."

Isaiah looked away and tried to find David's far off distance to maybe try and explain. When he composed himself he could do nothing but hold up *Grandeur of Illusions*.

"Sorry to bug you. But this book is really good. You can go back to your reading."

David did not say anything, but the book seemed explanation enough, and he actually gave Isaiah a slight smile before looking back down. Isaiah was not surprised nor no longer annoyed when he did just that and ignored him to continue reading. The monotone bell shook them with the building's will. He got up in unison with David and walked beside him as if he could protect him from the machinations it had started. Braces girl was still silent and did not look up at him. As a boy David had carried his book bag the same peculiar way as he did now, as if he was barely aware of it. He put the constant stubborn face upon his silence, his lids drooping again even as his eyes were intently in the distance. Isaiah was fearful of what he really thought of him. They were first into the empty hallways. Characters moved peacefully in the shadows like memories. In contrast the befuddled faces behind them moved in confused wanderings. *Pull the fire alarm, pull the fire alarm*, Isaiah thought, *smash the clocks in*. He wished he had caused this chaos to briefly alter the day as they parted wordlessly into opposite hallways.

PIERCE HIMSELF TILL THEY HURT

How did you celebrate a normal day? What words were there to commence it? Things had been going good. Isaiah exhaled smoke through the toilet paper roll out of his screen. He flushed the roach and hid the baggie back in *Leaves of Grass*. He hadn't smoked the joint English had rolled, but he had become skilled at rolling his own. The G.I. Joe t-shirt he found in the back of his closet he had not kept for nostalgia, it had been too big as a child, but now it was perfectly snug on his biceps.

He went back to studying his history textbook. But the dead did not care if the dying knew their language. He lifted his screen and stuck his head out to stare at the ground. It would also come of its own accord. The toilet paper roll worked for a cigarette also. His ash was a remnant of the past he flicked into a glass of water. He was not afraid of the pressure against his nostrils, or the romanticized letting go to the pulling forward to the end of the years. The unclean man who had accosted Isaiah as a child was still screaming on the street corner, not caring how his spittle landed on small children. He was drunk on eventuality, his cold dead eyes finding their only amusement as a seer of death.

"The world will soon end so you better enjoy what is left of your petty life," he still screamed at frightened children.

Isaiah picked up the textbook by the corner as if grabbing a child's ear and carried it to the porch. He put his lighter to it, watching the flame as he eagerly awaited the flare. In the flames he wanted to see the fall of Rome. When it burnt a father had carried his cherub son between large pillars that crumbled in a ruined civilization that had seemed as steady as infinity. The flame briefly engulfed the cover in chemical colors. When he took it away the burnt smell and a slight warping was all that remained. He put it to the pages and they caught, but the burning red lines smoldered into the pages to leave only a line of black ash to crumble away. Again he held the flame so the blue lighter fluid ran up the cover. It rearranged goops of dye and left a brown stain but the cover did not catch fire even as the lighter burnt his thumb. History was imperishable.

He walked back through his house. The living room was where his dog Turner had walked around in circles like a four legged top out of control, and then had stopped to lick Isaiah mercilessly until he bored of petting him. It wasn't until he threw up neon foam that Isaiah realized something was wrong, and by the time he got to the vet his brain had already been fried by the fever.

He stared at Rachel's large oak frame bed, he wanted to disrupt the clean lines of that refuge and lie down. His parent had started using the space for extra storage, in it were his father's golf clubs he had received one Christmas. Christmas morning he had kissed the purple suede head cover of the putter. His mother's left over miniatures in a box contained the stone naturally shaped like the state of Ohio. When she had pocketed it at the state park they had teased her for being a criminal. He closed the door gently.

He stared at the white walls of his room unfocused. He didn't want to imagine a future like this. He took a small sip of vodka, then another. He liked the heavy feel of the bottle, like a full gas container swishing around. The rest of life was just momentary blurs in between this, but he couldn't imagine anything different. He couldn't think of anything but commercials. With a pang he remembered Chris and David and he sitting under the stars and laughing at an unexpected joke while that small universe expanded.

He took a bigger drink. Not to belong. Not for mild rebellion. He wanted to swallow until something shifted, the future shifted, the whole universe shifted into an alternate dimension. He opened his throat. He turned his stereo on and danced to exercise the fumes.

"I am not drunk. I am tearing away the peripheral to meditate."

He wanted to see the world through a spider web of red lines. He wanted the room to be spinning so the walls of his box would blur. He inhaled hard like the cigarette was a joint. He inhaled harder. He breathed like friction. In a fury he jumped around his room like performance art. He chuckled at nothing for a long time; he ignored the dull ache almost as long.

"I will paint myself red dot like a target. I will wear my G.I. Joe shirt. I will pierce myself until you hurt."

He swallowed.

He took the knife from underneath his pillow. He toyed with its weight. He wondered if Chris had considered the razor blade he had used to sever veins and his gaze. From the kitchen Isaiah had chosen a steak knife. He wanted to feel the melodrama in his heart just a bit to clarify it. He parted forearm hair to rub the blade against the soft prepubescent skin underneath. He ran it between his lips to kiss the cool steel serrations down to the tip. Caressing his face he pressed its tip against his temple. He pictured Chris with the razor blade parallel to blue veins underneath the pale skin of a wrist similar to his. What did those eyes see as they stared out of windows in buildings creaking like the moaning ghosts of their childhood?

For a while he paced with the knife held at his side. Then he stopped in the middle of his room and closed his eyes to slide the knife across his forearm. Drums crashed. The pinch he felt was something. If he could disassociate himself from the pain the sensory world would shimmer in transcendence. He would dispel the illusions they had about him. But when he opened his eyes he saw just a scrape on his arm. *Pussy.* He cut himself again quickly, and then again, but no matter how hard he tried to press he could only add scratches. He frowned, wondering if his torturous emotion was nothing more than mild loneliness. *Pussy.* He tried to find intensity in the bottle of vodka until he gagged. He smoked to burn stale life in quickly growing ash. He rolled his sleeve up and with eyes wide open brought the knife again to his skin. He screamed. This time the bite of steel took his breath away. Drunkenness dissipated. He looked in wonder at the blood running down his arm. For him alone the perfection dripped on the carpet. He cleaned the blade on his shirt. He turned his arm so his palm was facing up. His melodramatic muscle pumped. He jerked the knife. The red scratch just below his elbow pit was not worth the bite of pain. He scowled, wondering if his loneliness was nothing more than sadness at being ignored by the masturbation queens. With a rush of adrenaline he sliced so hard the knife felt like it brushed his bone. He looked at the white meat curiously. Then blood came in a gush. He held his hand limp and walked over to his computer desk to examine the red streams flowing down his wrist under his lamp. It dripped on his computer desk until its surface was thick with blood. He took his G.I. Joe shirt off and cleaned the blade, then held it to his wounds as it buttered up crimson. The blood coagulated on the laminate of his desk. He used the shirt to clean it then wrapped it around his arm. He went to the bathroom. The afterglow was for his alabaster smile alone. But soon the adrenaline faded and he was numb. He cleaned and dressed his wounds in fear his dad would come in to find what his coward son had done. He washed the blood out of his shirt and guiltily scraped fingerprints of hardened blood from the faucet with his fingernail.

BIG HEAD SKULL CRUSHER

An oxford hid his shame. But he didn't notice the discomfort from his wounds in this habitat of like-minded creatures. Where did these rare species waste the rest of their time in the building? He was a computer left on standby looking around the classroom with his eyes blinking like a cursor so an unimportant thought wouldn't burn into his mind. Mr. Quinn and Tim were at the center of their combined computing power dipping space-time. But even the mathematical recesses of their thought had residual humanity in their shared looks.

Isaiah was glad his mind had something to occupy it. The emotions that had almost caused him to drip drop away last night were now opposed by thought. His brain sparked as he pondered the question Tim had posed for them. Kurt pressed his pinky into the springs of his afro to itch his head. Stanley looked to Isaiah.

"What is reality?" Ronald said.

Isaiah ignored Ronald's egghead look of confidence. Isaiah searched Tim's face. He had asked if science had proven reality. He wanted to know the measurements, how he had formulated his theories, the consecrated hypothesis, and if in that light shining from his calculation he had found God.

"Faith," Isaiah said hesitatingly.

Tim's head stopped its rolling orbit as he looked at Isaiah with his mouth open, his eyes fixed as he tried to formulate an answer. Ronald rolled his eyes and shook a frustrated fist at Isaiah.

"We talk about the laws of the universe. But what I mean is, doesn't that still leave so much unexplained that we still have to take on faith?" Isaiah asked.

"That is not what I meant."

Isaiah flushed at Tim's curt response. He felt as inept as nebulous space dust compared to the planetary certainty now pulling Tim's gaze back towards Mr. Quinn. Mr. Quinn laughed.

"Interesting. Tim science hasn't disproved reality. But so far the data stands up to the theory that there are actually multiple dimensions, or realities."

Tim took a lecturing tone seemingly for Isaiah alone.

"We have to take into account the quantum map of probability giving us a greatly pixilated map the more experiments we perform. It is kind of sophomoric to say because something isn't disproved completely that it isn't proved."

"But doesn't that still leave something about our world that we have no choice but to take on faith?" Isaiah asked.

Tim got up and walked to the chalkboard and picked up a piece of chalk.

"May I?" He asked and Mr. Quinn stepped aside courteously.

He dropped the chalk on the ground and it broke into pieces.

"I'm pretty sure man instinctively came to terms with this phenomenon well before Newton. Schrödinger's Cat doesn't really care how we philosophize, it is either meowing for some milk or dead."

Tim had no gravitational attraction to the weak force of Isaiah's uncomprehending look and he again orbited away.

"Well then let's party, let's hop, if all our thoughts are going to end up piles of worm feces anyways," Isaiah responded.

"Whoa, whoa, don't go and drown yourself in the frat beer in college. I didn't mean to scare you with my talk of the end of the universe. Entropy is a true bogeyman isn't it? But anti matter, electrons and protons and neutrons, there is much to this life we still don't understand."

"Haven't we already discovered it? It is God," Ramona said with rapture.

Ronald broke the hushed silence.

"Whoa."

"No, no, it is all right. We can speak freely here. I don't know if I have an answer to that. I have my personal beliefs, but I think maybe that is a question we all have to answer ourselves."

They waited for him to continue.

"We spend our days doing these experiments. We spend our days in this experiment. I try and teach you what I can. But I am but a dorky old science teacher. I can but give you things to ponder."

Ronald hit his head like he was crushing his skull.

"There are rules that need to be followed. The world is set, and we don't exist in another dimension. What is the point in talking about it?"

"Only God would be able to see beyond the Heisenberg uncertainty principal, and therefore if there is reality there has to be a God to observe it," Kurt said and scrunched a handful of his spongy afro.

Tim sighed. He looked at Isaiah like he was a naïve child.

"Just because we can't be 100 percent certain doesn't mean that we can't through the power of intellect and the science of observation determine that by the nature of the proof, these things are self evident."

"Hhhuh," Stanley the biological factory said.

"Should we give the priests a chemistry set and send them to work? They may prove more useful in their gospel," Tim said.

"Reality itself is a leap of faith," Ramona said.

"I have a dragon in my garage," Tim said.

But as they continued their debate all Isaiah heard was 01001010. They had gone beyond where he could follow. If they found a universal theory their greater computing power could spend a lifetime arguing that. They might just all be in a bubble formed in the wad of snot spit from a dying deities mouth. He shared Mr. Quinn's pleased smile. It was fun to think of quarks going back in time, and Isaiah felt hope again that there were still things to keep his curiosity for hidden in the routine of every day. The dead didn't care how the living philosophized.

"Sometimes—"

The bell cut in.

"Awk! And there again is inevitability. Maybe one of you can go on to discover time travel please? In the meantime, if it isn't too late, one piece of advice, find a college without bells!"

EVOLUTIONARY SNOT

His silence was confessional. On a whim Isaiah had invited David to the arboretum. He had been surprised he had said yes. Turning the opposite way from the familiar drive home from school Isaiah had felt vulnerable. Bringing him here was opening an intimate part of himself. He wondered if David marveled as he did at the road like thin fingernail paint upon the great path of the glaciers, boulders deposited by the slowing ice age leaving hills undulating in the distance.

In this rolling countryside arrowheads were in the mounds covered with grass, but nature was quick to swallow the gravesites hidden amongst their suburban neighborhoods, refreshing history and leaving no ruins to sift through.

Leaves on the path made wet sloppy sounds as they created Nike footprint that would become fossils in the mud. 500 years ago as today from this bosom boys told stories underneath the vast massing timeline of the primal clouds.

"I wonder if Tecumseh walked this very same place," Isaiah said.

The small furnace of life within David coalesced in his breaths and altered his face with a healthy flush of blood. They were explorers as the rest of civilization huddled. In the pond larger ducks bullied smaller ones as they fed in a frenzy of dipped heads. Bird chirps were muffled as the chill crept into their brittle bones. Only the pines held green, the rest of the tree skeletons seemed to sag as if they had sopped up the melted snow. Through them the railroad mound and the neighboring houses were now visible. Crows perched upon telephone poles cawed as if they had evolved for this melancholy season. He observed the blue ash, too shy to share his wonder with David by asking him if he thought its name was derived because when staring up in a winter forest the sky gave their light bark a bluish tint. He wanted to point out to him the plaque dedicating the Winter King Hawthorne to the city arborist. He wanted to tell a story about the lonely patriarch who found solitude bearable amongst his royal arbor court, naming friends in common nomenclatures that sometimes didn't fit, troll oak, poison oak, southern nigerwood, like the slurs of ignorant oppressors.

He sat on the corner of his favorite bench and David sat on the other corner. Partially iced over the creek sped by in wobbling wavelengths where the rapids once had been. The knobby little tree had begrudgingly given up its leaves and left piles of cherry bomb fruit broken and rotting with the bitter smell of poison apples. A swarm of flies buzzed at the feast. They did not talk as they followed an airplane's line of condensation. A fly bothered his hands and face before biting him. It arrogantly landed within easy striking distance, waiting for another chance to attack. Isaiah waited completely still then smacked at it. He wasn't even close. It landed again in the same spot between them. David snorted hard, cleared his throat, turned his head and spit. His aim was perfect and before it could react he had trapped it in sticky green phlegm. He picked up a rock and smashed it. Isaiah leaned forward to peer at him with an incredulous smile. David flipped the rock and shrugged. For a moment David followed the rocks descent to stare at it on the ground, and then he looked back up unable to repress that wide smile finally plumping his cheeks again. Isaiah took out his pack of cigarettes and packed them as he shook his head and smiled.

"That was amazing."

He lit his cigarette holding eye contact lest David retreat back within himself. But here he again seemed of the world.

"I got lucky."

David looked at his cigarette.

"Want one?"

He took it casually. Isaiah pretended not to pay attention as he smoked with the look of discomfort he remembered.

"You have a pretty sweet weapon against flies. Do you think that is how the first spitting lizards evolved?"

Isaiah cleared his throat and spit towards the swarm of flies before continuing.

"Like there were these outcast lizards that spit too much. Then this, like, lizard malaria came on that was passed on by flies, and the only ones who survived were the ones who could kill them with well aimed spit?"

They laughed even harder because they weren't supposed to talk this way.

"Too bad it doesn't work in Goldenwood," Isaiah said.

"There are other evolutionary traits to help survive school."

Isaiah could tell David was trying to tell a joke, even if the timing was wrong. He waited as David looked in the underbrush to gather his punch line. That other people would think them weird, that they wouldn't understand, made the bond of outcasts even stronger.

But before he could continue they heard voices, huffing as they approached. David flicked his cigarette and again escaped in the far off distance. The approaching bellow took form in words.

"She has not been saved. I am certain they couldn't bring her to the light."

"But they lifted her up. She certainly is a pretty woman though isn't she?"

The second voice had a slight hope for kindness, but it just seemed a prop for the first voice to sound off upon.

"In a fake manner. But pious eyes can see well beyond that. I am certain she has not found the light yet."

The voice booming sanctimoniously he realized belonged Mrs. Lumpinsky. She was with a heavyset friend in a similar sweat suit as they speed walked around the bend. He lowered his face. It was too late to put his cigarette out, so he tried to keep it still so it would be unnoticed smoking behind the bench. He had to resist covering his eyes with his arm. Hiding his eyes to escape the world, with maybe a finger creeping to his nostril, was an essential memory of childhood. David retreated like a human potato bug.

"And she is always changing the color of her hair," the second woman said.

"I'm sweating like a pig even in this cold. It's running down my body," Mrs. Lumpinsky said.

The invading laughter dominated David's posture.

"Yeah Sister. Lord knows I feel the wet slickness in my thigh folds."

He understood why David hid. He wanted to protect him. Who gave a damn if Lumpy's mom saw him smoking. He had vomited in her toilet, had been drunk at a party she knew about while her son was in her bed urinating in a drunken fifteen-year-old girl's mouth. He took a tremendous drag form his cigarette and stared up at her.

He was surprised at the little girl in a pink sweat suit trying to keep up with them. Their voices had overwhelmed the innocence of hers but now he could hear the excited questions that ran over each other without answer in a complete conversation of wonder. His smirk changed into an unthreatening smile for her.

"Aw mommy that man is smoking."

Mrs. Lumpinsky hadn't noticed them on the bench until the girl pointed. Her face stiffened and she grabbed the girl's hand.

"Quiet Danielle."

"Hello," he smiled at the girl.

It was obvious the girl was Lumpy's little sister, but with the lumps smoothed out their familial bone structure was fine, without zits to distract from them her big blue eyes were magnificent, the malice of Lumpy's intelligence replaced with an even sharper kindness as she smiled back at Isaiah. Her tight brown curls bounced as she swung her head in harmony with Mrs. Lumpinsky's arm pulling her along.

"Hello," she said as Mrs. Lumpinsky gave him a curt nod.

He kept smiling in the face of her firm stare. He flicked his butt on the ground. He watched their retreating backsides, two heavy cheeks on each plow horse bottom stretching their sweats, and was disappointed that even though the little girl's body was small in contrast her mother was regurgitating her lifestyle into her, and her sweat pant bottoms were already starting to become overstuffed. They stirred the flies from their feast and they again smacked into him.

"Come on, let me show you something."

He prodded David to follow him and hurried around the path and up the gravel to stand on the railroad tracks. After a minute David reached the top to stand next to him. He watched his reaction, for here the childhood he hid intersected the real world, and he did not need to hide. They stood above the men of their village as boy kings.

"Cool," David said and started walking along the tracks two by two.

"Isn't it?"

Isaiah was pleased. David didn't need to speak of elves because they were already in an enchanted land. It wasn't until he was a ways down with no sign of stopping that Isaiah hurried to catch him. The railroad ties were a blur underneath him as they strode towards the horizon. Past the clearing where trees closed in David led him beyond the furthest point he had ventured. When he detoured down the gravel Isaiah didn't know how he had noticed the path leading through the trees. It ran alongside a streamlet that joined the creek through a large steel tunnel. He followed him to the field on the other side. In it was a large black rock that drew David. Its darkness absorbed the gray winter light into its volcanic center. David put his finger upon it as if tethered and orbited. Isaiah followed him with the finger of his glove absorbing the occasional jabs. The atmosphere spun around his mind and looking at the ground made him feel queasy. He focused on David like they were spinning the wheel on the playground, gasps of wee in slow motion.

"This doesn't seem real," Isaiah muttered.

"Why?"

"I feel like if I take my finger off I am going to go spiraling out of control."

"I'd just fall on my ass."

"Let's do it."

Isaiah let go and took two stumbling steps as his balance shifted, looking up at the trees that kept moving in a blur that he could not focus.

"Whoa."

They had seemed to be circling fast, but as his vision righted itself he watched David spin alone slowly, leaning slightly towards the rock with each revolution as he pondered the unseen center of oblivion.

"Bad idea," Isaiah said.

"You didn't go spiraling off into space."

"I'm already there, man, I am already there."

When it seemed that David had no designs to stop Isaiah spoke up.

"Ready to go?"

"Sure."

Equilibriums still wobbly they struggled up the slope to go back along the railroad tracks.

"The cold is invading my ass," Isaiah said.

Their laughter was a comforting sound. But as it faded again into the ethereal quiet Isaiah could no longer ignore the ghost of Chris between them. In their silence was where he would have been. Memories found their way in like the cold wind invading his coat to chill his bones. In the deeper shadows of the trees he searched for his ghost. The barren branches shook and he could not imagine the Garden of Eden on that barren ground. What insanity made him remember the summer breezes when Chris had still been alive?

Far off on the tracks he noticed a small point growing. He discerned bright headlights just as the train horn sounded off in the distance. David panicked as the far off chug a chug sound became discernible. He looked side to side for an escape route, inhabiting the world of unavoidable eventuality now, and then started to run along the tracks. But his body had been too often ignored when he was off in his mind, and it didn't respond correct when now called upon. He tripped and fell hard on the tracks. He tried to push himself up but could not defeat gravity. Isaiah hurried to help him up. At the complete mercy of the world he looked at Isaiah with humiliation. The train was still distant and Isaiah pointed at the entrance to the arboretum a mere 8 railroad ties in front of them. They descended and Isaiah grabbed David's shoulder to keep him from tumbling along with the avalanche of rocks they had kicked down. He turned him and kept his arm around his shoulder. Embarrassment replaced the fear in his expression.

"You all right man?"

They watched the opening as the sound increased furiously to hit a crescendo. The freight train filled their view as it sped by with the roar of steel wheels and smell of oil and smoke. The last car had windows and was full of men dressed in gray suits like gentleman going to the country. All of them focused on each other, but for one solitary man staring at them perplexed before disappearing.

"Were alive!" David suddenly yelled as it passed.

Isaiah laughed in wonder at his quick revival. He wanted to walk further down the tracks with him and pretend for a bit that they would keep going, but he knew when the gray skies turned to night the cold would seep in and he would feel the barren harshness of survival.

THE JOY OF PROCRASTINATION

Every weekday Isaiah woke unnaturally early to do not much at all, and he relished the autonomy of the weekend mornings. On this Sunday morning Isaiah stayed in bed until the sun was almost directly above. On the seventh day even God rested. There was willfulness to his laziness as he played video games. He ate, but nothing else held precedence. As the day wore on he was aware there was something he needed to do for Monday, something he had been putting off, but thinking about it made him realize how blissful a nap would be.

He awoke still in the joy of procrastination. Today he savored the anything but. He flicked the rosary that had inexplicably ended up on his lamp and watched it wobble. Tomorrow a bell would ring but it was not ringing now. The rosary came to rest. On the television a dog rolled side-to-side on its back and snorted. Then for some unknown reason it shot up and ran in loops in the backyard. It stopped to pant, then again sprinted off towards the gate barking with its tongue lolling in the required antagonism dogs relished.

Outside airplanes sped against time zones around the shifting axis of the earth. Small feats of time travel were being accomplished in journeys back towards the lavatory. Stars were light that was wasted food for ignorant solar systems. The dog would be lying in the shade now. He lied in bed to do nothing more than think. As the evening progressed he again felt a brief pang of something unfinished. The unrelenting red minute hand of the classroom came to mind. But he picked up *Grandeur of Illusions* to instead measure the angles of time with puffs of pages. The second chapter brought the world crashing down upon Caldrid. When he finished the chapter he put the book down already anxious of it ending. He resolved to take only a chapter of daily ink to tinge every day.

NATURE VERSUS NURTURE

David came down the steps singing in a strong voice Isaiah would have never thought could come from him. He stopped as he entered his basement.

"I have to go. Dad forgot his lunch again."

David hadn't seemed to mind when he invited himself in after school so he felt comfortable asking him if he wanted some company for the drive. He shrugged.

"Sure."

David cheerfully kicked icicles off the back of his hatchback as he tossed the lunch pail in. Isaiah had never been in his car before, there were scattered soda cans and wrappers on the floor and the grubby sheen coating the interior made his hands feel dirty. He rubbed his thumb against his fingers to rub caked dirt and imagined boogers into balls that dropped on the floor.

"Lately dad has been forgetting a lot. This is the third time in two weeks I've had to bring his dinner to him at work," David said with the cheerful contentedness of a caretaker.

Isaiah could not distance himself from all his car's surfaces as they drove with his speakers barely holding up to the loud music. The guitar splintered as the bass was lost in a rattle and the moaning voice distorted like it came from an old man's throat.

"Isn't my dad's building creepy? Goldenwood's sadistic architect must have also designed it. Hold on a minute, I'll be right back."

The building swallowed him into the gaping glass maw of its lobby. The scattered refuse of David's life made Isaiah need to get out and stare at the sky. Not even a minute later David was spat out of the doors looking chewed.

"Did you talk to him?"

"No. He can't talk to me at work. I left it with the security guard."

"What does he even do in that prison?"

"You know, he never talks about work," David tried to regain his former cheer as he sheepishly looked at Isaiah. "He does tell me about the things he sees on that path when he walks on his breaks." David pointed at the path circling a pond besides the building. "Do you want to walk the path a little?"

He nodded hoping his enthusiasm could prop David's shoulders back up. As they walked David explored the brambles on the side of the path.

"Dad says in the spring rabbits are everywhere. At that bench ahead he sometimes eats lunch, and he said one day baby rabbits came out of the underbrush close enough he could have reached out and petted them."

Isaiah sensed this place was as sacred to David as the arboretum was for him, and this opening up was what he had been waiting for, but his hushed tone and the need in his earnest look had come on too sudden. Isaiah became aware of the evil puss still surrounding his soul as he looked away to hide his pang of mockery. He didn't deserve this trust. He should tell him their brutal peers would ridicule him with disgust for talking like that. Isaiah barked a nervous laugh out.

"What?" David asked.

"Just picturing it. That is cool."

And it really was. He repressed his fading wickedness. It was like the faint twinges of nicotine addiction he felt now when he went a day without a cigarette. He could see the father in the son, Mr. McCormick walking solitary with his brow furrowed and his mind swimming with the memories of an old life.

"Over there is where the beaver nested this summer. One day Dad said it didn't see him and he sneezed and it almost had a heart attack. But after jumping away a few feet it looked at him, and continued to eat. Then it gathered a few saplings for its dam before plopping back into the water."

With affection Isaiah completely gave himself over to David's world. The frozen creek that fed this pond was easy to imagine as the same one at the arboretum. Green slime stained the plastic bottles frozen in the pond, and cigarette butts were ripped apart with the expanding ice. The building was still visible as they reached the far end of the small loop, callous windows from which the bare branched trees would seem barren trapped inside the Tetris murdering of hours. The constant sound of the freeway didn't fade.

"Dad never mentioned this side path."

Isaiah thought he was just pretending as he stared into the brambles. But then he noticed the path also. It was hidden in the underbrush nearly blocking it. David ducked through branches and held them for Isaiah to follow. They reached a small bridge over a streamlet that looked like it led to a dead end in the tangle.

"It looks like it doesn't go anywhere," Isaiah said.

"No there is something ahead."

"How do you know?"

"Because of the no trespassing sign."

David burrowed through. He ignored the scratching branches that pulled up his shirt and coat to expose pale fat rolls. Isaiah followed with the reward of branches in the face.

"There are strange creatures at the edge of the world," David said.

On the other side it did spread out to a wide bike path that was in poor repair. It wound towards wilder places. But as they hurried along it curved and came out of the trees to a highway overpass. A blind semi truck rattled it as it thundered overhead.

"I thought we would be led to someplace a little more magical," David said disappointed.

The path ended on the other side but still they had to follow it to its end underneath the overpass. There was something forbidding in the scattered trash amongst the rocks and along the concrete in the dark shadows. Only David's momentum kept Isaiah from following his instinct to stop. He looked up when he heard a sound. With a jolt of fear he saw a man with tattered clothes. A hat with earflaps covered the sides of his brown dirty face. He stared at them.

"Hello my friends."

Isaiah stopped and pulled David back as the man hunched up from his perch.

"You can't pass the troll under the bridge without answering a riddle."

His mirth exposed stained teeth as he lurched a few steps down. Isaiah knew that expression, and did not need to know him to recognize he was drunk on madness. David took another step back. His threat was most powerful in the fear of being touched by his filth.

"I'm just joking. Could you nice boys spare a few dollars?"

David reached into his pocket. Isaiah grabbed his arm. Anger surged at this man's righteous insanity, he had seen it too often before, and it always smiled slyly as it begged something of him.

"No, don't give this slob any money."

The man took a step down then stopped and spit. The spittle sped past Isaiah but drops landed on David. Enraged Isaiah took a few steps as if to charge. The man took a step back and cowered. Disdain was the only thing he would understand. Isaiah threw a rock at him and it bounced to strike his leg as he shuffled back into the shadows.

"Why don't you disappear from the world you false prophet? Cower in the shadows where you belong," Isaiah roared.

"I'm sorry young sir."

"Go."

He shirked back into the recesses of the underpass, into the shadow like some creature banished back to its lair in fear and festering resentment, whatever humanity once there again repressed in an animal survival instinct.

"You ready to get back?" David asked.

Displaced they walked back towards the office building with the receding bellow of the freeway. There was litter strewn all along in the underbrush. Everywhere they turned the world was hemmed in. The demons on the outskirts had a world paved for their mad wanderings, and they were everywhere to force their leprosy upon Isaiah. He still quivered with battle rage as he plodded along with his head down.

He was a ways down the path before he noticed David had stopped. He stared at an unpaved path shooting off in the opposite direction. It may have just been a stretch of dead soil, or maybe it was the path of a stag, leading to another world. They shared a smile. Before he turned to follow David along this new path he turned to the office building and gave it his middle finger.

DUNGEON HIGH

Isaiah had no stories that would stimulate their lethargy of hibernation. They would sit quietly in David's basement until either spring came or another dark ice age began. David's fluffy Cleveland Browns sweater looked like the plume of an NFL logoed penguin as he bobbed his head to Radiohead.

But Isaiah did have a plastic baggie of marijuana in his coat pocket. After they listened to half the CD he had the courage to hold it out to David.

"Want some elvish bread?"

Isaiah thought maybe the concentrated taboo would bring some strong reaction one way or another, but David just looked at it and shrugged his ascent. When Isaiah passed it to him he smoked the joint like a cigarette with no spectacle or cough. The pungent smell of smoke replaced the faint whiff of urine in the basement.

"Have you had this potion before?"

He handed Isaiah the joint not looking the least bit impressed and shook his head.

"No."

So of course Isaiah had to smoke the joint like he was training for the pot Olympics. When they had finished Isaiah waited to see how the basement would shift, to see if the years of distance them would dissipate with a goofy grin. David's head bobs took on an impassioned slowness, but otherwise there was no transformation.

After three songs Isaiah finally spoke. "Does your dad have any alcohol?"

Isaiah bobbed his head harder for yes. Then he closed his eyes for another song. Finally he stood and beckoned for Isaiah to follow him as he traipsed up the stairs. Isaiah's subconscious finally started to waft up fresh familiarity. He remembered this cupboard, and the cups were in exactly the same place as they had been when Mrs. McCormick would give them lemonade. She would tell them jokes and ask them questions as they sat at this counter keeping her company while she finished dinner. In the living room David pointed at the family portrait hanging on the wall with a smile.

"Look at that hideous sweater."

It had large obnoxious squares in mismatched colors. But underneath it was the same David, just a little less of him. Mr. and Mrs. McCormick had their arms wrapped around his shoulders. She was a bloated version of Isaiah's memories, but the distorted reflection of the photograph had captured the glee of her smile.

"I had no hope from the start."

He led Isaiah up to his father's office. Isaiah had never been in here before. A large model airplane hung from the ceiling, shelves had model cars and replica handguns, medals were in cases, and a large broadsword hung on the wall next to a gun rack with shotguns and rifles.

"This room is awesome."

"Dad put all the models together himself."

The liquor cabinet was full of bottles that made Isaiah's father's collection seem sparse. Isaiah took a full bottle of whiskey and sieved water carefully back to replace the whiskey he poured in their glasses.

"Your dad will never know."

David took a key and with a mischievous grin unlocked the gun case to pull the shotgun and rifle from the rack. Isaiah had seen guns his whole life on TV, but they were just toys like the replica handgun in David's basement with the red tip. The shotgun David handed him had a taboo weight and he felt a sense of awe holding the tool he had never imagined he would feel. David cocked the rifle and rested it on his shoulder as he aimed at the wall and pulled the trigger with a click.

"You hold it like this and aim over the sight. That lever on the shotgun is how you open it to load it."

Isaiah clicked it open to look down the empty barrels. He wondered how the explosion would feel as he rested it on his shoulder and aimed it at the wall to pull the trigger. David stuck the tip of his rifle between two blinds and aimed. Isaiah did likewise and sighted a rock on the ground.

"Bang."

Isaiah jumped at the sound David made. Then they laughed with youthful exuberance as they made shooting sounds.

"It is a bit harder to hit a moving target. Like if we were defending the house against zombies. We should go shooting with Dad sometime. It is a blast."

"I feel like an action hero, all kinds of movie scenes are running through my head," Isaiah said.

"The ammunition is locked up in dad's bedroom."

"Well, God, we really don't need that."

Isaiah set the shotgun back in the rack. David remained standing straight. "Bang, bang." Isaiah imagined red sprouting in special effect bursts. Then David put the gun back and locked the gun cabinet and put the key back.

"Of course," David said.

Back in the basement David dropped on his stomach and plucked grains of dirt from the carpet as he sipped his whiskey. Isaiah plopped his leg on the armrest of the chair and drank. The singer cried out how he used to fly like Peter Pan. David sat up and fingered his ear lobe. Then mad jabberwocky sentences started to come out of him.

"Wonder what I would look like with an earring… My mom bought me that sweater… I guess I really don't know how to dress myself…"

"We all look funny to ourselves."

Isaiah felt dishonest. David's molting hormones had awkwardly transitioned him from a blond toddler. The sheen of intoxication had not made him elegant. But Isaiah could not explain to him that despite this he saw strength forming underneath his awkward layers.

"Although that sweater was pretty bad," Isaiah said.

David laughed. But when he stood up there was a wet sheen on his eyes that held more emotion than Isaiah had seen since he had joined him at his lunch table. He looked at Isaiah as if to be sure that at least someone could see the pain overcoming him. With anguish he then looked up. But there was no hope in his eyes for answers to his asking why. He coughed out a moan and a tortured sob asking for mercy.

"Life has been so lonely."

Isaiah could only look at him with sympathy and hope the echoes rippled outwards to maybe touch upon some greater power than him.

"It is like I haven't changed from that child. How am I supposed to live in a future where she is gone?"

His words clumped upon him as another layer. The silence in between was thick with aching.

"It has always been a feeling more than a thought. I want to reject anything that is not then."

He hunched over to gulp the rest of his whiskey. Then he paced the room, staring at a poster of a dragon as he blew fumes out his nostrils. Isaiah pictured the prayer group at church, and wondered why he only imagined thin hands devotedly clasped in prayer, never stubby sausage fingers. He wanted to dispel the judgment for David's wobble of baby fat, childish gluttony he did not deserve to be crucified for. But it did not matter what he said. The world's reaction to him rarely allowed human connection to the person underneath all his layers.

"Do you think about Chris a lot?" Isaiah asked.

He regretted summoning him as soon as he had spoken his name. David stopped to stare at him.

"Of course. But you don't get it."

Isaiah stood up and finished his whiskey. He pulled his sleeve up to expose to David that which shamed him with every shower. The scars weren't as severe as he hoped, he regretted that the gashes weren't fresh with ugly red rawness but instead a pink that was quickly fading.

"I feel pain too. I have demons too. Everyone thinks I am just straight laced Isaiah Templeton."

"Yeah."

David looked at his arm without surprise.

"I feel pain too," Isaiah repeated.

He had spent weeks trying to decipher a stare, to understand the subtlety of a laugh. He had befriended David for signs of how he could help him, and now when he had opened himself up there was not even a flicker of understanding. Isaiah was defeated. He prepared to leave.

"You are right. I was a jerk. We made a bet at my table, sat around joking about who would kill themselves next, who would fulfill the curse of Goldenwood. I picked you. I didn't mean to, but I chose you. I betrayed

Chris in our friendship. I know I did it on purpose. But I am not a bad person. I made mistakes. But I am sorry for what I did."

"Dude, don't be so melodramatic."

"What?"

"Do you think we were such pussies? That he killed himself because you didn't talk to him? That I care what a bunch of dickheads talk about at their bored lunch table? You just don't get it."

Isaiah looked at him waiting to be admonished like a child. He wanted the full force of David's rage to punish and cleanse him with the penance he owed.

"Do you think he was just a pussy?" David asked.

"No. It's just that…"

"I've heard the jokes. A pussy so wet he fingered himself to death. A pussy so sweet he pricked his little peach virginity out of the world."

"People are dumb."

"Conditioned," David grimaced as he stared at Isaiah. "They called it social anxiety, the counselors his parents made him see for years. Do you think they ever asked him what he really felt?"

David's intensity was focused in the clarity with which he spoke.

"He felt a lot," Isaiah whispered.

"Damn right. That little boy, that sensitive child, that pussy."

His jaw jutted from his double chin.

"That amazing friend of mine who taught me you have to come to terms with silence. That solitude is a gift, silence a blessing, a break from cruel humans incessantly filling the world with lies. But Chris wasn't as angry as I am. He came to terms with being ignored, with silence, as the way he heard the world. He interacted with it without the constant interruption of the half completed thoughts of language. I am not quite as good as him. I can't ignore it completely. All the mean petty jokes, people like Barrett kicking me in the ass, people like you laughing. It is this static I can't quite ignore, every day forced to hear it, stirring up latent negativity in me, even as hard as I try I can't ignore it."

"I'm sorry."

"You were blind to him too. Even his so called friends didn't understand. His social anxiety was because he was constantly interrupted when his mind was somewhere else. He had bigger thoughts, was in different worlds, his mind was wandering beyond the small-minded building. We were lucky to hear a little of what he saw."

"I understood."

"Even teachers, supposedly the adults, interrupted him purposely even though they already knew how he would react. They would force him back to their world, hatred in their eyes that for him taking no notice of it. The silence at first was him trying to register what context he was even supposed to answer in. Quickly you are conditioned to the awkwardness, the mocking, and the laughter. Do you not think that sensitive boy knew every cruel thing said about him?"

"He heard," Isaiah muttered.

David bellowed and whispered as he paced. His arm movements would have made Isaiah laugh, shooting out like a drunken penguin, if it wasn't for the progression of broken expressions.

"But here is the part that people don't get. He had bigger balls than any of us. He knew he should pay attention, he was trained to pay attention, so the mockery would stop, but he did not give a damn. He continued in the worlds of his thoughts despite the humiliation, he had the strength, that sensitive little prick, to not be beaten into paying attention. He didn't give a damn about any of it. And that is not why he killed himself. I don't think it was the boredom of being forced to sit every day in a place feeling unwelcome, his very way of existence mocked, reality defined for him. He could get through that. Honestly I wish I knew why. I wish I was strong enough to follow him where he went."

"I am sorry," Isaiah fingered the craven tracks on his arm.

"His friends meant the world to him. Do you know that when you started ignoring him—"

"I know."

"Oh I don't give a fuck about that. He didn't either. Do whatever the hell you want. He didn't want your pity. What I was trying to say was that he actually was concerned that he may have done something to upset you. What you don't know is in every silent moment that you ignored him he was concerned that he did something wrong. Because you were his friend, he blamed himself, but he didn't know how to approach you and ask. I told him to forget about you, cursed you, but all he wanted to do was to apologize to you."

David sagged, the energy leaving him in the folds of his misfit clothes.

"Suicide. Sad, cliché, as real as the morning bell. Mortality, death, drama, who cares? To most people he was just a symbol of the act, the experiment in mortality. The melodrama. Chris himself was just an afterthought. Why is it any of our business to make judgments? It is an existential argument made literal, a conversation with God turned into an argument, a finger to a stern father, a demand for answers, a fatal attempt to gain control and stand face to face with the truth, an attempt to escape illusion."

"I feel pain too."

"So? They say Jesus sat on his cross for 3 days."

Isaiah left.

JOKING WITH GHOSTS

With a joke about suicide David ended their standoff.

"The why is pretty easy to understand. He didn't want to have to spend another day in this prison."

Isaiah's depression had been a growing autoimmune response. Fed a lardy soup of cynicism it had grown until it was a gorged tumor choking out all other emotions. David's joke released the valve to a gush of insane laughter, tapering off to chuckles like the creek gurgling at the arboretum.

"It's a lop stop in a Trollock's pot," with wild unkempt hair David waved his arms around to admonish the lunchroom. "It's the top of Sauron's tower."

As children the illusionary nature of the world came as natural as losing track of time playing, and David cast a spell with his odd words, allowing the ghost of Chris to be free between them.

"Remember when Chris pretended we battled monsters that squished lightning bugs for the joy of destroying them?"

Isaiah recollected he had felt boyhood heartache at being reminded of the senseless killing of insects, but had never admitted his guilt at playing whiffle ball with smacking explosions of light.

"It's all hearsay. Maybe Chris just found a way to transcend life," David said.

"No more school," Isaiah said.

"Why not sever the bounds of what makes you miserable. We live like we are already dead. Who cares what people think? We should live without consequence."

"How?"

"I don't know. Do whatever we want, as long as we don't hurt anyone else. Think about it, it is the gift of freedom."

Isaiah nodded.

"Why kill ourselves when we can search for God."

"Screw God," David said.

"Yeah. Well, we should live that way anyways right? I mean, have more fun."

"Is this our last supper?" David lifted his tray. "Heaven will have to do very little to fulfill our expectations."

With relish Isaiah released his wild goofy expression.

"What we see as cold little stars are really distant unlimited cabins in the outer space of loneliness."

"Chris is warming his boots right now at the bonfire of the heavens."

"We would roast marshmallows. But, does Chris remember us at this fire?" Isaiah asked.

"Yes. Yes he does. And I think he is calling for us. He always was an elf. He could converse in mythical tones with the world."

"And he will translate for us?" Isaiah asked.

"Yes. Elves, after all, are just evolved humans."

Easy lunchtime rebels, he leaned back with David and was beyond the outskirts of the lunchroom. His old table no longer even acknowledged him and for that he was grateful. He looked at them from a distance as they let misery control them. Barrett was still at the complete mercy of his short attention span. He forgave him the strange twitching glances of passing in the hallway. Lumpy's violence was limited to spinning his tray in front of Ronald with milky ketchup splashing drops onto his face. Ronald avoided looking up as he yelled at the tray. They accepted the parameters, as they pretended rebelliousness with curse words, drinking and smoking and breaking through some imaginary hymen to relief, all the while becoming more miserable in the fight to come of age, the myths of manhood coursing through their bodies. They forgot stories told around the roaring fires in winter, repressing joy in a hibernation they didn't believe would ever end.

"A life of adventure," David said.

Isaiah hadn't noticed Carrie Ann's approach until the force of her hips stopped in front of him. She faced him with contempt.

"Stop staring at me freak."

"What?"

"You heard me. Stop staring at me you freak."

She spoke loud to try and humiliate him but it was easy to feel nothing as he looked back at her.

"Whatever."

"And tell your fat little pervert friend to stop staring at me too."

She started to turn away but Isaiah matched her sarcasm.

"What would you do if people didn't want to fuck you?"

She planted herself back in front of him confident in her easy victory. "But people want to fuck me, Isaiah, so I am nothing like you."

"You're just an animal."

"What did you call me?"

He was calm in the face of her false confidence, gaining power with his every word coming out calm and definitive.

"You know the thing that a Doberman wants to mount in the ecstasy of its heat is called? A bitch. Same for a Poodle, a Chihuahua, or whatever that little piece of shit dog of yours is that Barrett hates. A bitch."

He made a feral face and pretended to nibble.

"Rats like to fuck too. I feel sorry for you. All you aspire to be is an animal."

"You are a freak. Weirdo. You probably fuck your weird little friend. Stop fucking staring at me!"

She could barely whisper at first but ended with a scream.

"Whoa. Calm down there sparky."

She leaned towards him with her hand raised. He drew in all her rage. He had never seen her vulnerable before, but now tears welled up she was unable to hide behind her sarcasm. He did not look away. He hoped she would strike him.

"Fuck you fagot."

She stormed off. He smiled triumphantly at David.

"We definitely need to escape this place."

Freezing rain limited the world and the only place Isaiah thought to go was the mall. The pale clerk disregarded them with a flash of teeth. "Welcome to CounterCulture." Her black lined eyes flickered upon them with disdain as obvious as the vampire bait expanse of bosom from which a gothic cross poked out. David gave a shrug at the clothes Isaiah chose for him. Isaiah walked along the denim and t-shirts choosing outfits by recalling being stoned. David's only showed a flash of interest in the Kurt Cobain poster he grabbed.

"I don't really care either, but it is for the ladies we clothe ourselves. There has to be a girl at Goldenwood you notice?" Isaiah asked.

The clerk looked at them like they did not belong, and it would have intimidated Isaiah if not for David beside him making it feel as if they were the only sentient beings in the world.

"I guess I am waiting for the girl who makes it through."

"Who?"

"I guess really no one."

"Seriously, there has to be a girl if you had nothing to lose you would talk to her?"

"Your mom."

"I see. The girl who makes it through puberty as a hermaphrodite."

"The girl who makes it through…I don't know because I am not even sure who it is. It is the girl who after high school everyone will wonder why they didn't notice her before."

"That is genius actually. Like the playboy pin up model that was a dork in high school and never had a boyfriend," Isaiah said.

"Something like that, I guess. But she will stay nice."

"I like it. Unsullied, unslutified, her fertile ground not sown with bitter seeds like that one."

Isaiah nodded towards the clerk.

"Those that blossom early become tainted. I could help you find her."

David drew away from the pink Led Zeppelin t-shirt he had been rubbing and spoke with a noncommittal voice.

"My fat ass isn't going to be that chick from Clueless no matter how hard you try to pick me out the right clothes."

Isaiah thought maybe he had invaded his pain again until David's laugh came into the vacuum with such power that the clerk looked at them annoyed.

"Maybe you would like me to ask her out for you?"

They laughed as the clerk affectionately folded clothes and made them wait at the register through two choruses of guttural screams on the music overhead. Only when the singer again whimpered to an acoustic guitar did she sulk over to help them. Beep. She piled the clothes into the bag as if they were tainted when she scanned them, beep, greeting them with only the sound of register. She was gentle with the poster out of the bare observation of her duties.

"280.37."

She ran his mother's credit card with moony eyes, clicking her tongue ring on her teeth. Isaiah let out a thick silent fart. As the register spooled out their validity the funk mixed with the musk of incense and Isaiah grimaced happily at David. She handed him the bags and finally caught a whiff with a disgusted face. He flicked the signed receipt back at her.

"This store smells like ass."

They laughed at her utter confusion. They laughed hysterically through the mall full of people who pretended not to notice them. In his car Isaiah took the leftover Halloween makeup and glued himself a beard. They laughed at the bored people in other cars with destinations as routine as their expressions. The gas station clerk didn't pay attention to him so he walked out with a case of beer without paying. Only at a stoplight did someone finally notice him, a strange little girl with curly puffs of red hair who stared at him from the backseat window, showing no surprise at his ridiculous disguise; from far flung worlds she kept his eye contact until they sped off through the green light.

Safe in the basement David taught him about music through steady bars of ownership. A pile of burnt CDs piled up stolen from Napster. The black and white poster of Kurt Cobain had an intensity of emotion crinkling the corners of his eyes in an otherwise blank expression. Masked underneath his intensity of indifference it was a slight acknowledgement of absurdity. It almost formed a smile underneath the grim set of his lips. Isaiah sipped warm beer as he searched the depths of apathy. Their cigarette puffs merged with the bands of hazy smoke in the background of the poster coming from the cigarette Cobain held disregarded between two fingers.

The photographer had captured a black and white extreme, ignoring the laughs between songs to frame an Arian symmetry of features.

What was in the way?

What did Kurt Cobain joke about before there were any journalists to care? Who were his nerdy friends on random Friday afternoons? Was his school daze like David's? His blonde hair and delicate lines hidden in the shadows reminded Isaiah of Chris. Would Chris's shy eyes have eventually morphed with an intensity summoning up worlds from the very nothingness itself? Isaiah emulated Kurt Cobain's stare as he paced. He harnessed its power that had followed him through the camera and the printing press through the mall to now watch him pace in the basement.

He belched out fumes.

Erratic guitars breached his trance, the mass of emotion quivering now inside him like indecipherable screams. David's eyes followed him. He imagined Chris's also. He wanted to scream. He wanted to froth at the mouth. He tried to stare frenzied for a new state of mind. He took the beer can to his lips. David got up and followed him.

What was in the way?

With the guitars they banged their heads. Twitch, his head in quick procession, bang, bang, banged. At first they smiled like it was a joke. But soon the sonic force stirred familiar energy and they lost all awkwardness as they thrashed. Like a music video they heaved and stomped, twitched, stomped, twitched, head banging with their feet tapping, cha, cha, cha, then their movements became unique seizures around the room. They breathed smoke like friction. Cobain, Hemmingway, the tales of suicide were macabre and romantic, Chris, Phil. They shook with the music to come closer to those who at the pinnacle still stared up. They banged their heads for a view unobstructed from Everest at the heavens. Their voices screamed like they had finally ascended the top, growling in their throats, till they sang along raspy at the skies. Just a blink, cursing gravity, just a blink, from the pinnacle asking God if there was anything more, just a blink, before the tumble down.

The computer shuffled a new song. They sat down and Isaiah chuckled at David, flushed with adrenaline and his wild unkempt hair like waves escaping. They chuckled at their near weightlessness. They chuckled at nothing for a long time. They ignored the dull ache almost as long.

"Pearl Jam," David muttered.

The guitar hit a deep note and every sensation collapsed into its resonating tone. The tingle was not from chemicals in his veins further accelerating his heart's pounding, but from the guitar stimulating the center of his warmth. The deep note hit again. The bass hit a measure lower as the bluesy whine of strings teased a soft cry. The drums struck to lead the way for a delving baritone. It followed forgotten tracers into the thick syrupy mass of frustration and loneliness and pain. He did not understand the lyrics but emotion formed and disappeared in pulses. It filled the place within him desperate to feel something, anything. The voice begged at last with rich elongated tones, and Isaiah also ached to leave, understood the daily catacombs in which he didn't want to stay. Two last high pitch notes were plucked at the end of the song, as if a transcendent angel shrugged her shoulders and said fuck it.

JUST DON'T DO IT

The bell reasserted time. Isaiah tried to steal a few more moments with his head down. It was not exhaustion as much as a groggy inability to relate to a day moving at the speed of lectures. Karen recaptured the minutes as she started her lecture.

That morning fresh snow had culled white out of the gray skies. As the world huddled into the fleece of their meekness, David and he had walked out onto the blank sheet, their typewriter head footprints circling as they imagined their path leading away. But now David did not even glance back at him from his corner in the classroom. The ruddiness had faded and the delight was gone from his eyes as he started to take notes. Salt melted snow on the concrete and gave its pulp to industrialization in a dirty mush refrozen at the edge of the parking lot. In his new clothes, his book gone, David was only recognizable to him in the slowed down furrows forming on his forehead as he scribbled in the margins in the pauses of the lecture.

It wasn't innovative for Isaiah not to pick up his pen and take notes, but for him it felt like a revolution: Just don't do it.

He would go someplace else also. Cocksure he took out *Grandeur of Illusions* and blocked all but a corner of the cover in case David happened to look over. With the book open he had a more intimate angle from which to understand him. But the words would not register. With an ominous feeling he looked up at Karen. Memories of the overpowering scent of her concentrated nature let no other fantasy immerse his senses and overpowered the forest smells evoked by the book. He tried to ignore her beauty, noting the sheen robbing her eyes of light as she read from the overhead, blue oblivion focused on role-play as grotesque as any kids playing with dragons in a dungeon. He reread the paragraph but her voice made the characters disappear. He was impressed by David's endurance to escape.

He could not read. Neither would he take notes. So he just stared at the book. Here were words, English, distinct foundations from the middle ages, around which Arthur and Merlin had sat; inventions that lived longer than any bishop or pawn, royal caricatures on histories checkered chessboard. Yet in this school he shivered as in the bleakest stone dungeon. Unable to understand *Grandeur of Illusions* his notebook rendered a past without imagination. The ventilation system stirred cold drafts in the graveyards of time. Karen lectured only so at night eventually Romeo and Karen would sit content in the suburbs, while Juliet was strung out in sitcoms of pornographic reruns in the outskirts of Hollywood. Unable to decipher the runes, the power of Juliet's enchantment, in the future she would lie down amongst the wildflowers and stare back at the ruins waiting to join them.

He felt a pang of fear when he noticed Karen staring at him omniscient. There was no doubt she had noticed the book he hid. He would have been able to resist her anger, remembering how she had humiliated David. But he could not resist her flirtatious smile. He blushed. When she started reading the next page of notes he closed the book and started to follow along.

GOOD OLD BOYS

David barely had time to flush the joint down the toilet. Isaiah wondered if he should hide in the adjacent bedroom that he had not entered since coming back to David's basement refuge. Footsteps thumped down the stairs. There was not time for the open window to dissipate the smoke, and in the haze Isaiah's paranoia increased as he waited for Mr. McCormick's reaction. The ridge of his brow raised thick eyebrows showing no expression above his long wasp nest beard. His eyes were like David's, but the playfulness Isaiah remembered in them when Mrs. McCormick had been alive was gone, along with most of his hair. Time had hardened him like a pudding rind as his hairline crept up the thick plate of his baldhead, only wild tufts of hair remaining on each side the same brown as David's residue of escaping brain waves.

"Hello Isaiah."

"Hello sir."

Father and son looked at each other in contrast until the smoke dissipated.

"What are you doing down here?"

Isaiah waited for the punishment. But his father had never looked at him this undecided. The confusion was especially tender upon Mr. McCormick's hardened face.

"Just kidding. Your pops isn't stupid. I know that smell. Your mom and I did the same thing down here before you were born. I guess my boy is growing up."

His smile was a grimace as his mind tried to create new pathways for lightheartedness through his corroded memories.

"You guys look like I scared the crap out of you. Don't worry. I had to leave work. I just couldn't take it anymore today."

Sadness was underneath his laugh.

"I was going to drink some whiskey with the television. But it looks like it is time I have a drink with my boy. You guys mind having a drink with this old man?"

He trudged upstairs and returned with the same bottle of whiskey they had stolen drinks from and looked at them with a raised eyebrow sending tectonic shifts up his skull.

"I thought I smelled smoke down here a couple of days ago but I figured I was imagining it. Hell, when I found some beer cans I tried to figure out when the hell I had drunk them."

He laughed wholehearted. He took a swig of whiskey straight from the bottle.

"God damn I needed that. How are you Isaiah?"

Isaiah was shy to respond even as he waived for him to take the bottle. He didn't trust if this was a stoned hallucination or if this was really happening. There Mr. McCormick stood as wild eyed and unkempt as Isaiah had envisioned he would be after his wife's funeral, but he had never imagined him passing the bottle to him with jubilation. Isaiah took a tentative drink and passed it to David.

"It's about time I had my first drink with my boy."

David took a swig without reaction.

"Let me tell you boys, don't grow up. It isn't just that my boss is an asshole. But when he is bored he goes on these rampages and refuses to be ignored to let me get through my damn day."

He took the bottle from David with vigor and drank again.

"Oh well. Forget him. Who wants to hear an old man complain about work? You're in this basement all alone. Where are the ladies?"

David looked away embarrassed, leaving Isaiah to try to explain.

"Eh. There aren't really any girls at Goldenwood that interesting."

"Come on, there have to be some beauties still in high school these days. Things haven't changed that much."

"I mean, there are attractive girls. But most of them are ruined by being complete bitches."

"Do they start that young nowadays?"

"Yes."

"Well then boys were in trouble."

He handed the bottle to Isaiah again.

"Don't worry. You guys will eventually meet plenty of fine young women."

A thoughtful expression came over David's face as he drank.

"Was mom the girl who got through?"

Mr. McCormick paused and looked at David before taking a long swallow.

"What do you mean son."

As he eyed his son their features seemed to meld, David becoming more prominent underneath his superfluous layers and Mr. McCormick softening with boyish putty.

"David has this theory, how there is a girl not noticed by anyone now, but after high school she will be the type of girl we will all want to be with," Isaiah said.

There was no mockery behind Mr. McCormick's laughter.

"I feel like I am in high school again."

In their silence the music again came to the forefront.

"When I met your mother I was your age."

Isaiah imagined Mr. McCormick's hair growing back with the euphoria of his expression.

"We had so much fun. That is what is important. Find yourself a girl who you can dance with, who you can enjoy life with. Who you can get stoned in a basement with."

He winked at them. A trickle of whiskey slid down Isaiah's chin.

"How do we find that girl?" Isaiah asked.

"I wish there was some magic advice on that. But honestly, just be you. Have fun. The rest, the universe will decipher for you."

"Dad, have you ever thought about trying to meet someone else since mom?

Mr. McCormick was thoughtful as he looked at this child formed from the woman he loved.

"Oh I have been on dates. Even met a few interesting women. But I soon get bored with the power struggle. I wonder if that is all I missed out when I spent my life with your mother. Maybe I was the lucky one after all."

"Quoting another love song dad?"

"They are all love songs son," Mr. McCormick said with childish wonder. "I thought I was the lucky one when I was you boys' age. Enjoy it. Hopefully for you the illusion will last forever. Hopefully you won't end up in a cubicle with someone who douched his way through business school talking to you like an idiot." He put the cap on the bottle and set it aside. "One thing I learned is to treat this with moderation."

"I took Isaiah to walk around your path at work the other day."

"Yes. I do have that. We get a few breaks to walk the yard. That is the best thing every day."

The crinkles on his baldhead relaxed so you could see the crags in his skull.

"God how the years have piled up since your mother has been gone," he said matter of fact. "I don't want to measure life in this way."

"Yet life is measured," David matched his tone.

"Only our crying changes. I still remember you in the crib. How your grandparents once remembered me. Only your mother could soothe you. Our crying has changed. And now there is no longer anyone to come hold us in the night. How our crying changes."

He uncapped the whiskey for one last swig and handed it to his son. When David passed the bottle to Isaiah he looked at him with a start.

"Oh. Sorry Isaiah." He laughed.

"No problem."

Isaiah drank hard of the burning distraction.

"Could you pause the music?"

Mr. McCormick took the guitar off the stand. The wisps of his scraggly beard spread on his shoulder as his fingers tested each stiff string.

"Dad come on," David said.

"Sounds like it is in tune. Have you tuned it recently?"

"Yeah I think."

"You guys continue talking. I just want to pluck a little."

"Maybe if we try hard we can both find the girls no one else notices. Some litmus test could…"

Isaiah trailed off when Mr. McCormick's fingers became fluid. Isaiah had never before heard these simple six strings create magic in the same room as him. When Mr. McCormick finished he looked at them. His skin was not absent wrinkles nor his bone softened of expressions, yet Isaiah could imagine him Mr. McCormick a baby looking in his ageless eyes, seeing that light which even before religion made him believe in such a thing as a soul. He handed the guitar to David.

"Play."

"No dad."

"Come on. He is real good Isaiah. No? Ok, no."

But as Mr. McCormick told them of the memories that made him fall in love with Mrs. McCormick David started to strum softly. Mr. McCormick again capped the whiskey.

"Enough for today boys. Isaiah…You know, don't tell your dad… Well, your dad isn't the type of man to come over to kick my ass I think. Still you probably shouldn't tell him for your sake."

 He laughed but there was no humor left. David started to hum an accompaniment to their conversation. The pleasant sound pulled more emotion out of Mr. McCormick.

"No one can give me any answers. Except that I can't deny that you are here. Our son. Most days, I feel very little hope. And I am sorry for that David. Because you are here and you deserve more. I am sorry son."

"It is ok dad."

"Well. This old man got drunk on you boys. Don't drive anywhere, try and blow your smoke out the window, and have a good night."

"Good night dad."

Mr. McCormick creaked up the stairs to his room, the lonely sound made much more haunting by the chords David played on his guitar.

APRIL DOESN'T BLOOM IN SPRING

I *too will show you the world my friend.*

David walked so close to the wall his shoulders sometimes brushed it. Isaiah walked beside him protecting him against the people rushing by. Thoughts were so thick they created an ever-forming furrow on passing brows, unaware that they were dispersing possibility as they disappeared into the hallway, to eventually form again into jeans and sweaters and materializing the familiar faces of Barrett, Wadsworth, Aaron, and others, returning apparitions he would feel affection for even if they had ceased to pay much notice of him.

Even though the March skies were still those of winter, Isaiah envisioned seeds unfurling underneath the soil and becoming green buds readying to open in the light, just as the girls beckoned an early spring underneath their sweaters.

He would conduit this energy into David's sadness, for even if he had not buckled from the weight of solitude his spine was bent with the burden. He put his hand on his shoulder to stop him.

Braces girl was jabbering to her pretty friend with thick swimmer's shoulders in front of their lockers. The straps of her bra were visible through the back of her pink shirt. Her friend was cute in the non-intimidating way that you ignored unless really paying attention to her.

"How are you girls making it through the day today?"

It was all nonsense. He danced a slight impromptu jig and gave them a goofy smile. Braces girl was beautiful again as she looked at him fearful.

"I just wanted to tell you that you look really nice today."

For a moment he wished it was Karen in front of him shaking. But she would not be shaking. She would be devouring him in her smell.

"I am sorry. I didn't mean to scare you. I have never introduced myself. I am Isaiah. This is my friend David."

He waited silent until she had no choice but to fight her nerves and answer shaking.

"I'm, I'm April. This is Camille."

"Do you girls like to party?"

She shrugged.

"David has a cool house. His dad is never there. We have a good time there. You guys should come over sometime."

He leaned closer to her, knowing she would timidly answer yes to whatever he wanted just to escape this moment.

"Ok."

"Give me your phone number, so I can let you know when we are hanging out. You know, in case you guys are bored and looking for something to do."

"Ok."

He handed her his notebook and she wrote her number small in the margins of a blank page.

They both knew at the end of the night he would be holding himself over her like this. Her jaw quivered, and she tried to look grown up as she negotiated the wave of hormonal aftereffects. He wanted to make all the uncertainty go away. Her smell was fainter than Karen's. It did not mix with a slick layer of stink and latex like Stephanie's. Other remembrances he did not pay heed to. In her warmth he understood that which her voice could not communicate. All night she had warbled with the burden of conversation. She had talked and talked and talked but he could see in her face her reserve. Now her heartbeat pounded her life, which had been barely perceptible in her shy movements all evening as she pressed her hips into the counter or rubbed her hands nervously on the tabletop as they drank. The blind fumbling, the acts of secondhand desperation she had allowed him, all of it was surreal, only in her scent and heartbeat remained the reality of what they had done. Where before he had felt numb and disconnected, remembering an athletic event, her shyness had sucked him in until he still felt like the intensity of her textures were wrapped around him as they lied there. He wanted to comfort her, but when he brushed his hand along her chin she shrunk even as she tried to feign affection. He knew she was waiting for him to move, to give her permission to quickly cover her shaking body.

He rolled off of her taking the blankets so she couldn't cover up. She stood up bravely, and he tried to capture in his mind her pale skin and the translucent tuft between her legs darkening in the center, hoping it would remain with the smell in his memories of the intense moment. Gloriously fragile she was naked of even the words she surrounded herself with. Quivering even harder she could not move or look at him. He could do nothing more to comfort her than to trace his finger along her hip and down the side of her leg.

"You can get dressed darling."

Her blonde hair was wild and loose now around her shoulders, her scrawny calves led to the soft skin behind her knobby knees, out of the whole of her beauty the pink hues of her nipples and lips and the hint between her clamped legs came as a sigil to his blood. But he desired more to protect her. He glanced away for her comfort, because she wanted to be clothed and safe from what they had just done. Her body was not to be worshipped, it was not where her secret was held, but still he could not help looking back at her with his heart trembling as she faced the wall and took her pink shirt from her ball of clothes to put it back on. She pulled her lace thong from inside her jeans. She had trouble pulling her jeans on, panicking for a moment as she tried to get the legs straightened. She finally yanked them on so hard it looked painful.

"You are beautiful."

She cowered and covered her body even though she was clothed.

"Please."

He got up and dressed. She still stared at the wall, so he couldn't take her face and kiss her softly. She followed him downstairs. He could see the remnants of what had been going on with David and Camille as they immediately retreated from each other relieved at the appearance of their friend.

TRUANTS AT INDIAN MOUND PARK

Would you rather spend the next four years of your life in a cell, an hour each day to exercise in the yard, no prison rapes or anything crazy like that, but then after those four years you would be ridiculously rich the rest of your life. Or would you rather have the hottest girlfriend in the world for four years, but then afterwards have one ugly wife the rest of your life?"

"Damn. That is a tough scenario. Can you kill yourself after the four good years?" David answered.

"No."

"Let me think a second about that one. What would you do?"

"I would choose the prison. Because at least the hope of the future would get you through."

Isaiah showed him the joint he thought might bake the morning in observation.

"There is no hope."

David looked off into the distance with mock solemnity that only lasted a moment before he laughed.

"Always there is hope," Isaiah said.

"The drugs, they makes you feel better," David looked at the joint. "And then of course they makes you feel worse."

"Yeah. It was just an idea. I guess I actually don't really feel like getting high."

"Yeah. I also don't really feel like going to school."

David gave him a mischievous look that considered the world's potential.

"You call off for me, I call off for you?"

And as easy as that they called the school secretary pretending to be each other's father and trying not to laugh. They didn't discuss where to drive. Dusk had not yet revealed if the day was going to be sunny or gray.

"Are you actually going to finish the book?" David asked.

"But I hate endings."

"There are more books my friend."

"I promise it is good. I have just been really busy…with school work."

"You mean drinking?"

"Yeah I mean drugs."

"Maybe we'll never come back."

David said as they parked at the arboretum. On the railroad tracks David walked towards the horizon opposite the one Isaiah always went. David didn't hesitate as they approached the road they would have to cross. They hunched in the shadow of an empty building as the blind cars passed over the tracks. In a break they rushed across the street hunched over like infantry invading a foreign city. Back into the county a few miles ahead was the start of hills. The sun rose east on their shoulders to hide in the overcast clouds that spread over them. The horizon remained light blue and it seemed as if they went far enough they would come from underneath the clouds to walk into spring.

"I want to follow this creek till its end," Isaiah said.

They stopped to observe the creek alongside the railroad tracks. David swallowed hard a few times. Adam was always a boy until the apple. He spoke when he caught his breath.

"We are at the beginning of the Mississippi."

"Well then onwards to the ocean."

Isaiah opened his arms wide to the view. They started walking again and David picked a stone up to toss in the calm water. Dying wavelengths disappeared to leave the cathedral glass reflecting trees and the sky. David picked up a larger stone and launched it into the trees. It clunked from branch to branch then fell into the brush with a rain of twigs creating new ripples in the water.

"Goodbye Goldenwood," David muttered.

From small beginnings little tributaries not worth marking on a map joined the creek. The city behind them spread out into America's heartland on a dried out parchment. Roadmaps couldn't trace their adventure.

"Why were you friends with those guys?"

There was no accusation in David's curious glance.

"They aren't all assholes."

"Pleasant fellows indeed."

"I know Barrett was a jerk to you. But it wasn't personal. Most everything to him is an impulse. Lumpy now, little Greggy poo is an evil bastard. I guess to be honest, I probably hung out with them mostly to get girls."

"Just think. They are miserable right now and we are free!"

They had reached the hills. A sign up ahead on the road again entering this world read: *Indian Mound Park*.

They stepped down the gravel and stood underneath the soft nettle world under a line of pines bordering the railroad tracks. The first steps through the threshold had to be taken with a wild yell. Unfortunately that also meant their running barrage into the sacred world brought them crashing through the rough underbrush of brambles and burrs and an unseen stump that caused David to stumble. They slowed to a cautious walk as they fought their way up the hill avoiding branches to the face. They shunned the paved path. They climbed a fallen tree and up the hill the underbrush gave way between deciduous trees. These silent spaces between the old growth, with fallen trunks becoming mossy logs, and the matted leaves muting their footfalls, made Isaiah feel like a native entering the park. The empty brown branches were haunted in muted sunshine. But he was not afraid of the spirits. He had read how farmers had plowed over most Indian mounds, but their intimate worship of the land remained; he felt it in the earth beneath his feet.

"We should have brought tents" David said.

"And bows."

"We would never have to go back."

"I wish I knew how to build a shelter. I wouldn't know how to survive out here. I guess school does teach us some things," Isaiah said.

"But could you imagine us huddled in a classroom, burning books to keep warm, roaming the hallways as we waited out the end of the world?"

They entered a clearing. No limited lens could capture the breadth of the wall of trees surrounding them. Only in awe inspired glimpses surveying its entire length could his brain recreate the entire glory of the vision. Above them the clouds did not eliminate the light but rolled with it underneath their condensed gray centers. Through the trees on the other side they had to cross the path to continue up the hill. They looked both ways, then hunched like stalking Shawnee they hurried across. They climbed one last difficult ascent and breathed hard on the top. Through the trees they glimpsed miles of the surrounding countryside, acres of farmland dotted by red and white barns.

When their breathing slowed they rounded down the opposite direction to rest upon a felled tree trunk. Its branches had accumulated dead leaves to create a den. The tree beside them had a split with shadowy recesses that could be a hibernating animal's hidden world. Up in its branches was a thick spider web full of twigs and leaves. Cigarette butts on the ground were a disappointing reminder of the civilization Isaiah had brought along in the Marlboro pack in his pocket.

David climbed the tree, pulling himself up clumsily with scurrying feet to precariously sit on the lowest branch. He scooted to the crook of the trunk and spread his arms playfully, wobbled and grabbed the branch again.

"Hye ya ya, hye ya ya."

Joking Isaiah started to sing. But laughter faded into singsong when David began to bellow along. With his palm he thumped a heartbeat into the trunk of the tree. Isaiah joined him to play the hallow log like a native bongo. Did they stir up dust atoms from the past to form in his regenerating cells? Was latent hallucination burning with the fat in the back of his brain? Or as the wordless melody continued did his peripheral shimmer with ghosts circling in a pounding rhythm?

He didn't need to see Chris dancing for him to be there. If one needed to they could picture him at the edges. If fondness needed it his degraded remains could concentrate in the warm apparition of a boy flesh and bone. But Isaiah did not need to picture him.

"Hye ya ya, Hye ya ya."

Their voices rose and the beat increased its pace until his whole body bounced and his hand stung. Never had boys dressed like them played this rhythm here. Always boys like them had chanted this song. It was a prayer and atheism smiling in the darkness. If you wanted it could be nothingness. But he didn't need it to be anything. The dark mood had been an illusion waiting for this, and he diminished to a quark in his center, where there was neither heat nor cold, big nor small, not even his mind' infinitely smaller till this all encompassing energy superseded the laws of time and space.

David's legs swung in a pendulum. Or they did not move at all. And then he fell out of the tree.

"Oh crap."

The world expanded back out when he lost his balance and scratched at the trunk airborne. As he fell Isaiah observed the tree's twisting sheaves of bark as unique as a fingerprint. Outwards in the forest ever reaching fractals shoved hopeful skeletons up. David's legs pumped like he was running mid air, but unfortunately this caused him to tilt forward and he landed hard on his stomach with a grunt. When his moans let Isaiah know he was alive he started laughing.

"Are you ok?"

David grunted and rolled over holding his stomach. His first ragged breaths were pained with laughter. Their hysterics returned them to the circle as they had left. Isaiah helped him up and held his arm around his shoulder. He tried to make sense of reforming thoughts.

"Dude, I'm not even stoned," Isaiah said.

"We are weird."

He did not need to stare in his eyes to see his affection. Isaiah still clasped him in the silence.

"Wow, I didn't know you had a crush on me."

David pulled away from him and started walking down but Isaiah was not ready to leave. A question formed that he knew he shouldn't ask, but he could almost speak of things to David he couldn't communicate.

"Do you ever pray for Chris?"

"No."

"Oh. You know some people are so hateful they hurl him immediately into hell. Can you imagine him as a demon coming back to haunt?"

"No."

"I guess I would be the one he would torment," Isaiah said.

"I wouldn't say that dude."

"But I find it ridiculous that there is any such God that would turn his back upon a child just trying to find his way closer to him."

"Yeah."

FRIEND OF THE DEVIL

David's face scrunched up to tell a joke but trampling footsteps interrupted him. They jumped at the walky-talky blast as if the blind tentacles of Goldenwood were approaching them. Like spacemen in an alien land they two people jingled and clinked as they plowed through the vegetation. David and Isaiah scampered into the underbrush. Isaiah took shallow breaths, trying to be like Chris and fade into silence. His heart pumped. David's fearful face did not look defeated; instead he stared towards the noise as if the malevolence he had always felt was now proven real, and it was time to do battle with it.

"God damn it."

A man cursed as he crashed in the trees close to them. Isaiah stiffened as two policemen passed by them searching with dimmed eyes. They were awkward animals close enough for an easy arrow in the neck. One was sturdy, his angular hat contrasting his doughy cheeks. The other was lean, his hat in his hand exposing a shaved head that made his angular face look skeletal. It held no kindness. Isaiah prayed they would disappear without a trace like characters in one of David's books.

"Boys. Enough. We know you are here. Let's make it easier on everyone."

Skull Face's threat came out his nasal passages. Then this friend of the devil turned around suddenly and stared right at them, his omniscience shattering existentialism and filling Isaiah with fear, for he had discerned no sound, no movement, not even a breath out of David or him to give them away.

"Get on the fucking ground now."

He unlatched his handgun. They lied down in the underbrush like sacks of dead meat. It scratched his hands and face. Skull Face had hatred in his eyes as he stumbled, a desire to hurt them as he rushed towards them with his hand on his gun.

"What do you think you're doing? Put your god damn hands behind your backs."

Skull Face grabbed David's arm, snagged on a branch, and yanked it behind his back, pressing his face hard into the dirt and scratching nettles. He violently patted him down. The other officer patted Isaiah down much gentler.

"Do you have any weapons?"

"No sir we don't have any weapons." David's hallow voice was muffled by the ground.

"Relax Pinkerton, they are just boys."

"What are you guys doing out here? Are you doing drugs?" Officer Pinkerton yelled.

Isaiah wished he had something to admit, fearing that Skull Face would delve into him with his supernatural power.

"Speak damn it, what are you doing?"

Skull Face stepped over to him and blows stung his defenseless body as he started to pat him down before the chubby officer grabbed his arm.

"I said calm down Pinkerton. Do you have anything in your pockets boys?"

"Yes. Our keys and wallets," David muttered.

"Ok, you boys can sit up now. Go ahead and empty your pockets for us."

"Slowly now, or I will break your nose. I asked you guys what are you doing hiding out here?"

"We were just walking sir," David said.

"Don't lie to me. It would be different if you were an old man here walking your dog. But you guys aren't on the path. You are trespassing. So what were you really doing out here? Tell me."

He pushed David's shoulder. His keys and wallet went flying onto the dirty ground. Isaiah emptied his keys and wallet on the ground and then set the pack of cigarettes on top of them.

"Stop Pinkerton. Look at them, they are terrified."

The chubby officer stood them up and pulled their pockets inside out. Skull Face peered at them.

"Why aren't you in school?"

"I don't know," David said.

Then Skull Face noticed the cigarettes.

"I think you were out here doing drugs. Are they in your cigarettes pack? Don't lie to me, I will find them."

Skull Face emptied the pack of cigarettes. Isaiah almost wished he hadn't left the joint in David's basement. He took Isaiah's face into his hands and peered into his eyes. The mint on his breath made the stench of halitosis overwhelming. Isaiah couldn't breathe, he couldn't think, they could do with him what they wanted, for he now knew the true extent of his powerlessness. Skull Face turned to David and peered also into his eyes, but he just looked into the far away distance again. Isaiah wondered if he was playing dead.

"You look high. Your friend here seems mute. Where did you hide the drugs? Answer me!" He screamed into David's face with incessant hatred in his voice.

"Sir we don't have any drugs."

"There are truancy laws against this sort of thing. You can't just skip school and do whatever you want. You can't just come to a park and trespass wherever you want. I think I am going to take you back to the station and lock you up and come back and find your drugs. I swear if I find any drugs you are not going to like it."

He got back into Isaiah's face.

"And you have cigarettes. How old are you boy?"

"He is eighteen. Check his I.D," David said.

"Enough," Skull Face hissed. "If you have stashed drugs," he sniffed the air, and then sniffed again peering in David's face. "I will find them. We are going to the station now."

"Officer Pinkerton, come here," the chubby cop said with an official tone.

He pulled him away and with an effort made Skull Face smile as he patted him on the shoulder. They had a laugh and returned with the chubby cop on the lead.

"Which one of you is Isaiah?"

He raised his hand not surprised they had known his name without even looking at his driver's license.

"We ran your plates at the arboretum. We called your parents. They are worried sick something happened to you. They told the dispatcher never in a million years would you skip school."

He stepped away and got on his walkie-talkie.

"Dispatch, could you call Isaiah's parents and tell them we found him and he is ok. Thanks."

"You ungrateful little curs," Skull Face peered in David's face. "What is your name?"

"David."

"Your last name?"

"McCormick."

"Do your parents know where you are at?"

"No sir. My dad does not."

"Like we wouldn't find you."

"You didn't."

"What? What? Don't talk back to me. The only reason you two have for being here is mischief. Where did you hide the drugs? Just tell the truth."

"We were just talking."

"Talking. Talking. Don't raise your voice you little chubby punk." David had whispered. "What are you two out here doing then, boy-boy stuff?"

"No," David muttered.

"I said lower your voice fat ass. You know, playing doctor with each other's little peckers while your parents were worried sick. You can't just disappear. There is such a thing as truancy laws."

"Pinkerton stop. Listen boys, Isaiah's parents are worried sick. David I'm sure your parents will be upset when you get home."

"Parent," David said.

"Shut up," Skull Face hissed.

"So we're going to walk you down to our police car. I want you guys to think about your actions."

Walking down the path the magic place became just a park, and Isaiah looked at his feet to not see it from this vantage point. For a moment he had believed they were somewhere else and didn't ever have to go back. The officers did not speak to them as they put them in the back of the police car. Quick they returned to the known world, just a short drive led back to boredom.

"What about your dad David?" Skull Face scoffed.

"My dad?"

"Yes. Your dad. That troglodyte needs it explained that there are laws against this sort of thing and he could go to jail."

Isaiah did not care where they took him. But when they parked beside his vehicle there was a pang at being reconnected to a world he now knew he could not escape. The chubby officer took a joking tone.

"If you are wondering how we found you, we got a call from an old couple who heard you hollering and hooting like madmen in the hills. You boys put quite a scare in them. The poor old souls were half frightened to death when they called. We're going to release you this time to your parents. But I want you to go straight home. Do you understand?"

"Yes sir."

Skull Face spoke in an official voice without looking at them as his partner let them out.

"This is serious business. I don't know what you were doing out there. I sure hope it wasn't something stupid like drugs because we are going to search the park. This is your last chance to admit it. No? But. You. Should. Not. Have. Been. There. Understand? Isaiah your parents are loving people. Remember that next time before you pull a stunt like this. Go."

They got out. The chubby officer patted Isaiah's arm.

"Straight home now. You be good boys. You have no criminal records right now. Remember, that is very important for your life. Make sure you keep it that way."

He got back in and the cruiser drove away. Their omniscient presence lingered. The covered bridge now only beckoned an insignificant respite in his grid locked life. Following orders was his only impetus. He dropped David off without speaking, jealous of him having no parent waiting for him.

He didn't hesitate at his doorway and his parents were waiting for him at the kitchen table with the worried faces he expected. His mother's hand stifled her sharp intake of breath and covered her mouth, agape like a soap opera. Then her hand covered her whole face as her pinky scrunched her upper lip. Questions, anger, fear, happiness, all these emotions were in the novelty of his father's focus upon him. It was too intense for him, and he shielded his eyes.

"Hello," He mumbled.

"Hello?" His father said incredulously. "Ha. Nice try. You'll have to do better than that."

All the emotion Isaiah had repressed came out now as he looked back at them. Were they but a part of the force that repressed him? His parents were supposed to love and cherish him. Yet he was unsure as he searched them whether they would believe there was any excuse for his actions.

"What's the big fuss about?"

"You skipped school," his father said. His voice rose. "Your mother was worried sick."

"So."

"So? So? Come on Isaiah. Don't try it. Speak to us."

The candor of all their emotions barely held in check caused Isaiah to sit down with a desire to try and explain.

"I know. But it was just for one day that I acted irrational. I needed a break. I don't know how to explain it. I had to step outside of the limits of my life. It was just one day."

"That is how it always starts. The first time makes it easier to do again."

"Oh for Christ's sake," Isaiah yelled.

He was unsure how they stayed calm in the face of his wellspring of emotion.

"Come on. It's a joke anyways. Why are you being so melodramatic? It's not a huge deal. I...it is just a joke. All the bullshit, you have to see the bullshit. Don't tell me you can't see all the bullshit."

"Eloquently put," His mother said.

"I understand cutting loose occasionally. But not like this. How could you do that to your mother?"

His father slapped the table.

"And don't think we are stupid. We notice you have been acting different. I know you have been drinking. I can tell a hangover when I see one."

"This was something different."

"You have to understand Isaiah. With all the horrible things your classmates' parents have had to go through, and the way you have been acting weird, I couldn't help but think the worse," His mother said.

She looked at him with raw concern. He scoffed out an emotionless laugh. He stood to get a cup from the cupboard with their eyes intent upon him. Ice clunked into his glass and then water filled in a precise stream. When the water was a centimeter below the rim he sat back down and took a long drink.

"Mom, Dad, I am not going to kill myself," he spoke with all the common sense he could muster.

"Oh, we know. You know, they were just crazy thoughts," his mother said. "It's just, when I got that call from the police that they had found your car in the park. My heart just stopped Isaiah."

Her eyes filled with tears, and even though she tried to blink them back from the brink of her eyelids they started to run down her face in tracks of mascara. He couldn't remember seeing her cry, and he never wanted to see it again. When her husband put his arm around her she looked to him as a friend, and he could envision them as young lovers. As she cried in his father's arms, the dying flower of DNA, that momentary complexity that formed their family, could have crumbled its fragile inner structures and left only the light of her soul to break his heart.

"Who were you with?" His dad asked.

"David McCormick."

"What were you two doing out there?"

His father looked at him with openness that for the first time made him feel like an adult. He took the chair next to his mother and held her moist hand.

"I promise we did nothing but walk and pretend to be on a great adventure. To be honest at one point I worried David might be the next one to kill himself."

"Is he ok?"

"Yeah. Yeah he is. Actually. More than a lot of people, I think."

"Good."

"Yeah," Isaiah said with the first shudder of emotion. All the thoughts that would not let him be, the pain, the guilt, came out as he spoke. "Chris was David's best friend. I was so cruel to Chris before he died."

His mother held him now and shook as he cried. His father lost his last trace of sternness and wrapped his arm around both of them.

"Oh Isaiah."

"You guys don't know. Kids can be so cruel. David has this long off stare, you can tell everyday he wants to escape. Kids pick on him. Kids picked on Chris. David pretends like he doesn't care. But people otherwise barely even speak to him. I barely even talked to him for years. Even the teachers barely notice him. How could he not be sad? So miserably sad."

"Oh, son, everyone gets picked on. I was such a chubby little punk, everyone picked on me until high school."

"That doesn't make it right Ernest," his mother said as she tried to catch her breath.

"You don't understand. If David kills himself it would be my fault."

"Your fault? You can't really believe that son."

"Barrett, Lumpy, all those guys, we made up a stupid bet one day on who would be the next to kill themselves. We all picked someone. And I picked David. They all laughed as I cursed him and he was my friend. I felt so guilty, because I could tell how sad he was even as we laughed at him. How sad a lot of kids are. It was people like me, my fault. So I have been trying to be his friend again. I wanted to take it back. I prayed so hard for him mom. But I feel…I feel…"

He held his mother and cried.

TRUANT'S PENANCE

Distance couldn't have reformed this quick between David and Isaiah at the lunch table.

"Did you tell your dad what happened?"

"Hell no."

"You are lucky. My parents had themselves a scene. I'm grounded."

"That sucks."

David went back to reading. Isaiah had been wary when he said he would drive himself to school, just as Barrett had, but he refused to believe it was anything more than a mood. He left him to it so it could take its course. He forced himself to study for his parents, but it was difficult, as it seemed David and he huddled again underneath oppressive walls with Mr. Stigler patrolling the lunchroom. So it was back to chewing with an occasional page shuffling, silent as conversation surrounded them. He felt guilt for envying the happiness convulsing Barrett as he flourished his hands to the rest of his old lunch table.

April was no longer shivering and vulnerable. Every passing observation was precious as she filled her lunch period with words. Her braces had not been exposed once in her naked womanhood like they were now.

The words of his textbook would be forgotten, but the order of the type in two tight columns would remain.

Wadsworth puffed his cheeks and lifted an imaginary gut from over his groin, as Aaron relished a sneer at Dixie Winn walking by. Even Lumpy, that hateful creature, was laughing at his joke. Hoss always shook his head but he never sat anywhere else. Barrett stood to dance over Wadsworth as they laughed as if they were the center of happiness.

April had to feel Isaiah's stare but she did not glance over at him. He wondered if her words comforted her as if she were still a child, or if she played at being grown up as she spoke of lying underneath him. He couldn't remember any blood, or even if she had made the slightest gasp of pain.

There was not a hint of loneliness anywhere he looked except for in the boy sitting across from him. David didn't care for any of it anyhow.

It stayed this way until the minute hand clicked on the verge of disruption. Only when the bells urgency pressed on her did April search Isaiah out. She motioned him to meet her at the entrance unable to hide her desperation. He could not decipher David's emotion as he walked past them without a word.

"What are you doing tonight?" She implored.

"Nothing. I am grounded. My parents won't be home until late though. You could come over and watch a movie."

Neither of them had mentioned a movie. Her courage was reserved for bragging about the Lexus her daddy had given her for her sweet 16. But as the minutes clicked on his wooden clock, closer to the time she must leave, she squirmed as she talked. She pointed again at his senior portrait and their family pictures on the wall and giggled.

"You guys are so cute. Look at your sister's plaid skirt. Precious. And oh my God, in your senior picture you are so hot."

She ached to give in again now, a subtle supplication for him to kiss her. But in the presence of his family pictures he could not help but see her as her father's daughter. He did not want to betray her innocence again in his home. He put his arm around her and started talking as much as she had been. She did not respond. Her silence was willful, as she leaned to enlarge his opening. He knew the desperation in her eyes to not let time pass empty into the past.

It was to rescue her from spending the rest of her evening in this agitated state that he gave in with a kiss. She whispered slight breaths against his lips. Passion came quickly over him as he became aware of her smell under her perfume. She kissed him, sensitive to every minute change of pressure from the outside world. As if scared of this breadth of time ending to alter her world again she opened her mouth and guided his hand down. She played off her writhing as if she were shifting her weight on the couch. The temptation was strong to lead her up to his bedroom, where a girl had never been naked, and bring her to his innocence. Just softly at the edge, calming her cocoon walls, the world fluttering as they combined to redefine its slow rhythm. But then as a nervous reaction she pushed his hand away and peered at him. He liked how when her jaw was shut she looked ancient and wise. Just as quickly her desire took control again and she pressed back into him with a wild kiss. She supplanted again to his hand and he knew she would let him in now after her first balking, but he resisted the pressing need.

He pulled away. He left his hand on her hip so as not to abandon her, feeling her shiver from a touch stolen from her ancient line into past wombs of existence. But he resisted the heat of their blood ready to gush the biology he had tapped into once. Like his family watching him from the walls there were pictures too of her family. Her submissive yes, the girl contrasting the woman she bore exotically underneath, he instead answered like a whispering holy man, no, as he looked into her eyes to feel that part of her that was out of time. It was time for her to go home to the mother who had shaped her good looks, back to the place where her father protected her, in her familial line the years that separated them seemed an eternity. He moved to the end of the couch to protect her chastity against the desire pounding within them. He wanted that timeless creature to come out of its nest of its own accord, it was a thing no force of will could pull out, but instead only press deeper within under the illusion of possessing all of her. He never wanted to see that scared stricken look on her face again.

"I'm sorry. My parents are going to be home soon."

As he walked her outside to her Lexus he could tell she was going to feel the impending sadness anyways. He was only eighteen yet he could already feel his youth passing.

"It is strange to think I am soon about to graduate."

"I know. It makes me sad."

"Don't worry. We are all immortal."

She looked at him uncomprehending.

"Damn your ass looks good in those jeans. I wish my parents weren't coming home."

Her eyes sparkled as she laughed. He wondered if it was the same way she laughed at her father's jokes. At her car door she held on to the moment by refusing to turn. She pressed up against him and opened her jacket so he could feel her underneath her t-shirt

"I notice you in church. I believe in Jesus too. Have you ever seen me there in a dress?"

"Yes," he lied.

"We are so bad," she giggled.

The she was on him so franticly that for the first time he became aware of her braces as they kissed. He finally pulled away.

"I can't wait to be married in that church. And to baptize my babies there," she said.

He didn't believe any of it, but she was pure and her perfume smelled wonderful and her thin shoulder blades trembled so he kissed her again before opening her door. She got in her car, her jaw quivering, shaking now as much as she had underneath him. She rolled down her window.

"Are you my boyfriend now?" She whispered.

He knew he was looking at her the way a scientist would a specimen, but he acknowledged how sweet and beautiful those innocent thoughts played on her features, even though those innocent eyes would tear away from him soon enough. In this moment she still believed, and he could almost make himself believe what they had shared meant something more. So he said yes. Her smile was so radiant that he knew the boyishness in the soft features of his face had lost too early the ability to smile like that. There were so many sins in his life and he wished he had never needed forgiveness.

LOL.

Of course in the dull evening afterwards she instant messaged him everything that crossed her mind like the computer was linked to her delicate forehead. She hinted at what they had done together, then the next minute typed about class and homework, only to return again to their indulgence in the same way she had asked if Isaiah was her boyfriend; as a plea for him to make it right.

MEAT

Lumpy hovered over David like the Death Star, two big blue eyes feigning benevolence as they took aim upon a primeval being. Barrett pounced upon the chair next to Isaiah.

"How is it going buddy."

Barrett seemed friendly, but his unexpected arrival at their lunch table after all this time seemed to come from the same malevolent force that had brought the cops upon them at the arboretum.

"What cha reading there buddy?"

Lumpy tilted over David's shoulder. A new pattern of zits peaked in the corner of his eyelid in a place where the whitehead could not be popped. David ignored him, as impassive as he had been when Isaiah had tried to converse with him at the beginning of lunch period. His disregard just included two more voices to ignore. The happy conversations around him were insubstantial. But Isaiah was tempted by Barrett's smile, and it felt like betrayal to feel grateful for his voice after weeks of David's prolonged silence. Still he was able to stare defiantly at Lumpy.

"What do you want?"

"This animosity is so stupid. I have some big news I want to tell you," Barrett said.

"What?"

"I leave for Parris Island, MCRDPI, boot camp, right after graduation. I finally did it."

Barrett's alteration was evident in the intense stare his mood swings would not have been able to maintain before. It was as if a stranger stuck out his hand for Isaiah to shake, so open was the exuberance in his expression. From the vantage point of their former intimacy Isaiah could not help but feel affection, picturing this wild and uninhibited boy shaped till his clean cut energy quivered in uniform. He shared his congratulatory handshake as if meeting a new friend. His plans to join the Marines after graduation had always seemed a whim to Isaiah, but now he had actually signed the contract and defined himself.

"I am so fucking ready."

"The Marines will still be looking for a few good men," Lumpy said.

"Listen, I am sorry I let some chick get into my head and convince me I shouldn't talk to you. Screw Carrie Ann's skank ass. Friendship is more important. You can come back to our lunch table."

It was not like Isaiah woke every morning desiring to keep a sullen face all day. He could not resist smiling back at him, and his rebuke was unconvincing.

"I like sitting here."

Lumpy rolled his eyes.

"That's cool, I can understand that. I know I was a jerk man, but we can still be friends. We're over it. We have a lot of partying to catch up on before I leave for boot camp."

Barrett gave Lumpy a hard stare.

"I agree," Lumpy said.

Lumpy's will bent under Barrett's set jaw and joker stare.

"Yeah man. I'm over everything. We miss having you over. You are always invited to my parties," Lumpy forced the words out. "Hell, I thought you sat here because you were trying to make sure you won our bet."

David didn't glance up. But when they glanced at this statue of a boy could they not see he had the same orifices as them, he could hear, his blood flowed life just the same as theirs to every inert extremity; could they not tell his heart was already broken.

"Don't be a sack of lard."

But Barrett's voice was just a flinching reminder of his foot kicking David in the ass.

"Oh come on man. I was just joking. We are all cursed, we're all cursed." Lumpy flinched from Barrett's stare. "Hey, I am sure he is a cool dude. Why don't you bring David with you to one of our parties?"

Barrett put his hand on Isaiah's shoulder and he almost believed the bet was nothing more than the price of their entertainment. But they glanced again at David as if speaking of an effigy.

"Come on man, bros before hoes," Barrett said.

It wasn't like David thought I want to feel apart, alone, every day that he dreamt of escaping into his books.

"Come on say it with me, bros before hoes."

"Bros before hoes."

Isaiah responded because it seemed the only way to end this. He tried not to take comfort in his good humor.

"We don't fight our wars for vagina. Speaking of hoes. I see you have a new girlfriend. A cute young thing. April. Did you finally pop that cherry you were looking for?"

Isaiah blushed.

"You have haven't you? Don't lie. I know how you like popping cherries. I'm glad you finally found one. Steph' told Carrie Ann's dumb ass that you slam danced with her again, and that backstabbing skank obviously can't keep a secret. I know you are a freak on the down low."

"April is different."

"Different huh? I hope so, if she actually is you are lucky, but most girls are business sluts so be careful, don't get your hopes up."

Barrett's face for a brief moment clouded with the betrayal he had learned in Carrie Ann's true nature. But it quickly passed, for the future held more women to look upon him as an 18-year old boner.

"Who would have thought that our valedictorian is a degenerate like the rest of us? Come tell us about it over some Buds at my house tonight," Lumpy said.

"I can't. Believe it or not I am grounded."

"Grounded? Mr. Valedictorian? For What?" Barrett asked.

"Skipping school."

"That is stupid. Come on Isaiah," Barrett said.

Isaiah shrugged.

"How about you, you strange little fucker? Are you boinking one of her friends?" Lumpy asked David. "Come over. We'll introduce you to some drunk sluts."

David's silence was only interrupted by the turning of a page.

"Oh come on. Believe it or not, at church I actually prayed for you."

Finally David looked up.

"Don't you love it when someone says I'll pray for you? Like you are God's problem now. Guess what asshole, I already was. So save your prayers for yourself."

"Hey," Lumpy growled and leaned over David. "I was trying to be nice you—"

Barrett grabbed him and pushed him away.

"Shut up Lumpy. No one wants to hear your mouth. Puss stick and I will leave you two to your reading. Call me later dude," Barrett said.

When they left David continued to read as if they had never been there.

"Sorry man," Isaiah said.

David looked up with his contemplation settling on Isaiah from the distance.

"Do you ever wish someone was reading a book about you? In their pajamas rooting for you to meet your star crossed lover, or following you as the hero, enjoying your every triumph, panging for you through every defeat, always with that underlying trust that there would be a happy ending?"

"I guess. I always imagined—"

"But of course we always picture ourselves the protagonist. Only stock side characters are moronic bullies, only flat characters go off and waste themselves away addicted to heroin, only nominal roles kill themselves off, as the story continues."

NO NARNIA BEHIND THE MIRROR

Isaiah's reflection studied dutifully ahead in his bedroom mirror. There was no fantasy hidden behind the frame, no adventure would open up out of his imagination into a fantastical world as he had prayed for in childhood. *Grandeur of Illusions* lied next to the Bible on his nightstand, both unfinished as he memorized pages spent.

His father had given him a reprieve from grounding for this last weekend of spring break. Barrett right now probably had his arms interlocked with friends singing drunken lullabies to the crashing waves. Isaiah could have convinced his mother to let him go along, but he had been using his grounding as an excuse to avoid all Barrett's invitations. He regretted that today.

As the time approached for David to meet him he paced by the front door like a cat stuck inside. It had taken a lot of convincing, but finally by force of will he had convinced David to have a get together at his house. The knock finally came and he opened the door and bounded out. David was wearing the clothes Isaiah had recommended he wear to impress the girls. His hair was even combed. It was too late to do anything about how he had gelled his hair tight to his head with a part exactly in the middle.

"Ready for a new adventure?"

After a bout of silence David feigned excitement when he realized Isaiah was waiting for a response.

"Yeah."

"Looking good buddy."

David shrugged. Isaiah took him by the shoulders and shook his excitement into him, refusing to let him retreat back into this mood.

"Let's go pick up the ladies. Do you still have the joint I left at your house, or did you smoke it in a fiendish fit?"

"It's there."

"Sweet. First we're buying a pack of cigarettes. I have been dying for a smoke."

Isaiah wasn't going to let him stare out the window at some imaginary land as they drove, their youth passing in musty tomes while their peers reveled in the sunshine.

"You actually going to talk to Camille tonight?" Isaiah asked.

"Yeah."

He did not sound convincing as he hunched inwards like a coward trying to hide from a world he pretended didn't exist. He only rolled his potato bug shoulders when Isaiah asked him what kind of cigarettes he preferred. Finally when Isaiah got back in the car and the silence continued as they drove he could no longer hold in his disgust.

"Dude. What is wrong with you?"

"What?"

"Why are you acting like this?"

"What are you talking about?"

"You know, as a child I actually once believed there was a magical place I would find. Shit, that Chris, you and I would find it together. Where the battles were more real than fighting boredom, that there was good versus evil, and the good guys always won. Maybe even an elvish princess for me. But guess what? There is no Narnia behind the mirror. Only your reflection staring back at you."

"Duh."

"If you are so sad, do something about it. You can't live your life hiding in books and fantasy. If you don't face the world, how can you go around blaming everyone? You don't even try. Life is more than reading about it. Every day you will wake up in this world and the mirror will only show your reflection. Do you want to see only a pussy?"

"Damn dude, I was just thinking. Relax."

The three girls did not realize it was Isaiah's car that had pulled up in front of the mall. They stood outside still in the disinfected safety their unassuming parents had dropped them off at. But as they chattered on the edge of their comfort they glanced into the parking lot, curious of what was on the other side. The dark heavy mood in the car contrasted them.

"Listen I'm sorry. I didn't mean it like that. I just want you realize I am trying to be your friend."

With a cheerful honk and wave Isaiah got their attention. April was more confident than the two girls following her, Camille, and a heavy set girl Isaiah didn't recognize.

"If you expect me to take that one I'd rather read a book," David said.

He laughed in relief at his sudden turn of demeanor. They scrunched in the backseat.

"Having fun at the mall ladies?"

Isaiah winked at April. She turned to her friends.

"David's dad is cool. He lets them do whatever they want and doesn't even bother them. He isn't going to be home right David?"

"Oh who knows with the old man?"

"He works late. So he won't be there when we get there. But he said we could have a party," Isaiah said, noticing their look of concern. "You guys ready to have fun?"

"Paint me pink," April said.

"I haven't met your friend. What is her name?"

"Yolanda."

"Nice to meet you Yolanda. Let's go get crazy."

Yolanda laughed and played with her long black head of curls. But her bashfulness was just waiting for the rest of her to mature into her bully face. Isaiah joked as they drove and her giggles only mimicked the other two, her beady eyes calculating, her upturned pug nose just needed a bit more confidence to bark out sarcasm.

"Nice house, but my parents could help you with some landscaping," Camille said politely when they parked.

The girls were hushed as they entered the house. David's exuberance surprised Isaiah as much as the girls as he merrily turned towards them and with a grand gesture motioned them towards the basement.

"Welcome to my humble abode. Good times are this way ladies."

Camille's broad shoulder placed her in the room. But her pretty face was bored as she looked around and then back at David, pouting as she ascertained every detail. Isaiah handed her a beer to thwart the distinctions he saw forming. Yolanda grabbed one from him before he even offered it to her.

"Now April I don't want your dad showing up and kicking my ass for giving you a beer."

April tried to hide her braces with a smile that only plumped her lips. She pressed her padded bra out as she cracked open her beer. She spoke in the serious tone of an adult.

"Oh no. Don't worry. We each told our parents we were sleeping at the other's houses."

He tickled her side so that her braces showed, her delicate ribs clenching half in fear and half in excitement.

"Little do they know you are going to be a bad little girl."

Before they were halfway finished with their first beers their giggles bubbled and their faces flushed.

"So your dad doesn't really care if you drink down here?" Yolanda asked.

"Nope. Isaiah and me smoke and drink down here all the time." David finished in a slurred Irish accent to Isaiah' surprise, "sometimes he even pours us some whiskey."

Even Yolanda's laugh was sincere. The look of a girl did powerful things to a boy, and as Camille flushed with the full glow of her attention on David, appraising him, exuberance flowed into him as he chugged his beer.

"Hmmm. I see the beginnings of a great friendship developing," Camille said.

David reddened in pleasure.

"Speaking of smoke," Isaiah said.

"Oh yeah. It is in my bookshelf behind *The Devine Comedy*."

"Have you read all those books?" Camille asked.

"Well most of them, my dear, most of them," David said with mock sophistication entering his Irish accent.

Isaiah flourished the joint in front of the girls, appraising their good humor. He winked at David. The world indeed had potential if David would just embrace it.

"Well light that thing up." David had gained confidence in his voice with Camille's attention.

"Yes sir. David, why don't you impress these ladies with some of your stellar tunes to get hazy to?"

Isaiah brought the joint to his lips. Intent upon him, the girls were uncertain, their curiosity contrasted with the fear instilled by Goldenwood's D.A.R.E. to keep a kid off drugs program.

"Don't feel any pressure. You don't have to smoke."

April pressed her push up bra out even further.

"Oh, I've always wanted to try it."

He brought the lighter to the joint and waited for the music to stare. But David was having a dilemma choosing something that would impress the girls.

"Whatever you pick will be perfect."

"Well then, I think, hmmm, this will do."

As David mumbled to himself with self-doubt Isaiah lit the joint to bring their attention back to him. The familiar pungent smoke entered him with new relish with their innocent eyes upon him, and he hit it hard in a performance they would always remember. When he passed it to April she took it tentatively.

"Just like a cigarette."

"I've never smoked a cigarette before," she giggled.

"Just put it to those pretty little lips and suck."

A solemn bass note began long and mournful. David sat down and scanned them for their reactions.

"Good choice," Isaiah said.

Bluesy notes filled the room like molasses. April made a valiant attempt at smoking, even though she could have taken no more than a mouthful into her lungs. The cough that wracked her delicate body took a while to turn back into a giggle.

"It tastes funny."

"Puff again and pass it," Isaiah said.

She took in less smoke this time. Camille politely waved her off. Yolanda took the joint hungrily and inhaled. She blew out a cloud of smoke and hit it again.

"It looks like someone has done this before," Camille said.

Yolanda was mesmerized and for a moment didn't acknowledge her and April's laughter.

"No, no, I haven't. I never told you guys, but when I was fourteen I used to smoke cigarettes. I know, I know, don't look at me like that. But it does taste funny."

David took the joint and smoked while looking at Camille. As if on cue the singer's voice became impassioned and the music quickened its tempo. Isaiah got up to take the joint from David when he was done. He smoked with less enthusiasm now that the desired transition had been achieved.

"I feel funny already," April said.

Her fearful look caused him to pass it to Yolanda without offering it to her. The taboo alone was powerful; even Camille's mood was under its influence. Isaiah puffed the roach hard as he had seen others do, burning his lips and inhaling no smoke, but they wouldn't know he hadn't done it right. He handed out more beers. It didn't matter if they actually enjoyed the music, for it was exotic, and they slithered their necks trying to be worthy of this new dance. Isaiah pulled David up to dance with him as idols for their reverence. Life dilated David's pupils as he pretended not to notice Camille's attention. At the end of the song David bounded up the stairs.

"I'll be right back."

He skipped back downstairs with a bottle of whiskey and shot glasses. He poured four shots and passed them out.

"To a new reality," David said.

He held the bottle out and Isaiah tapped the bottle with his shot glass, without time to even ponder what they were doing the girls followed his example and they all drank. Even after the girls had finished appreciating each other's flurrying aftershock David kept the bottle to his lips. He drank for what seemed an entire guitar solo. Isaiah had never seen anyone swallow so much. When he finished he gagged and his complexion paled.

"Oh my god, are you ok," April said.

He shuddered before he could speak, but then responded again in that sophisticated air.

"Why yes, milady, never been better."

Yolanda looked at David with her beady eyes. She danced with pounding movements unconcerned with their lack of grace, confidence in her voice as she looked at David with distaste that was already starting to fill in the harshness of her features.

"Don't think you can get us drunk and take advantage of us. We're not those types of girls."

He meaningful stare deflated David but still he managed to answer nonchalant.

"No. It's not like that. We…we're just trying to have some fun."

"Except for April of course. She may be that type of girl," Camille said.

"Shut up."

April blushed and wouldn't look at her friends as they cackled at her.

"Can I get us another beer Isaiah?" She asked.

"Certainly my dear."

She swayed into his lap and pressed a beer into his chest. She pretended she hadn't done it on purpose and gave him a piteous look.

"I feel funny."

Yolanda and Camille talked amongst themselves in discomfort. Spurned, David had moved away and from the other side of the room he stared at April on Isaiah's lap. He could not hide his jealousy, and Isaiah realized what had been lurking underneath his animosity. Isaiah was disappointed, for he had started to view him as the noble outcast, bereft of the petty emotions that caused others to throw tantrums. Isaiah shifted his face away from April to focus on David.

"Dude I am not ready for school to start again Monday."

"Hopelessness drains eternal."

David took a swig still staring at them.

"Maybe we should skip again."

"Yeah."

"Those cops were evil. I wish they would have tripped and fallen down that hill. Bastards."

"Yeah."

"Did April tell you girls what happened? David and I got caught skipping school by the cops. We were lucky not to get arrested. That is why I got grounded."

Isaiah tried to get Yolanda and Camille's attention. April turned on his knee him with excitement to face them.

"Oh yeah. I forgot to tell you guys. The cops put them in the back of the car and everything."

"Neat. Hey does anyone have a cigarette?" Yolanda said.

Isaiah reached in his pocket to toss her the cigarettes. April squirmed closer. Yolanda smoked like there was nothing else in the room. Camille saved all her prettiness for pondering the walls again. David drank. April brought her face close and peered at his mouth. He eyes implored him to kiss her. And just like that things spun out of control as she gave up waiting and kissed him. He kissed her back not to be rude. When he pulled away David was ignoring them with fervor. Camille estimated David by the things in his basement, Yolanda's quick rebuke of him echoed still in the distance they kept from him. Isaiah could not resist April's repressed passion when her swollen lips were wet on his mouth again, her soft bottom seeming to grow heavier with desire. Only when she paused to catch her breath could he pull away again. Yolanda smoked, Camille had a serendipitous pull towards the wall, and David solemnly drank, as they all pretended not to notice. April grabbed his shoulder and the padding of her bra pressed up against his chin and she didn't even breathe in her fervor. Again with an effort he disengaged. David was now standing in the middle of the room with Camille and Yolanda watching him. He put the bottle down and ripped his shirt off. It got caught on his face before he could get it off. The fat of his pale body did not descend in folds, as one would imagine from the way his clothes bunched, instead it was one solid mass that bulged at his love handles as if a mold of lard had been plastered to him. He spun his shirt around his head.

"Woo."

He threw it at Camille's feet. April turned. Isaiah scooted her back onto his knee. David's smile faded as he looked at the girls. He jiggled his bottom roll, the whole mass of fat bouncing.

"Look at me. Aren't I disgusting?"

But they were only confused, there was no more disgust for him than if he were a chubby little boy at the swimming pool. He glared at Isaiah and chopped at his fleshy upper arm like his hand held a knife.

"Maybe I should cut myself like Isaiah. Maybe if I get me some nice scars girls will like me. Has he shown you his wittle scars April? Yeah, I think I'll do that. Hold on, I'll be right back, you guys can watch."

He started to turn.

"David stop. There is nothing wrong with you. Calm down," Isaiah said.

He continued towards the stairs.

"You're not that fat David. You're attractive in your own way. Let's just have fun," April said.

He turned back with a wobble at her voice. He gave her a drunken smile and grabbed his fat roll again with two hands, shaking it violently so that tremors again jiggled the whole mold.

"Such a sweet Christian sympathy. This is the way god made me ladies. Isn't it disgusting?"

April looked at him with sadness.

"Clueless, Isaiah, you can't dress this up and cover what is underneath."

Isaiah didn't know how to respond.

"Oh, come on, I'm just joking. But you don't have to lie to me. The only girl for me is in the pages of a book."

He picked the shirt up and swung it around his head again.

"Woo."

He laughed again and this time the goofiness in his drunken grin released the tension and they joined him.

"You're hilarious," April said.

"Hey David, why don't you put your shirt back on and play the girls your guitar."

He slammed his shirt down. "No." Then after a wobble, "I will play my guitar though."

"Oh. You play the guitar?" Camille asked.

"That's hot," April said with hope in her voice.

He turned the music off, picked up his guitar and sat down. He looked at them and after another wobble plucked one string.

"Ooooooo pretty," he wailed.

"Stop it. Play us something," Isaiah said.

"Ooh, do you know how to play 'Don't Speak' by No Doubt?" Camille asked.

"Shhhh," David put his finger to his lips.

"I know just what you're saying," Isaiah said.

David stared until Isaiah's chuckles silenced. He gathered his wobbles and looked at the guitar again. This time all the emotion that had been sloppy now concentrated in one chord strummed solemnly as if they weren't there. He let it hang in silence, and then struck another, and then another until a slow rhythm formed.

"Wow. Who would have ever known?" Camille said.

"He has a really good voice too."

But David was lost to them. He brought Isaiah beyond where he had ever led him before in the progression of chords. But he was only interested in the guitar. Isaiah hoped he would surprise them by starting to sing at the perfect point. He was waiting for it when something went wrong. He misplayed a chord. Then he tried to play something else, but he plucked the wrong strings. And he became aware again of his audience. He looked at them in a new-formed wobble.

"I suck. Stupid guitar."

He stood up and swung his guitar at the wall. It made a loud crack. Isaiah had seen it done a thousand times in music videos, but it didn't look the same in real life, this beautiful instrument was a rare tool of magic, and it looked sorrowful with the crack at the handle cutting into the body. They were silent as they looked at what he had done. Then there was stirring upstairs. Petrified the girls looked up to the top of the steps when the footsteps started. They hadn't even heard Mr. McCormick come home.

"Hey. What is going on down there?"

Mr. McCormick didn't yell, there was no anger in his voice, but still the girls cringed as he softly tread down the stairs. When he looked around at the girls, Isaiah, his son, none of it seemed to be able to penetrate the plate of his baldhead scrunched in confusion. Only when he noticed the guitar in his son's hand did he finally focus. Isaiah could tell he had been drinking also; he did not wobble as David had, but he anchored himself as stiffly as his son. He seemed to fumble for some sort of emotion as he stared at David.

"What have you done David?"

He could only find sadness. He walked over to his son and gently took the guitar, examining it briefly before tenderly placing it in the guitar stand.

"All right. You obviously have had too much to drink. We'll talk about it tomorrow."

He then took David by the arms like a willful child and walked him towards the hallway. David went limp in his arms.

"Come on son. Let's get you some water."

He mostly carried him as they trudged up the steps.

"One step at a time son."

The sink faucet ran. Then David and his father trudged up to the second floor.

"Well that was psycho," Yolanda broke the silence.

"I've never seen him like that before. He is usually cool," Isaiah said.

"Real cool."

"Why do you have to be such a bitch? He was just trying to have fun."

He wanted to obliterate that expression from Yolanda's face now before she became the mean woman she was destined to be.

"Like you have a right to bully him. Look at you. Big boned as a linebacker from Notre Dame."

April gasped.

"Stop Isaiah."

"I'm sorry. But she shouldn't be so mean to people."

"Whatever," Yolanda said.

Mr. McCormick trudged back down. The girls raised their fearful eyes expectantly, desiring a parental force to take control and reprimand them. He sat down in David's chair and laughed.

"I'm sorry ladies. Don't think my son is crazy. He just overdid it. He doesn't know how to handle drinking yet. Mind if I have a beer?"

He cracked one open.

"Go ahead. I assume none of you are driving. Don't be scared, finish your beers."

It wasn't the order they were expecting but they were obedient all the same.

"I hope his display didn't ruin the evening. I put him in the spare bedroom to sleep it off. There are plenty of couches, and one of you can sleep in David's bed. I'll get you blankets. I definitely don't want you driving home."

He drank his beer pondering them.

"It is so strange to see such lovely ladies here. David didn't tell me had such pretty friends. What are you girls' names?"

They answered quickly.

"April. It is almost your month. Aptly named, you are as beautiful as the springtime."

"Thank you. I am Isaiah's girlfriend."

"Way to go Isaiah. He is a nice boy. Been David's best friend since they were boys. Does David have a secret girlfriend he hasn't told me about?"

Camille avoided his smile so he turned it to Yolanda.

"Oh no sir. We barely know him," Yolanda said.

"Well, such lovely friends. I was his age when I met his mother. She was around 18, same as you girls."

They mistook the intentions of his open expression and shrunk from him. They didn't see this lonely man was just trying to briefly be a boy again. Isaiah for a moment thought he should be a child again with David, with him in his room when the rage sputtered into the same sadness in his eyes.

"You girls are so pretty, I can see why he went a little crazy."

He did not notice them looking at him like a pedophile as he pondered the guitar.

"But I can see how that boy is just like his poppa in a lot of ways. We all go there sometimes."

He couldn't help that his wild beard and hair shooting out form his skull made his features primal when he stared at the bottle of whiskey. He didn't mean to scare the girls. They just couldn't see the boy Isaiah saw underneath.

"Your son was playing for us so lovely Mr. McCormick," April said.

Isaiah looked at her grateful. He again glimpsed the ancient line hidden under her girlish guise as she gave Mr. McCormick a motherly smile.

"He is good. I taught him myself you know."

"He just got mad because he was too drunk and made a mistake," Isaiah offered.

"Yeah. We are going to talk about that in the morning. He is a very calm boy, but we all have anger sometimes and he is going to have to learn how to deal with it better. Hey," He perked up. "David's birthday is this week. I'll have a party for him next weekend if you guys want to come?"

"Sure," Isaiah said.

"Ok." April was a girl again as she demurely winked at Isaiah.

"I don't know, I'll have to ask my parents," Camille said.

"I can't," Yolanda said.

"Well, we can have a party. Isaiah, if you want invite some other people. April, invite whoever you want. It is his eighteenth birthday after all."

He winked at Isaiah.

"I'll leave you kids to play. Have fun. No more craziness tonight."

Their beers no longer were sweet with forbiddance, and they set them down when he was upstairs.

"Creepy," Yolanda said.

"Shut up fat ass," Isaiah responded.

"Will you drive me home? I don't have to take this."

Camille nodded. They looked at April. She glared at them then implored Isaiah not to leave by rubbing his thigh.

"I am not driving anyone home," Isaiah said.

"Fine. I'm calling my parents."

"And tell them what Yolanda?" Camille sighed. "How are we going to explain we were at a boy's house drinking?"

"I don't care."

"Shut up Yolanda. It's fine. Isaiah is sorry. Right Isaiah?" April said.

"Yep."

"Let's just drink and try to have fun since we are already here," April said.

Yolanda shook her head and pouted with her arms crossed. Isaiah would have been glad to be rid of her and Camille and their cruel judgment, but for April's kindness he forced a smile to appease her.

"I'm really sorry. I just want you to give David another chance. But I have lots of other friends. I bet they would like you, what with those mammaries you've got on you."

She uncrossed her arms and her pout disappeared. "Stop it."

It turned his stomach to flirt with her after seeing her meanness but he sat down beside her.

"Seriously. How big are those yams, double D? I have a friend, Lumpy, who is obsessed with breasts. He would go crazy for your boobs. And Camille, do you like football players? I bet you both know who Barrett is? He is hot right? He is my best friend."

They smiled to remember having fun. Their giggles reaffirmed life after the density following David's outbreak. April looked at him thankful. They laughed harder because there was nothing they could do but be glad it wasn't them upstairs.

But then April gasped as she looked in the hallway. David had come down without any of them hearing him. The things that made him a person were still passed out upstairs in bed, escaped into the distance he stared off into. What remained, the only thing that could stay conscious in the sludge of drunkenness and pain, were the demons that tormented him. He took two heavy steps as if the demons possessing him were unaccustomed to operating the apparatus of his body, and he stopped in the middle of the room with the only emotions they could channel in the disdain of his eyes.

"Are you guys having fun?"

He would have crumbled under the force of the hatred if those evil forces weren't holding him erect.

"What are you laughing at?" The demon breath hissed out of his slack jaw.

"Nothing. Just being silly."

David looked at April with fury so strong it was like a blow crushing her jaw and leaving it fragile and quivering again.

"Isaiah is so funny, he is so cute, isn't he April?"

April couldn't look at him.

"It's not funny anymore. It's not a goddamned joke. This is the world. This is the fucking cruel world."

Those dead eyes focused on Isaiah.

"Isaiah the saint. Did he even tell you guys about my friend Chris? His supposed friend Chris? The boy who killed himself."

"David you should go to bed. Your dad will be angry," Isaiah said.

"Shut up. He turned his back on Chris when it wasn't convenient to be his friend. So he could get himself a little skin. Pussy. Isn't that what you called me today, Isaiah, a pussy? Do you want to fuck me? Pretending you are my friend."

David scrunched up and grotesquely dry humped the air.

"You, my friends, are the cruel world. You are the cold existence forcing itself upon the poets and philosophers. Your boyfriend, April, is the reason people like us kill ourselves."

"Please stop," Isaiah said.

"You forgive boys like him Yolanda? Who make fun of fat girls so that you will one day end up in the hospital, wishing you were dead instead of facing another day of their cruelty."

"Stop. I had nothing to do with Maggie and you know it."

"You forgive boys like him April? Does their cruelty make your little skanky vagina wet?"

"Please stop," Isaiah said.

"No," he hissed.

With belligerent fury he stood in front of Isaiah.

"No. Did he tell you he and his friends made bets about who would bleed for the curse of Goldenwood, who would kill themselves? Ha ha. Funny. His friend killed himself. But still he jokes about something like that. And you picked me. Isn't that right Isaiah? You picked me to end my life, you prick."

He swung his fist at Isaiah but he easily grabbed his arm. The force of his rage pressed forward and pushed Isaiah backwards in his chair. Isaiah fell with his arms tangled with his and he had no way to brace his fall. Their weight bounced his head on the ground.

"What if we kill you motherfuckers?"

Isaiah was more dazed by the words than the blow. He couldn't muster the energy to fight him off. It was Yolanda who yanked him up.

"Get off of him."

April was quickly at his side. Isaiah put his hand on the back of his head and it came back with blood. Yolanda stood protecting them

"Get out of here. Go upstairs or I'll scream for your father."

David looked at her unaware of what was going on. He meekly turned but was uncertain how to take a step.

"Go or I'll call the police you psycho."

Then he was gone and the girls surrounded him.

"Poor baby. Are you all right?" April asked.

"I need to lie down."

April led him into David's bed and sat over him. Camille closed the door behind them.

"The cut isn't too bad. I think you will be ok."

Soon he was on top of her in the piss and boogers and misery of David's grubby life. It wasn't Isaiah's fault. He pressed into her. It wasn't his fault. He would be happy. His fervor increased against her. He would feel good.

DAVID IS GONE

Happiness didn't always have to come from somewhere. Isaiah's alarm clock hammered its way into his dreams, waahn, waahn, waahn, blaring its dominion over the sun. He drove to school alone, the bass of his stereo turned up so loud it rattled his arms in unrelenting rhythm. He did not question the source of his euphoria. Routine offered the path of least resistance. The birds chirping that spring morning echoed in his mind in the hallway. Time passed with its old familiarity. In classes he was only aware of the mental lean forward, tick, tick, tick, the doodling slow murder of minutes between the bells. In high school you were often trapped in a world of your own thoughts, and not much really happened.

But leaving Mr. Quinn's class he lingered at the door. He closed it and turned around.

"Mr. Quinn, can I ask you a question?"

His beard swayed like it was taking the equations back into their source as he erased the blackboard. He stopped and turned.

"Yes Isaiah."

He sat upon the corner of his desk and crossed his legs, corduroy pants exposing a calf muscular from biking. Above the brown sock hair from his pale skin curled. His amusement turned to concern.

"What is the matter son?"

"Oh nothing is the matter," Isaiah replied.

Isaiah's questions were answered before he had even completely formulated them. His answer was in Mr. Quinn's compassion, the way he stroked his beard as if again readying equations that offered the hope of answers. Merlin was real. For with every talisman of science, every experiment repeated in day-to-day life, he found magic underneath. Claiming no omniscience he offered a new way to hope. Isaiah laughed when the silence would have been awkward with any other teacher. As a questing Lancelot Isaiah wanted to ask of his wisdom.

"Why can't you be my teacher all day?"

"It is important to have many different viewpoints."

"So Hitler could be my art teacher?"

Mr. Quinn's concern burst into a loud laugh that scrunched the squiggles of the equations in his beard.

"I guess I really don't know what I want to ask. What are your feelings about...about, anti entropy? But more than that. What are your personal beliefs?"

He let go of his beard with a slight smile remaining. The quizzical twinkle in his eyes faded into a serious look.

"Well Isaiah, in all honesty that is complicated. The administration wouldn't even want me to discuss it."

"I won't tell anyone."

"Oh I know, I know. I just don't want to be misconstrued. In this class we prove the 99.9 percent, etcetera, etcetera." He laughed. "If we all woke up tomorrow floating I think Principal Conjecture would have bigger problems than firing me. But anyways, I defer. I can tell you that even with science there is a miniscule part of reality itself we have to take with faith. And I do see something more. Will that suffice? Yes. That will suffice. I see something more, and that is a leap I am willing to take every morning."

Students crowded outside the closed door.

"Have you ever heard kids talk about the curse of Goldenwood?" Isaiah asked hurriedly.

"Yes. I have overheard mention of it."

"Do you believe maybe it is our fault?

"Son. Very little in this chaos of revolving universes can we control," Mr. Quinn nodded. "I am certain whatever it is, it is not your fault. As to the rest, we haven't come up with a theorem yet to test some mysteries."

He wanted to keep discussing it but the door cracked open and a head poked in.

"Sorry to interrupt, but I didn't want to be marked tardy."

"It's ok," Mr. Quinn looked at Isaiah for permission to continue. "Isaiah, I have another class. But why don't you stop by to see me here after school sometime. I don't know what I can tell you, but we can ponder over these questions together."

"Ok. I will. Thank you."

He gave way to the throng without regard for their faces. Out of the goo of confusion he tried to understand the molecular formation of the bricks stacked up to form the walls of the hallway. With a pondering smile he observed how the sunlight excited the youthful energy in the lunchroom. He ended up at his lunch table curious but still uncertain of the true nature of this milieu.

David was gone.

Isaiah stood with his tray looking at the 8 empty chairs placed expectantly at the glossy table. The lunchroom had never been so unbearably solemn. They would always be in high school. Sometimes he would feel that mass of emotion. Chris would have always been socially ill at ease. David would always be in the far off distance. They all would learn coping mechanisms, but underneath those formalities of adulthood the children hidden deep underneath would forever seek friendship in the loneliness.

April's shy look implored him. She defied the rubber bands hinging her braces, even though something may go unexplained, keeping her mouth closed with innocent adoration that sprouted like the first desperate pubic hairs. But he did not go to this mate, and there were no answers in her longing, only memories of her small chaste bottom blushing in his hands. He was full of a need to escape into the undefined future.

It was unfair that he could just return to the welcoming bosom of their generation. But he could not bear to sit alone thinking about David and the specter of Chris. So he returned to his old lunch table. It was as if he had never left. He didn't deserve their hearty greeting. Barrett patted his back like an old comrade in arms.

"Welcome back."

"What are you two fuck sticks so giddy about?"

There was less of Lumpy, even the animosity, as if there was no longer a goal for his cruelness to press its bulk against.

"Were off to see the wizard, were off to see the wizard, off to see the wizard who banged your mom."

Again the mandatory joke, again they pretended friendship as they shared a wicked grin. It was unfair that his zits were fading away, that he would graduate thinner and healthy, and go on to become a happy frat boy.

"Have you lost some weight Lumpy?"

He could not hide the pleasure as his long eyelashes fluttered.

"Yeah. This fat fuck has been working out with me so he can walk on at college."

Aaron's blank face would never appreciate his good fortune, all his success in life would just be common sense.

"I've been chewing my Slimfast."

Lumpy's arm wobbled as he shook the large plastic water bottle of tobacco spit stained in rainbow layers from the large bag of skittles.

"Disgusting," Hoss said.

He had missed that laugh, rumbling so he could feel his good humor.

"Angela must be pleased," Isaiah said.

"Forget that skank, I'm done with her."

"You mean she is done with you," Barrett said.

"I mean in college I am going to be banging Rachel. I hear she has become quite the slut."

He stared at Isaiah.

"Maybe you can starve your zits. About 30 pounds just there," Isaiah said.

"I can still mount you any day pansy. You're as pretty as your sister."

"I was always wondering why you stared at me so much. Hey Lumpy, do you know why life is like an essay?"

"Why?"

"It always ends with a period."

Isaiah pretended to wipe his face off. They hurrahed and hollered their laughter at this old war story.

"Whatever."

Wadsworth was the first one to sheepishly pull out his glossy yearbook, *Lasting Memories*.

"I can see you are the same douche," Isaiah said. "Give me that."

You had a sweet skinny little ass. Isaiah Templeton. He wrote.

Names cursed, names exulted, they pretended disinterest in the sentiment as they wordlessly slid their yearbooks around and sarcasm took over.

On Aaron' yearbook. *We drank. We did shit together. Isaiah Templeton.*

On Lumpy's yearbook, *I lent you a kiss from Stephanie's lips. Isaiah Templeton.*

And so it went, until Barrett handed him his yearbook. He slid his over to him and they both paused without looking at the other. He contemplated what to write as the others chuckled at what they wrote. What he wrote would guide the memories after this faded.

Good luck buddy. I hear in boot camp even an ugly woman looks attractive. You better keep me out of your fantasies grunt. Isaiah. They passed each other's yearbooks back without looking at what the other had written.

"Look at that cumquat," Aaron said.

Wadsworth hurried around Carrie Ann's table, giddy as he scurried to each girl with his yearbook. Isaiah signed yearbook after yearbook, faces materialized in photographs of days already lived, they laughed at jokes already told, as they started to blur. Mr. Stigler stood curt at the wall. Another year of the mustache faded, captured with him in band pants too high upon his belly, behind him the ever-changing band in high hats stepping to the echoes of lost percussion. In a moment of respite Isaiah looked from the ironic display crowding around their lunch table to the outskirts, searching for those forgotten faces nothing more than ghosts.

Carrie Ann's yearbook slammed down in front of him.

Look at this kid too cool for school."

She pressed her hips into his shoulder and her crotch was in his face, leaning over him to allow a glance up her low cut shirt to the lace of her bra. She smiled at him as if she could influence all the years with an intimacy that he would designate on her yearbook. She took his yearbook and signed it.

You were hard not to like. Carrie Ann's ☺ wink.

He ignored the tingle caused by her perfume.

You will make a good teenage mother. Isaiah Templeton.

He scribbled his name large and grinned at her disdain as she read. He received an equal expression from Stephanie after he signed hers.

Glad we could meat. Isaiah Templeton.

They gave him a dirty look and moved away with their yearbooks opened to the football team photo.

"There is no way any of you boys is getting out of signing our yearbooks. You made this cesspit entertaining at least. Our big star quarterback, yes, even you Mr. Cool, you have to sign my yearbook."

"Go ahead Lumpy, sign Stephanie's, you aren't the only boy who tasted her period blood," Isaiah said.

All sins were but ripples upon the surface tension of youth. They formed at these tables like falling raindrops to smack against Goldenwood's windowpanes, and ran down to be absorbed in the dirt.

ELEMENTAL FORCES

He avoided appreciating the spring sunshine coming through the blinds in Karen's classroom. Long ago he had been fooled by that tree-lined view through baseball diamonds and green practice fields. That hope had faded, just as the pang his parents had felt when they let their baby get on the bus that first time. School had changed from the nontoxic glue and crayons and nap times, through recesses, the parades and football games. The posters on the wall had lost their original gloss. Next year new ones would guide boys into men. The white paper of the clock had yellowed at the edges, draining numerous batteries to propel the hands counting out the statute of limitations. Soon the bell would disturb his calcified thoughts one last time. Twelve years would drop with one last guillotine tick.

This autoimmune reaction would pass, and he counted the ceiling tiles to keep his sanity a few weeks longer. Violent force cranked the pencil sharpener as it cut into virgin wood flat around a new pencil's lead. Nothing was really missing in David's empty seat. It was as if he had shed the fat rolls that were pressed daily over the chair-desk bar tight on his side, dissipating layer by layer to be in that far off vantage point. The class started oblivious to Isaiah sitting in David's assigned spot. Old hunchback now was he. The ventilation system like the breaths of some long dying beast stirred up smells that would be with Isaiah the rest of his life. It was no dragon to slay; there was no weak spot in mythical scales to end its terrorizing of youth. It was already expiring, had been so when it was created, but it would do so only of its own natural course. In the meantime it would digest whatever curt morsels lay within, regardless of who sat in this seat.

Where was David? Finally Isaiah looked out the window, seeking a glimpse of a yellow jacket zipping in quick autonomy. But he shouldn't have done so. A yellow jacket carcass was on the windowsill. Useless wings were attached to a yellow and black torso curled up in one last beautiful sting. Its pointy face was like a dead cartoon that had lost its animation.

He would never know how many hours he had leaned his head on his fist this way, of moments unaccounted for there were years, but he now amused himself by moving his stubble forward and backwards. He wondered if in the future relief from Karen's lectures he would miss watching her. Their vibration packed around her bosom, rising and falling. When the honey of the hive had dried out, but his life still rose and fell as an old man, how would he remember these days? Would he remember these days? Or her? Or would Karen disappear with only memories remaining of elemental forces. Tan from spring break she was like driftwood artfully weathered. Dredged up hormones were like traps full of crabs crashing into each other. Her iris made him imagine the sea far outside these walls. He did not look away when she noticed his stare, no more than one would look away from a wave, until she crashed in upon herself. It raised again in the curve of a smile, to crash again with a shake of her blonde hair, the elemental force teasing the weary shoreline of her lecture.

REVEL WHILE YOU CAN

Lawnmowers had brought order upon the yards full of dandelions. In David's yard the breed of manes thrived quickly to disperse skeletal seed in their reprieve. David's car was absent but Mr. McCormick's was in the driveway. Isaiah was sure everything was ok. Awash in sunlight the degradation of their house even looked hopeful, each step had chips in the concrete but they had remained sturdy through a childhood of disrepair and would remain so long in the future.

It took a while for rustling to answer his doorbell ring. Mr. McCormick's features like David's with the fat chiseled away had no fog today as he glared out. He relaxed when he saw David, and only desolation was left.

"Oh hello Isaiah. How can I help you?"

"Is David here?"

"No. He hasn't come home yet."

"Do you know where he is?"

"No. I assumed he was with you. I'll let him know you stopped by."

"Mr. McCormick, I am not trying to tattletale, but he wasn't at school today. I am worried about him."

Confusion pulled his skin tight on his baldhead.

"He wasn't? That boy. Come in, come in, let's talk for a minute."

No additional signs of chaos were in the kitchen. The whiskey bottle he took a sturdy swig from explained his haze.

"Not that I really blame him on his birthday. His mother's life insurance policy matured, he is one wealthy young man. I figured he would be celebrating with you."

"He never told me that…by any chance do you know where he might be?"

"No. No. Although Sunday he was withdrawn even for David. I figured it was just a hangover."

"When did you see him last?"

"I was like him when I was young. I reveled in the depression. Unique, relevant, I felt, I was alive, I was deep, I got it, and I could conquer the world."

He took a swig out of necessity.

"That of course was before I met his mother. Now when the depression comes, I am embarrassed. I rationalize it with pills. I accept this reality for my son, that part of life remaining from his mother, and I try to be a good father to her son. I fight depression so it shall never come again."

He looked at the bottle bored with his next dose. He snorted.

"I should go to the doctor and get him some pills. But he never complains. Hey those girls, do you think they will come to his party?"

He handed the bottle to Isaiah. He didn't want to drink in the shadows of the unlit kitchen, but he took a swallow to be able to look in Mr. McCormick's tired eyes.

"I will certainly try. Girls our age are fuckle cruel creatures. But where is he now?"

Mr. McCormick harrumphed.

"That hasn't changed. I can't speak for you, I pray for your sake you don't feel it, but that demon must also take its piece of him. No matter how I explain it away, before or after, when it is clutching me it cares little for all the bullshit. It will have its way with you no matter."

Isaiah drank and looked around the shadow of the kitchen, picturing how this room should look with the glow of the lights and Mrs. McCormick, but instead the empty shelves were the center of deterioration.

"I'm experienced," Isaiah could admit when the alcohol hit his blood.

"That is why I don't lie to my son. I don't tell him it is the fit will just pass. I know the demon I have passed on to him."

Mr. McCormick smirked at the bottle after drinking as if it was not enough.

"They tell you not to self medicate so they can sell you their pills."

He put the cap on the bottle.

"The world is beautiful. It is not what did this to me. Not even the oppressive mass of assholes, who grope at you, assaulting one like a swarm of douchbag zombies."

He laughed but the anger came rushing back

"I know they are raping David too. But it is when you have no stories to tell, no talismans of life to keep the assholes from you, that they surround you with their mockery until they are all you see of the world. They descend on all hours, bill collectors and recruiters, not even leaving you your damned solitude."

He handed the bottle to Isaiah.

"So I say let my son revel tonight."

"I don't understand, where is he?"

"Find him. Dance with him. Stand together against it all in your revelry. And dance like madmen around the flames. It is his birthday. He is a man. Be happy. He shouldn't have to drink with an old shriveled dick like me. It should be fun. Not like this. Learn to revel in these moments when the beast is new and seduces you with its contrast to life. Feel the world."

He left Isaiah with the bottle in the kitchen as he trudged up to his room and closed the door. In the shadows Isaiah blended in with the sorrow. He went to the basement and felt the hopeless ache alone there. The chair David had pushed over with Isaiah in it was still on its back. All the posters stared inwards at him. The shelves were as full of books as the school's, a library of boyhood hope left desolate now. Piles of clothes surrounded the unmade bed with all the sheets and covers in a ball. It was where April had absorbed Isaiah's disquietude. In contrast David had no respite from solitude down here with his lamp the only light of the world. On the bed a notebook lied open. Isaiah sat down to read it. *Drifter's End* was written in sharpie on the cover.

The last page was blank but for measured pen strokes in the middle:

> *'I dreamt of the words during a blackout, so beautiful I almost believed they would come true. But the painful part of the sobering, THE FUCKING HANGOVER, is there is nothing we can say to make someone love us, to make someone come back.'*

He read. David described his heart in colors like a child finger painting with words. Poetry was in between the desperate cries. He filled page upon page with wild emotion almost faster than the words could contain. Every margin of the ledger was filled. Isaiah drank whiskey so he could cry. A feeling was hammered upon him that everyone was afraid to admit even to themselves. His tears were a release, the only way he could honor the boy who felt so very strange as he cried to a God he wasn't even sure could answer. Then on an otherwise empty page he read the words he knew as a chant:

> *From room to room*
> *hall to hall*
> *can I write my way out of this hell*
> *if I start at the bathroom stall*

Of course it had been David. Isaiah should have known the words were his every time they greeted him in that bathroom stall. Isaiah walked back into the playroom. He grabbed the replica colt 45. Its shiny red tip was there to keep cops from opening fire on kids playing army with a smile they believed was eternal, bang, bang, mothers always watchful angels on the bench. He traced the gun along the stubble of his face into his mouth. He pulled the trigger. Boom. Almost like an accident. Boom. The playful scratches on Isaiah's arm were but the first taste of a new masturbation. They were trivial compared to hands shaking as they held a way to escape the pain. Reason was a hallow perversion of the living, it made no sense to a shot of steel that left emotion a slimy gooey mass, fragility left over bone fragments indistinguishable in the graveyard billions. Boom. David's stare would fade out of his face, outwards past all backyards, to the unexplored silence with Chris and his mother. Boom. The universe was created out of the pre dimensional goo. Boom. The trigger's spring pushed back and he imagined Mr. Quinn with his mouth pursed, boing. In the coffin the people who really loved you thought of you again with memories more alive than when you were sitting in the other room. *Don't make your prayers those of goodbye, but those of hello.*

THE SOLITARY SOUND OF CHILDHOOD

He escaped David's haunted basement with the bottle of whiskey and the gun. He did not holster it like Skull Face, whose megalomania drained everything away but his hissing judgement, but instead put it in his pocket like a toy.

A solitary basketball bouncing reclaimed the world. Isaiah hoped David grinned as he played hooky under this same blue sky. He hoped he smelled the renewal in the breeze as it flapped the shelves of his hair and ruffled tree blossoms as white as Chris's eternal tighty-whiteys with the pink hue of his pale bottom underneath. Barrett sat on his porch swing, a grin easily assuming humor even if he didn't understand the joke that made Isaiah pace wildly in front of his large suburban house.

"Dude, are you drunk?"

Isaiah reminisced upon their ease of youth. Before they could drive they used to play basketball late into weekend nights, the basketball lost in the lights with every shot as their sweat mixed fighting for the rebound.

"I'm not yet at the age of drunken desperation."

He avoided dwelling on Mr. McCormick's whiskey in his trunk. He wanted to enjoy his legs shivering like a stallion ready to run.

"Want to go play one-on-one?"

"I think I have dominated the past enough," Barrett said.

"Right! If I remember correctly our series is about even. Let me get you ready for the ass kicking you will receive in boot camp soldier boy."

Barrett swung on his sturdy porch swing in khaki shorts, his muscular calve flexing at every touch of the ground, laughing even if he didn't understand the euphoria.

"Dude. It is Monday. I actually have some studying to do."

Isaiah noticed the moon rising over the horizon, and even though he knew it was in the realm of possibility for it to rise this early in the day, it was an odd omen rising today in the suburbs. Their neighborhood seemed zoned like fallout shelters to protect them from the rolling topography, sturdy outposts well maintained because nature was waiting to claim their roads and creep back up their storm drains at any warning. It was more natural to be outside on this spring afternoon amongst the long living trees. As he stared up he almost tripped off the edge of the porch.

"Holy cow. Look at that moon. It is a sign. Let's have some fun, the time for studying is over."

His mind's eye filled the rest of the half moon in the blue sky, no definition of night as the white rock reflected the sun in the afternoon.

"It is not for school. I have to take the ASVAP this weekend and it is important I do well."

"What? What is this? Has the axis shifted? The moon rising in the afternoon, and you studying?"

"It is a crazy world," Barrett said.

"Clearly from the time of Sesame Street the man has been conspiring against us, always the sun and it's opposite the moon. The opposite of the sun is not and has never been the moon."

"Are you stoned?"

"They say the opposite of light is dark. But darkness is just the absence of light."

"Huh?"

"Some dark new tunnel's stink to hide my stick in."

"You've lost it. Where the hell did you get so wasted? And why do you have that toy gun in your pocket, weirdo."

Isaiah took the gun out of his pocket and aimed at the moon and pulled the trigger, pretending a kickback.

"Not me. I am just escaping into heaven. The moon is calling us. Look at that moon!"

Barrett laughed with jaws as solid as lunar rock and stood up to open his heavy front door.

"Yes that is the moon. And as fun as this is."

He hollered as he closed the door.

"Have April bring a cherry blossom to Lumpy's party Friday for me."

THE DEAD DON'T SYNTHESIZE SUNSHINE

A young mother looked at Isaiah from the arboretum's parking lot, laughing at her child's babble as she unfastened him from his car-seat, her jet-black hair falling around his face. She set him down and he sprinted to catch his sister entering the playground across from the arboretum. She strutted behind them, looking around at the otherwise empty parking lot with a smile. Their toffee skin was made to absorb the sun. Isaiah's arms were pale from winter, and he hoped David's even fairer skin hadn't lost the ability to synthesize the sunshine. He hoped his face was bright pink from a day in the sun. When he found him he was certain he would look like a native of this place in the full blush of life.

The makeup on Chris's face hadn't disguised how the pigment had drained from his hands across his chest in the coffin.

He walked across the covered bridge to stare at the creek they had followed towards the horizon; they had never gone far enough. The calm water floated at the top against the underlying current, seeming to complete a circle from the clouds and rivers and sea to swirl back to the gentle rapids in a fixed point of eternity. Isaiah tracked David by rubbing the soft texture of baby green buds in branches. He sniffed at them to catch the scent. On the tree's plaques ephemeral vowels translated Plato into Latin, as the leaves again grew into the form the evergreens always held, reforming from the abstract with purple and red and white flowers interspersed. Searching for David added poignancy, and he could see the richness of detail that made *Grandeur of Illusions* real, for it bled through here, that concentrated realm was connected and all Isaiah had to do was keep those kid dreams alive, the things the world told him he should grow out of, to see it concentrated again in magic everywhere he looked. He couldn't wait to find David, not just to apologize to him, but to tell him how he now understood that he had not been hiding from the world in fantasy but embracing its potential.

He had never been so desperate to find someone in his life, and he sat down upon their bench to concentrate on where David would have gone. He was certain he would eventually find a sign to lead him to him here, but still he lit a cigarette as he looked around to calm his nerves. If each cigarette shortened his life, as if every soul had a quota of pain, then he inhaled concentrated bursts of sadness.

He hyperventilated so he could fulfill his quota before those long last years when like Mr. McCormick he would watch nature in the long stretches between laughs. Maybe the ants and armies didn't mind much, but there were thoughts like asteroids from the dark outer reaches of the mind that could end this world, the same as squishing one ant torturously slow.

Amongst purple wild flowers was a sign Isaiah hadn't noticed before. 'Do Not Pick The Wildflowers.' Tree buds waving in supple supplication would richen in the following months before they fell. In the fall baskets of fruit would be ripe to let the sweetness of these fair months run down David and his chins as they laughed.

He fought through the bramble beside the bench and found clearing enough to follow the creek in this opposite direction. He expected he would find David where he just as easily could find Chris, in the comforting shade of the trees. He came to the other side of the steel tunnel underneath the railroad tracks where David had led him off the tracks. Where the small flow met the larger creek was a small sooty beach full of flat stones. He spun a stone across the creek, like a toe dabbling the water it crossed to clunk against a tree on the other side. The ripples were soon lost in the current. He cautiously leaned over to stare through the tunnel, expecting to see David in the light on the other side. But he was not in the field circling the black boulder. He decided against crossing underneath when he felt the cold water and the treacherously slick steel girders inside the tunnel. He splashed water on his face and it ran cool upon his lips parched from whiskey. He spit out the mineral tang with the residual taste of pennies and blood. If David was not here then he must have followed the railroad tracks. He scampered with joy up the steep gravel and pulled himself to the top triumphantly. He glared towards each horizon, unable to focus on anything at first from the sunshine glimmering off the tracks, seeking David in the far off distance. But he did not spot him with a backpack venturing off into the country, and the joy of that insane image faded.

"Chris, do you see our friend? Chris, where is he?"

He walked back to the arboretum deflated. He sought sign of him in the trees. He looked for some hopeful path hidden in the trees until he came across the point where David had fallen, betrayed by his body as the train's eventuality had thundered towards them.

As he walked there was a shift in the air and dark clouds massed on the horizon. Rivulets danced upon the creek in disorderly gusts as he crossed the bridge. His car was alone in the parking lot. Animals and leaves turned in preparation. A thick wet drop splashed off his forehead as he watched the storm come. Thunder reverberated in the houses beyond the railroad tracks, and he pictured it shaking the foundations where family tragedies hid and haunted. The bathroom doors slammed open and closed, debris stirred up making him no longer an uninvolved spectator to the chaos. He got in his car as storm clouds swallowed the light above the arboretum. The whipping trees adorned the milieu.

Sheets of rain pelted his car and it shook in gusts as he drove home. In his neighborhood an American flag flapped and smacked against the pole. Short grass bent uniform in each blast of air. The tall dandelions in David's yard whipped around. David's car was still not in the driveway. He hoped he had found shelter somewhere.

He sat in his driveway until sunshine was visible again as the storm quickly passed. He was embarrassed when he saw his parent's had been sitting the whole time on the porch. They did not hide their handholding when he noticed them. He forgot they were taking the day off to do spring-cleaning and yard work. Assorted gardening tools were laid in the mulch along with two pairs of dripping gardening gloves. He dashed out into the rain and alighted on the porch beside them. They smiled at him as they continued to hold hands. He was about to go inside when they pointed at the sky. Faint graceful colors from the top of an arc at the edge of the passing blackness became a full range of rainbow light at the blue horizon. He sat down next to them to watch the storm pass, expecting the rainbow to arch completely and maybe touch down where they sat. He allowed his mother to put her other hand in his. The must of spring was intoxicating as the water dripped around them in the storm's aftermath. Sheens of water covered the newly planted azaleas, and possibility bloomed in the flowers he could not name. The rainbow disappeared without completing to touch down on them. He gently pulled his hand from his mother's. He turned towards his car instead of going in the house as he had originally planned, and only then did his parents stir from their entrancement.

"Where are you off to now?" His dad asked.

"Just to wish David a happy birthday. I forgot about it until now."

"Oh ok. Don't stay out late. It is a school night."

"I know."

"Wish him happy birthday for us."

David hadn't sheltered the storm at home because his car was still not there. Isaiah drove to Mr. McCormick's work. Isaiah imagined he stared out the window of his cubicle with the same defeated posture as David, the effort of staying positive at work thickening the plate of his bald head each day with never enough time in between for the wild sprouts to regenerate. He walked through the parking lot past the second shift lunchtime crowd. It seemed no one he passed looked at their surroundings as their downward glances led them to and from the building. A man humming was propelled by some internal elevator music. A woman sped past him determined. No one paid heed to the boy in their midst until he veered off to take the path around the pond besides their building. The clean-cut vigor of the young man disappeared along with his smile as he passed Isaiah and straightened his tie to skulk into the entrance. He at least still was enough of the world surrounding them to feel there was some contrast to the malevolence of spending his lifetime in a hulking building that kept him from the sun.

He was not here to enjoy the path beside the hulking manifestation reminding him of the McCormick's unhappiness. Plastic wrappers and styrofoam littered the edge of the pond as if the storm had deposited a dumpster there. He started to run, around to where they had found the secret path. He sought David with trespassing so fast branches smacked his face. He welcomed the itching slices of discomfort, a vague pleasure in leaving his blood behind. In sight of the overpass he again slowed to a walk. His breath came in gasps as he turned from side to side. He was annoyed at his body's insubordinate jubilation at exercise in the spring air. Death in the wildflowers of spring seemed unnatural, but he had started to feel dread the moment he hadn't found David at the arboretum. He hadn't thought to ask Mr. McCormick to check his gun cabinet. And the pang he expected left him trembling as he saw clothing in an unmoving mess in the shadow underneath the dirty overpass.

"David?"

All his thoughts had stopped.

"David."

He screamed into the fury of traffic vibrating the bolts of the steel girders. Such a place to die and not be noticed until you were gone and all that was left behind was rot, such a place to barely to be noticed until you were known as nothing more than a story. This unmoving ragged pile was all that was left of a boy. This was where life had cruelly boomeranged his stare back to. Isaiah had to force himself to climb the incline to reach him. He was petrified of further entering the depths of human sorrow, all illusions would dispel into despair once he looked upon him. His body still in the joy of its animal heat would suddenly retch. The whole overpass shuddered above him with the engine roar of a semi as he approached.

"David."

His whisper was at the edge of hysterics. He tried to find the courage to take the last few steps.

"David."

The form shuffled. He was overjoyed at the movement but also afraid of David's judgment. There was a pile of wildflowers at his feet, dirtied and already rotting brown. The mass moved again away from him as if fearful.

"David, it is me, Isaiah."

But when the form shifted to face Isaiah he could see the irrationality of assuming the rags were David in the shadows. The familiar scowl came from the crazy man as he got up to hunch with a knife in his hand.

"Thought you would sneak up on me huh? Bash me huh? You little punks always try to sneak up on me. But I am too quick, you see?"

Isaiah stumbled and barely kept from tripping as he hurried down the slope. The man followed, moving much more coordinated than before.

"Maybe I should carve you up this time. Should I lord?"

Isaiah made it to the bottom before he realized the man had stopped halfway. He crouched with rage twisting his face as he stared down. Isaiah put his hand upon the toy gun in his pocket.

"This isn't some game boy. This is real life."

He took another step down.

"I'm sorry. I wasn't trying to disturb you. I thought you were my friend."

"I ain't your friend," he barked and took another step down.

"I am looking for a kid my age. My friend. Have you seen anyone?"

The madman looked up at the overpass as if quoting the traffic as he started to chant.

"There is no hope in following the dreams of the departed. This is a wasteland. Our path is with the stars in the night, so we will know how to rejoice when our star's intimate rising brings the blessed new day."

He shook his hands as if performing a summoning. His cackling was lost in the sound of the freeway.

"But that is a lie. You see, they always lie to us. There is never any hope. Your friend is gone. Your friend is dead. "

TRUANTS' BLOOD

He could think of only one last place to look for David. He expected Skull Face to be waiting gleefully with his baton in the parking lot of Indian Mound Park. But Isaiah did not care, let them all come, all the mad men with hatred in their eyes. Skull face was not there when he parked, but let him follow him as he trespassed up the route David and he had taken. Isaiah would pull the gun from his jeans pocket and aim it at him, bang, bang, and fantasy would become real one way or another.

"I should have told you I also am overwhelmed by loneliness sometimes."

He scoffed at time and space. God would grant him that the words reached David.

"There indeed is magic all around us," he yelled out through the enchanted forest.

This was the medium that he would reach David through. As Chris and David had learned the size of their hearts by knowing the emptiness where life should have been, so Isaiah would also discover himself. He would not heed those on the path who didn't care if they existed or not. To them his voice would echo and they would fear that this place had come alive to recapture the world with vengeance.

"Look at that evening moon. I never told you about the pathway I saw opening over me in the sky and beckoning me to a more exotic realm."

In the responding silence he remembered the nightmare fear in his heart as his spirit had traveled away in the line of ghosts. He pictured it again.

One ghost was Chris, discomfort gone from underneath the translucent hair hiding his eyes, no need any longer to try and explain what flowed freely through them all. One was David, the sorrow glimpsed in his depths when he had told Isaiah how much he missed his mother illuminated through with the light.

But Isaiah was still in time and David couldn't leave him here yet. He searched, desperate for a sign, for a moment like the madmen as he tried to re-forge the world out of his fury. He wished for a drunken disconnect to help him see, he wished he was high as the heavens to pry open the vision of something more.

Slowly he unclenched a handful of leaves and let go of the branch he had been clasping, ready to rip it apart. He ran his hand along the leaves. His breathing became calm, like Chris had taught him through that silent night of his boyhood, and he listened until he was aware of every birds chirp, the wind rustling, insects, and a distant car on the highway. As an oracle he needed to see beyond the tree shadows, beyond this brief spring cycling through the years. He would then be able to see Chris's ghost walking beside him as his guide.

"All of these illusions, all of this grandeur, through it help me find our friend."

No voice answered so he tried harder to decipher the sounds of spring. He stopped to reach through the prickly underbrush, the scratches on his hand barely noticed, to turn over a cloth. It was just an old rag. As children they had learned pain young. Everyone pretended it was just another game they played, a part of growing up, but life bestowed these wounds no matter ones age. Even now, as he pretended to be a man, it breached his walls and reached his innermost self. And as a child, absent the walls, they had felt the pain more fierce at its first sting.

"David," he screamed.

He felt so alone. At church they prayed that happiness may disperse the pain quickly with every bright day rising. But he did not plead. He did not beg. He just opened up his intimate places in hopes God understood. A boy could not disappear so completely.

"David!"

He looked up in the sky. They were born innocent for the promise of immortality. He sought answers all around these woods, the one place where this world intersected the wonder Chris had shared with him as a boy. Now he was gone? Dead? What for eternities sake did that even mean? And as if following him in line David had also disappeared?

"David."

It wasn't real. Isaiah looked down and concentrated on his center. If God was everywhere and everything, even if David wasn't free in the adventure Isaiah dreamed, if it was God that gave Isaiah warmth in his most desperate moments, then through his prayers David would also find comfort.

"Magic has to be real. Only with magic can we touch when even the atoms that form our bodies are distant from each other. Hello, goodbye, only with magic can we even have existed with each other between those words."

But as he had not answered Chris when he had called him on the telephone, but had met his desperation with cruel silence, so all sound seemed to silence again in the lack of a response. He was left with the broken places that no one cared about. But if there was no one, nothing else out there that could care, Isaiah vowed to care. The rich sounds of spring returned to him as he walked out of the wall of trees and crossed the field. He strode across the path as wild manifestation of the woods, imagining he crossed it with a sonic boom of nature. He didn't even glance at the view from the top of the hill as he went towards the hidden spot that was the last place he held hope that he would find him.

"David."

The branch he had sat upon was empty. The rhythm was lost that they had beat out to find other dimensions. Discarded branches were left to rot in dead and dying universes so the greater organism could twist its remaining life towards the sun. Pain and suffering imploded into the density at the end of the universe, Isaiah was no longer able to escape into the infinite point he had imagined his soul. Tears formed but there were no wet tracks of release down his face. They only formed because he wanted God to see. His head rested limply on his shoulder and he was unable to utter a sound. Every sob and question was sucked ever inwards unable to escape the mass. Only bird chirps remained in a lonely chorus at the end of the world.

He walked the path the cops had led David and him down the hill. The sun was setting, but there was no longer any joy at the thought of trespassing through the night, there was nothing here that he could reclaim.

But if this was an end of the universe, at the end of the world David and Chris also watched with him this atomic haze sunset. The strips of toxicity forming red clouds were the fingerprints of truant's blood. They didn't need to ask Armageddon's forgiveness. Finally the tears escaped down his face but he felt no undeserved relief. His left hand wrapped around his right pinky to clasp his right hand. His elbows pressed close to his sides. In the moistness he also clasped David and Chris's hands. All three of them as children held hands and walked down the path away from the nuclear tide. The path led glowing up into the sky. From the heavens they would see ringlets of smoke fall down the face of earth, and she would press forward to kiss the sun, lips parted, breath freezing in outer space.

www.ingramcontent.com/pod-product-compliance
Lightning Source LLC
Chambersburg PA
CBHW060911250626
47159CB00008B/2965